OCTOBER MEN

BY
ANTHONY PRICE

THE MYSTERIOUS PRESS

New York • London

For Elizabeth Simpson

MYSTERIOUS PRESS EDITION

Copyright © 1973 by Anthony Price
All rights reserved.

This Mysterious Press Edition is published by arrangement with
the author.

Cover design by Stanislaw Fernandez

Mysterious Press books are published in association with
Warner Books, Inc.
666 Fifth Avenue
New York, N.Y. 10103
W A Warner Communications Company

Printed in the United States of America

First Mysterious Press Printing: August, 1987

10 9 8 7 6 5 4 3 2 1

I

THE GENERAL SAT quietly in his car at the airport terminal, waiting for his mother and his mistress.

To have driven himself after dark was, he knew, an emotional action, perhaps even a foolish one. But then he had never attempted to impose on his private life that ruthless discipline which had characterised his professional career. Indeed, he was convinced that those with great power and responsibility must allow themselves a calculated measure of self-indulgence, which was then not a weakness but a safety-valve; as a student of history he frequently reminded himself that in matters that did not concern the state it was Caesar's wife who had to be above suspicion, not Caesar.

He drew on his cigar, puffing the smoke carefully out of the window. He wasn't supposed to smoke cigars either, in fact he had promised both women that he wouldn't smoke at all while they were away. Yet he felt only mildly guilty about his broken promise, for he had also never been able to resist the minor forbidden things of life, like smoking cigars and parking in the prohibited area right in front of the terminal. And from the number of cars parked around him the latter was clearly a national characteristic, and in his view a healthy one.

In any case, it was comforting to know that he had only himself to blame for being at the wheel when most sensible men of his age who worked as hard as he did were in their beds. For even if he might fret at his mother for her ridiculous economy in taking a cheap night flight he had to admit that she had neither asked nor expected him to attend her return. She had simply assumed that he would send his driver

5

—which would have been less embarrassing as well as easier, since he suspected that she knew very well that her companion was as necessary to his peace of mind as to her own.

In fact there were plenty of good, sensible reasons for his not being here at Leonardo da Vinci, truly. Only there were two other reasons, neither better nor more rational, which outweighed them all.

Quite simply and literally, he could not wait to get his hands on Angela. Not (somewhat to his surprise) in any lascivious way, but just in a strangely old-fashioned loving manner. All he wanted to do was to take hold of those splendid hips, one hand to each flank, and look at her. If it went no farther than that tonight he would not be discontented; it had taken him forty years and two marriages to discover that there was more than one kind of intimacy through which a man could enjoy a woman's company, and he was almost as excited about that discovery as he had been all those years ago about the other.

Physically, the feel of those hips would be enough. There was no denying that Angela's legs were long and elegant, her bottom shapely for a woman of her years, and her bosom magnificent. But the General had always liked hips, for they were the one thing about women that reminded him of horses. And Angela's hips were incomparable.

Yet if Angela was one indulgent reason for making this sweaty drive (though a reason more spiritual than his mother might suspect), there was also a contrary physical reason which no one suspected.

For the truth was that the General could no longer see very well at night.

He, whose military reputation was founded on those two famous night actions, one against the British and the other against the Germans, now feared that age was beginning to impair his night-vision. And characteristically he was fighting

6

this sign of incipient decay as furiously as he had ever done any of his human enemies.

So to have let anyone else drive this night, as he would have done without a thought a few years earlier, would have been to pass up a challenge to impose his will on his body. It was typical of him to dramatise this as a battle against odds, an immortal rearguard action, just as he saw his relationship with Angela as the bonus of a fully-matured intelligence. He would not let it occur to him that the spectres of old age and loneliness, which stalked ordinary men and women, would ever dare approach him.

So now he sat smoking happily in the No Parking lot, thinking of hips and screwing his eyes up in an attempt to watch the late night-life of the airport.

Anyway, the car was more comfortable than the lounge at the terminal, with its smart chairs architect-designed for discomfort and its depressing collection of waiting humanity nervous with excitement or querulous with tiredness, and with the bored cleaners manoeuvring their huge vacuum machines over the black rubber floors.

He glanced at his watch. The scream of the reversed jets he had heard a few minutes before would have been those of the Alitalia DC9 from Heathrow, which had probably left Pisa about the same time as he had set out from the villa. Any moment now the first passengers would be spilling out.

Not that they were any different nowadays from coach and railway passengers. The General could remember the old Rome airport in the old days, when the world was young and air travel was high adventure. He could even remember —how could he ever forget!—being presented to Marshal Balbo there at the beginning of one of his great aerial expeditions.

It had been one of the decisive moments of his life when the Marshal had shaken his hand and looked him in the eye and admonished him never to lead from the back—and had lived up to his own words moments later as the formation of long-range bombers roared overhead—

Here they began to come. But there was no need to stir himself, because his mother would be last. She always came last, and he could remember his father ranting at her for it on railway platforms halfway across the world.

Balbo had been wrong, of course. There were times to lead from the front and times to lead from the back. And the hardest times of all were when it was prudent to let others lead. But Balbo had changed his life, nevertheless—though less by the example of his career than by the manner of his death. For it had been on the day that the Duce had murdered the Marshal in the air above Tobruk because he knew the truth about the armed forces and wasn't afraid to speak it that the young Captain Montuori had ceased to be a Fascist. . . .

He nodded to himself philosophically, watching the travellers congregate outside the terminus, idly sorting them into their proper categories with half his mind, natives and foreigners, holidaying couples and rucksacked students—only the unlucky, the ignorant and the young braved midsummer Rome!

Except his mother, naturally, who behaved in her own way, regardless of everything and everyone.

The General watched a pale-coloured car farther up the parked line to his left slide forward smoothly, curving in front of him in the wake of a big grey Fiat into which the blonde woman with the baby—

His thought was extinguished by the fierce headlights of another car on his right which for one blinding instant illuminated the driver of the pale car moving across his front. It was like a photographic flash, so brief was it, but still long enough to transmit an image through the General's eye and etch it on his brain, to be instantly registered, identified and remembered.

8

Remembered!

He sat rigid with excitement: there was no possibility of mistake, not one ten-thousandth particle of a possibility, no question of failing night-sight playing him false with the vision of that profile, unremarkable but unforgotten.

Or unremarkable on this side, anyway. And since the years had changed its hungry outline so little they would have done nothing to erase the scar on the other side which ran from cheekbone to jawline—the General's own parting gift, delivered with the raking stock of his sub-machine gun. And he would not have misused a good weapon so if there hadn't been a company of German Alpine troops on the hillside less than three hundred metres below them: he would have used it as the Beretta company had intended, and good riddance!

But maybe he should have taken the risk at that—he thrust the hot memory down as the car passed out of his range of sight. The Bastard had been out of his territory then, just as he was out of his territory now. Only now he was out of his time too—sitting there alone in his car, sitting alone like the General, waiting for someone, also like the General. Except that he had driven off smartly having met nobody—the flashing headlights had shown that too.

So someone hadn't come?

The General swore and reached for the ignition. Someone had been here right enough—but the Bastard had not been here waiting to say "Hullo" to him!

He slammed the gear selector over, flicked the light switch and jammed his foot on the accelerator. There was still just about time enough to catch up with him—

Except that his mother was standing directly in his way.

He jammed down his foot on the brake pedal even more fiercely than he had done on the accelerator. The car tyres squealed and slithered.

"Mother, for the love of God—" the General began despairingly. "Mother—"

9

"Raffaele!" The General's mother had a remarkably deep voice for so very feminine a woman, and although her admonitory tone towards him had changed over the course of fifty-eight years, it was fundamentally still that of a long-suffering mother to her slow-witted son. "Don't sit there with your mouth open, Raffaele!"

"Mother—"

The General's mother turned her back on him. It was a well-dressed back too, he noticed bitterly; after four years of widowhood black still dominated her wardrobe conventionally—but it was always the black of Antonelli and Mila Schoen and Valentino (and God in His heaven only knew what English horse she had probably found by now to spend his money on).

"Angela!" The General's mother did not shout, she simply projected her voice. "Tell that fellow to bring the cases here."

He reached out and switched off the engine: when the odds were hopeless even the bravest man could surrender without discredit, and these odds, as he had good reason to know, were infinitely too much for him.

"Raffaele! Are you going to sit there all night?"

The General groped for the door handle. Already it had a quality of unreality, that sudden vision of the past. And he was really too old for these night games, anyway: there was something more than a little ridiculous about the idea of tearing through the night after his old enemy. And finally, it was too late now—his mother had seen to that. It had been too late ever since he had used the butt instead of the bullet twenty-eight years ago.

And then, as his fingers touched the handle, the General was pricked by that ancient instinct, that atavistic feeling of unease which had once been like an extra sense to him, as to be relied on as sight and hearing and smell.

He had thought that it had atrophied during his long spell behind desks of increasing size. But here it was stirring his innermost soul again : *too old*, it was saying, if you are too old, then so is your enemy. Too old to be waiting in the darkness unless there is really something worth waiting for.

"Raffaele !"

So the grey Fiat was worth waiting for—or rather the grey Fiat's occupants, who would be on the passenger list for all to see.

It was as simple as that.

"Coming, Mother !" said the General happily.

At the precise moment that General Raffaele Montuori put his foot on the tarmac at Leonardo da Vinci Airport, Mrs Ada Clark put her foot on the worn piece of carpet beside her bed in her cottage on the edge of Steeple Horley.

It had been the gammon steak at her sister-in-law's, which had been salted enough to preserve it until Judgement Day and which had dried her mouth until she could bear it no longer—it was a wonder to Mrs Clark that Jim looked so well after so many years of bad cooking, of over-salted meat and under-salted vegetables, and altogether too much out of packets and tins.

And that line of well-used sauce bottles told its own tale too, of flavourless food that went begging for a taste of something real, no matter what.

Mrs Clark searched irritably with her toes for her slippers in the darkness, looking out of the window as she did so. It had been clear earlier, but had clouded over now in preparation for the further rain which the BBC weatherman had forecast, so that it was impossible to see where the dark sky began and the roll of the downs ended.

Suddenly the foot stopped searching, thirst was forgotten and Mrs Clark was wide awake, staring breathlessly out of her window.

There it was again, only longer this time !

Decisively she reached across the bed and shook her husband by the shoulder.

"Charlie, wake up!"

Charlie Clark groaned unbelievingly.

Mrs Clark shook the shoulder again. "Charlie, there's someone up at the Old House—someone breaking in! Wake up!"

Charlie rolled on to his back, blinking in the darkness, grappling with the unpalatable sequence of information.

Finally he computed an answer, or at least a delaying question. " 'Ow do you know? You can't see nothing, surely?"

"I can see a light, a flashing light—like a torch going on and off."

"Car lights, that 'ud be."

"That it's not!" Mrs Clark insisted hotly. "You don't get no reflections all that way, and there are those trees in the way. And besides—" she overrode his murmur of disagreement triumphantly "—there aren't no cars on the road, or I'd 'uv heard 'em. I tell you there's someone up at the Old House. Someone as don't dare switch the lights on."

Charlie grumbled under his breath and heaved himself out of bed, reaching for his pullover.

"I reckon it'll be some of those tearaways from the town," Mrs Clark said to him over her shoulder, the outrage quavering in her voice. "A gang of them broke into a big house down Midhurst way last week—it was in the paper. They said there'd been seven robberies round there in the last month."

Charlie felt his way round the bed until he was standing beside his wife. As he bent down to peer out of the little window she pointed quickly.

"There! You see where the flash came—"

"Yes, I see'd 'un." Charlie was not given to believing half he was told or a tenth of what he read, but he always believed his own eyes. And there had been no doubt about that pale light. "It'll be they young buggers right enough—young buggers they are."

Mrs Clark nodded at the vehemence in her husband's voice. It frightened her to think of them loose in the beautiful house she had scrubbed and polished for a lifetime—scrubbed and polished so much that she almost felt it was partly hers and she was part of it.

But also it angered her, and the anger grew steadily, crowding out the fear.

Charlie moved away from her.

"What you goin' to do?" She could hear him fumbling in the darkness. "Don't you put the light on, Charlie!"

"I ain't a fool. I'm lookin' to put me trousers on, an' then I'll get on down to the police house. Let 'em sort it out."

"What!" Mrs Clark rounded on him fiercely, her sense of outrage now dominant. The police house was at Upper Horley, two long miles away, and half of that uphill. "You'll not do that! You do that an' they'll be out an' gone by the time Tom Yates gets 'ere—out and gone."

A terrible vision of destruction rose in her imagination, compounded of all she had heard and read. They weren't like the old-time burglars she had known in her youth, men who knew the value of things and were interested only in what they could sell—they were destroyers now who did unspeakable, senseless, wasteful things. They were the invaders from a world she could not comprehend, the city jungle spilling into the quiet, ordered countryside.

Charlie stared towards her in the blackness, one pyjama-clad leg half stuffed into his trousers.

"You don't mean for me to go up there—?"

"That's just exactly what I do mean. An' I'll go and get Tom Yates meantime."

"Ah—and they'll make mincemeat of me meantime, too, woman. Them's young an' I'm not."

"Then you just take your old gun with you. They won't 'ave the guts to tackle you then, not if you stand up to them."

Charlie had the gravest doubts about the validity of this theory of his wife's—it was not the first time he heard her voice it, that young hooligans had no courage. But he could recall the way the rats had behaved at threshing time, in the days before the combine harvesters when there was still plenty of work to be had on the land : if you left the rats alone they soon made themselves scarce, pests though they were. But if you cornered them—they fought, rats or no, snapping at the stick as it broke their backs.

And that, it seemed to Charlie, was what she was asking him to do to these young buggers—to corner 'em.

"I dunno about that," he began doubtfully.

"Well I do," Mrs Clark snapped back, through the rustle of clothes pulled hurriedly over her head. "And I knows something else too : that I promised Master David that I'd look after the house while he was away—and so I will. So if you won't go up to it, then I shall have to. And you can go and wake up Tom Yates."

Charlie swore under his breath and wrenched at his trousers. Somehow he had been manoeuvred into a corner himself, a corner from which there was no escape except by doing his wife's bidding. He never could fathom how she managed it, but it was a position with which he was all too bitterly familiar.

He was swearing still, steadily and bitterly, as he edged his way up the lane towards the Old House five minutes later.

Of all the nights of this rotten summer, this was the worst for such tom-fool behaviour. It was pitch black and chilly and sopping wet, without a breath of wind. The rain must have stopped an hour or more since and the heavy summer foliage had had time to drip off its surplus moisture, so that everything was quiet enough to hear a mouse stir.

It was this stillness that made him swear now. He had tried two or three steps on the gravel drive, but the scrunch of his iron-shod boots had deafened him. His only chance of a silent approach to the house was by the rough strip of grass beside the high hedgerow on his right.

He thought he knew both the grass and the hedge like the back of his hand; he had walked beside the one and picked blackberries and hazelnuts from the other innumerable times. But now he stumbled awkwardly, his trousers already soaked to the knee, his face lashed every now and then by unseen twigs and sodden leaves.

And yet, perversely, this discomfort aroused in him a determination to do the job his wife had thrust upon him. When he had blundered out of the cottage he had been half decided to save himself the unpleasantness—and very possible danger—of catching the little sods in the act by warning them of his advance with a bit of well-judged noise. But now, as he moved silently from the grass verge to the springy turf of the lawn, the smouldering irritation inside him ignited into a murderous rage.

He'd learn they little buggers!

There was a lot in life that irritated Charlie Clark: big cars and noisy motor-cycles, long hair and short skirts, letters from government ministries asking him questions he didn't want to answer or telling him things he didn't care to know about, and the high price and the low strength of beer. And most of all being bullied by anyone in the world but his wife —he didn't like that much either, but he reckoned it was more or less covered by the promise he'd made to the vicar when they'd gone to the altar together.

But always the enemy had been either intangible or plainly beyond his reach—always except those two times.

It was queer that he could never remember either of those two episodes in any detail. He could really only remember what had happened before and what had happened after.

There had been the quick, clever boy at the village school, who had mocked him once too often. And then there had been blood on Charlie's knuckles afterwards, and no more mocking.

And the second time had been more like tonight, even though he had had a rifle in his hands then, not a cranky old twelve-bore.

Not unlike this very night, though it had been much warmer, as was only to be expected in foreign parts. Almost as dark, anyway, except that they'd been fools that time too, and showed a bit of a light to guide the patrol.

Charlie's eyes picked up the glimmer of the torch inside the Old House the moment he came out from the lane on to the springy turf of the lawn. They'd drawn the curtains now, but it was a powerful bright light, that was sure. Only trouble, it was in a first-floor room—he knew the downstairs pretty well, but wasn't so sure of the lie of the upstairs.

And there'd been more smell the last time, the rich smell of farmyard middens. But then it'd been a farmhouse, longer and lower than this one, huddled into the ground almost. There was talk in the platoon that the farmers kept all their money in boxes under their beds, not trusting the foreign banks—which showed they had some sense, Charlie had thought, seeing as he didn't trust the banks at home either— and also that it was all in gold francs, too. By the time of the raid Charlie had privately searched several farmhouses with those gold francs in mind, but either it was an old wives' tale or someone had been there before him; personally he doubted the story, for all the farms seemed to him poor and rough, without a decent suite of furniture between them, not at all like those he was used to in Sussex, where farmers were usually men of substance and very often gentlemen, too.

Still, they didn't ought to have treated that old farm the way they had, throwing the grenades through the windows and kicking in the doors, all shouting like savages.

Charlie knew he had shouted with the rest, and kicked too, but that had only been because he'd been angry, red, raging angry at being drilled and marched one way, then marched another way, and forced to cower in ditches in terror of bombs and bullets, with never a chance to get his own back—

But it'd never do to kick in the door of the Old House, even the old kitchen door and even if it hadn't been solid seasoned oak, which he reckoned wouldn't reward anyone's boot. And anyway—she'd given him a key, he had it somewhere, thought Charlie confusedly, fumbling for reality in his mind while he searched his jacket with his free hand.

He had to get it right, just like the sergeant had taught him, making him repeat it until he had the meaning by heart: *First you creeps up quiet-like, to take 'em by surprise —then you goes in noisy, to frighten the bollocks off 'em!*

And first he did get it right, with the key hardly scratching the keyhole it entered. But no amount of care could stop the lock clicking unmistakably, or the latch clattering or the hinges creaking—it was as though the whole door had turned against him, bit by bit, damn it.

Charlie clutched the twelve-bore against his chest and stood irresolutely, listening to the absolute silence of the house ahead of him.

It was a silence which confused him far more than it frightened him, until the memory of the flashing light in the upstairs room came back to him—the evidence of his own eyes.

The time had come to be noisy!

With a furious growl and in total darkness Charlie launched himself across the kitchen. The first chair in his way went spinning; he banged into the edge of the table, driving it back so that it overturned another chair. But the table's position orientated him to the passage door. Three more skidding paces, hobnails skittering on the stone floor, brought him against it. Behind him something breakable crashed to the floor.

Four more paces took him down the passage to the foot of the stairs—the last footfall was muffled by the carpet with the eastern writing on it that his wife had told him never to put a boot on. Well, he'd got both boots on it now!

The tingling silence abruptly descended around him again. And yet not a true silence any more, but the moment when the gamekeeper and the poacher sensed each other's presence in the same covert, the moment of held breath and stretched senses.

It had not been like this in the farmhouse, it had been just how the sergeant had wanted it, all noise and terror.

Charlie reached out for the light switch.

"I knows you're up there," he said in a loud voice. "You just come on down quiet, an' don't make no trouble. Police is comin'. So you just come on down."

He clicked the switch.

There was bursting paper-bag noise—that had been the farmhouse noise he'd never been able to recall—and a hornet stung his ear.

Same noise with same result: as the man at the head of the stairs sighted the pistol again, this time on Charlie's heart, Charlie shot him dead.

II

Villari's manners, or more exactly his attitude towards those whom he considered inferior to himself, had not improved, that was evident.

First the fellow had idly fingered the files and envelopes on Boselli's desk, disarranging their mathematical relation to one another. Then he had admired himself in the little round mirror beside the door, patting the golden perfection of his hair and checking his flawless complexion. And then he had sauntered over to the window to gaze without apparent interest over the roofscape towards the Vittorio Emanuele monument. And finally, when he deigned at last to speak, he didn't even bother to turn round to face Boselli.

"Who's this guy Audley then?"

Boselli stared at the well-tailored back with hatred. If looks could kill he felt that his would have materialised into six inches of steel angled slightly upwards just beneath the left shoulder blade.

"Audley?" The anger blurred his voice.

"The guy you're getting steamed up about, yes."

It was typical of Villari to use that aggravating and unfair "you", even though he'd come running across a heat-stricken Rome obediently enough himself. But then Villari had always known when to temper his native insolence with a shrewd instinct for the whims of his superiors. The feet that kicked the Bosellis of the world at every opportunity trod very carefully on the carpets of men like Raffaele Montuori.

"We're not getting steamed up."

"So you're not getting steamed up—fine." Villari moved

19

across the airless room, back to the mirror again. "You're not getting steamed up, but you're here."

That "here" carried the same disparagement as the earlier "you", turning Boselli's own beloved sanctuary, with its rows of battered steel cabinets and its signed portrait of John XXIII into an unspeakable slum.

"And you are here too," replied Boselli acidly. He mopped his brow with the big silk handkerchief his eldest daughter had given him on his last birthday, fancying as he did so that Villari had chosen even those words "steamed up" with deliberate scorn also. For all his North Italian, almost Scandinavian blondness, the younger man showed not a sign of discomfort in the swelter—it was Boselli himself, the Roman, who was already wilting.

But that bitter little thought raised another much more interesting one which momentarily chased away Boselli's private discomforts. There had to be a reason for the General to recall this gilded clothes-horse from his leave beyond the fact that he happened to be here in Rome. If the General had wanted someone from Venice or Messina—or Benghazi —he wouldn't have thought twice about summoning him. So it was Villari and none other that he wanted now. And since Villari combined fluency in the North European languages with the right colouring and an ability to withstand extremes of temperature, cold as well as hot, it must be that Villari was needed to check up on Audley in England.

Which meant that the General was committed to a line of action, or was at least on the very brink of commitment.

And that was a useful thing to know, even though he had not as yet the faintest idea what Audley—

Villari suddenly loomed up directly in front of the desk, cutting off this intriguing line of reflection. He placed his hands precisely on the two corners—the desk creaked alarmingly as it took his weight—and leaned forward until his face was less than fifty centimetres from Boselli's.

"Little man, little man—" Villari's smile was as devoid of good humour as it was of friendship "—I can hear the cogs and wheels whirring in your little brain but you haven't answered my question. And when I ask a question I expect you to provid. an answer."

Boselli sat up stiffly and drew back in the same instant, the faint smell of expensive cologne in his nostrils.

"I haven't been told to answer any questions," he snapped. "I have no authorisation to answer questions."

"Authorisation?" The grin became frozen, but there was a glint of anger in Villari's eyes now. "You have the soul of a clerk, little Boselli. A clerk you were born and a clerk you will die."

He straightened up slowly. "But I don't need to lose my temper, because I have my own way with clerks. It's a very simple way—let me show you how I treat clerks who bandy words with me. You could call it my authorisation—"

He put his hand in the middle of Boselli's desk and with an unhurried movement, before Boselli could even think of stopping him, swept half the surface clear.

A second too late, unavailingly, Boselli jerked forward in an attempt to stop the cascade of paper, grabbing desperately and clumsily, catching nothing. Villari watched him scrabbling on his knees for a moment and then, as though bored with the whole affair, turned away towards the window again.

"You're—mad," Boselli heard himself muttering in anguish as he sorted the jumbled documents. "It'll take me hours—hours—" He cut off the complaint as he realised that it would only give Villari more satisfaction. He had no dignity left to salvage and no hope of lodging any sort of complaint without further humiliating himself (the crafty swine had calculated that exactly). Silence was all that remained to him.

But silence did not seem to worry Villari. He merely

waited until the papers had been shovelled more or less into their correct files, and the files had been piled more or less in their original places, in a mockery of their original neatness. Then he advanced again.

Instinctively Boselli set his hands over the files in a pathetic attempt to protect them.

Villari laughed.

"If you could see yourself!" He shook his head. "Better death than disorder! So we start again, then: who is the man Audley? Speak up, clerk."

Boselli sighed. "What makes you think it is Audley who concerns you?"

Villari looked at him thoughtfully for a moment, as though undecided as to whether or not to assault the files again. Then, to Boselli's unbounded relief, he relaxed; the game of bullying had palled, or more likely the need for information from a beaten opponent commended itself more urgently.

"Well, he seems to concern you, little Boselli. His name is written all over your files—three folders all to himself, and one from the Foreign Ministry. What a busy fellow he must be!" The manicured hand pointed carelessly. "And isn't that a photograph too?"

He tweaked open one of the covers and twisted round the contents.

"Hmm. . . . Not a particularly prepossessing type. In fact he reminds me of a bouncer I met in a club in Hamburg— he thought he was a hard man." Villari sniffed at the memory, then held the photograph up at arm's length for a more critical look. "The suit's okay—you can't beat the English for tailoring—but he's filling it too much . . . a big tough guy running to seed." He nodded to himself. "A bit like that actor of theirs who's always getting into scrapes with the cops. Another tough one."

Boselli smiled inwardly then, permitting himself to be

drawn into the game at last by Villari's crass error of judgement.

"You're looking at the wrong half of the face. Look at the eyes and the forehead."

Villari blanked off the squashed nose and square jaw with his other hand and stared at the photograph again. He shrugged. "So—a hard man with a brain. But don't let him fool you, clerk : if you let him talk you into a dark alley he'll still break you in small pieces and feed you to the birds."

"Then he has kept that side of his character remarkably secret," observed Boselli with prim satisfaction. "He has a doctorate from the University of Cambridge in England—he is Dr David Longsdon Audley."

Villari flicked the photograph carelessly on to the table, so that it skidded across the open file and fell to the floor beside Boselli's foot. Then, with elaborate indifference, he turned away towards the window for the third time.

Only this time Boselli watched him with a tremor of satisfaction. It was little enough recompense for that act of vandalism, but it was a start. And there was more to come.

"He's been a member of Sir Frederick Clinton's self-styled Research Group for quite a few years," he went on with smug innocence. "I'm rather surprised you haven't heard of him."

Villari appeared not to have heard. For several minutes he remained gazing at the distant skyline as though it interested him, deepening Boselli's pleasure appreciably. Of course he would have heard of the old fox Clinton, and possibly even of the Research Group. But the records showed that he had never encountered either of them personally— perhaps another reason why the General was using him now —and he was too puffed up with his own importance to admit it to Boselli. Conceding ignorance would be unthinkable for him, very different as it was from brutally demanding information.

Finally Villari spoke, only to Boselli's chagrin he did so in almost accentless English.

"This Dr Audley—is he a *dottore* doctor or a *professore* doctor?"

Boselli struggled with the mixture of foreign and Italian words for a moment, and before he could quite disentangle the sentence Villari had grabbed the chance of explaining it with deliberately patronising helpfulness.

"An historian," Boselli cut through the explanation irritably. "He is an historian."

"A historian?" The interest trickled out of Villari's tone. "...istory?"

"He writes—he's written a history of the Latin kingdom of Jerusalem. And he's written books on medieval Arab history. He—"

Villari waved his hand. "Okay, okay—he's a real historian too. So what has he done to interest us?"

Boselli looked at him unhappily for a few seconds. Then he shrugged—there was no way of skirting the question and no way of answering it. "I haven't the faintest idea. He—General Montuori, that is—he instructed me to examine our information on him—on Audley, I mean. He didn't tell me why."

"And naturally you hadn't the guts to ask him. That figures."

"When the General wants us to know, he'll tell us. He knows what he's doing."

Villari reached over and hooked the telephone off its cradle with a finger. "And I like to know what I'm doing." He started to dial.

"It's no good ringing the General's secretary," Boselli stood up in alarm. "She promised to let me know the moment the General was free."

"I'm not phoning that old cow—tits to her! I'm phoning the General."

Boselli was appalled and elated at the same time. The General's private number was sacrosanct : this Clothes-horse would be hanged, crucified, flayed and impaled. But it was his—Boselli's—phone on which the unthinkable crime was being perpetrated, rendering him an accessory. At the very least he would be banished to some far-off province still ruled by the Communist Party.

"Hey, General—Armando Villari here, General—"

"Armando—good to see you again, my boy!" The General came beaming from behind his vast desk towards Villari, without even a glance for Boselli.

"General." Villari acknowledged the enthusiasm as though it was nothing less than his right, but with a touch of caution now. "This is a hell of a time to want anyone to work."

"Hah!" The General embraced him, keeping his arm round the broad shoulders as he turned back towards the desk. "I know you, boy, I know you! It's those big German girls of yours—you like the big girls, eh? I know it—don't deny it, boy—I remember them myself when I was your age. Fine breasts and wonderful hips! What hips they had!"

The bitterness rose in Boselli's throat like bile as he watched the hand squeeze the shoulder affectionately. He recognised the whole vomit-making scene for what it was : through some ghastly aberration of judgement the General was identifying himself with the Clothes-horse, or at least his youth, part of which had been spent back in the Duce's day training with the German Special Forces in Bavaria. But that was something which was never mentioned now, an episode very carefully overlooked, if not forgotten—that the General should even indirectly mention it now was an extraordinary personal gaffe.

"I'm too goddamed busy for girls, General," said Villari easily. "You should know that—it's your fault."

The General chuckled. "You don't fool me one bit, boy. You'll stop chasing when you stop breathing, not one moment before. I'm much more worried that you aren't keeping up your skiing. You'll never make the national team now, you know—not a chance of it. And don't say you haven't had the leave for it, either."

Boselli, greatly daring, cleared his throat.

"I have the Audley files here, sir."

The General still didn't look at him. Indeed, neither of them gave the least sign that they had even heard him speak. It was just as though he didn't exist, or that he existed in some other space and time, a shadow man with his armful of shadow documents desperately waiting for someone in a warmer, more real world to notice him. He had a sudden pathetic desire to scream and stamp and throw all his paperwork into the air, and shout rude gutter words.

Instead, he felt himself shrinking, the sweat on his forehead cold in the General's air conditioning, and he knew he would stand there, meek and eager, until his turn at the end of the queue came. There was nothing new in this, it was the very pattern of his existence. Rather must he watch patiently for the arrival of his moment, when the General and Villari came down to earth. They would need him then —they always did in the end.

"Not a chance is dead right," Villari gave a snort. "Nobody who works for you has time for fun—or games. It's getting so a chap can't even slip through Rome for a day without you catching him. And it's the wrong season for trouble—this Audley of yours has no breeding."

"Audley? So you know about him?" The General's arm delivered a final man-to-man slap and then fell away from the shoulders. He turned abruptly and bent a fierce eye on Boselli at last.

Boselli tried for one second to match the eye and the hard

set of the mouth, but his face instantly turned traitor on him with an expression of total obsequiousness.

"I—" Boselli ran out of words after the first squeak, looking helplessly from one man to the other. From Villari he expected—and received—nothing, neither explanation nor even recognition. And from the General—with the General it was always the same : there seemed to lie between them (at least in Boselli's mind) unasked for the knowledge that when he had been a pimply youth toying with the idea of the seminary the General had been a daring Bersaglieri captain, raider of British airfields, and then the leader of the Partisan group which had ambushed Panzergeneral Hofacker in the mountains.

And hot on that memory came the comparison of his wife's sagging body with those of the gorgeous creatures the General always had at heel, despite his age and disabilities.

The General couldn't help it—he rarely even barked at Boselli. The trouble was, he didn't have to.

"I don't know *about* him," said Villari off-handedly. "I know *of* him, of course."

"What do you know of him, boy?" the General snapped.

"Not much, to be honest," Villari gave the General a sidelong glance. "The British don't concern me directly—or do they?"

"Just answer the question," repeated the General with a small cutting edge in his voice now which warmed Boselli. This was more like the real man he knew.

Villari sketched a shrug, unsnubbed, as though the matter was of little importance to him, ignoring or pretending to ignore the danger sign. "He's a university professor, or that's his cover anyway."

"He has been attached to a university, that's true. Go on."

But only partly true, Boselli thought gleefully. The Clothes-horse was already giving himself away.

"Go on," repeated the General.

"Well, he writes history books of some sort—about the Arabs, I seem to remember. Or something like that. And he's one of Sir Frederick—ah—Clinton's group—"

"And what do you know about *that*," the General pounced hard.

Villari grinned at him boyishly. "Frankly, damn all, General. Am I supposed to? I didn't think the British were in my sphere of operations."

"Where did you hear about Audley?"

"Hell, I don't know," Villari was something less sure of himself now, and something less than convincing. "I keep my ear to the ground—I hear all sorts of things."

Mostly bottles opening and bedroom doors closing, thought Boselli. That was the strength of it.

"You've never met Audley, then?"

"No, never." Villari used the certainty of his reply to cover the relief in his voice, without realising that he was thereby admitting that he knew what Audley looked like, Boselli thought with instant contempt. If this were the pride of the German section, then God help them: no wonder they gave him so much time off to ski. He gave himself away every time he opened his handsome mouth.

But the General was obviously not interested in pursuing Villari's incompetence any farther. He retired to the farther side of his desk and sat down heavily.

"Tell him, Boselli," he ordered dispassionately.

Boselli gave a guilty start. "Tell him what, sir? About Dr Audley?"

"The Clinton group first. And don't stand there sweating —sit down." The General waved a hand. "Sit down both of you. And make it brief, Boselli. I haven't all the afternoon."

"Sir—" Boselli faced the General, then Villari. The punitive gleam in Villari's eye drove him back at once to the

General. "The origins of the group go back to the aftermath of the Suez failure——"

"Not its history, man. Tell him what it does!"

"Yes, sir. Well——" Boselli began again nervously "——it doesn't exactly *do* anything. I mean——" Christ! He was getting himself as tangled as Villari had been, and with far less reason. He couldn't ski one metre, or hang expensive suits on himself, or fornicate with foreign women. But this one gift he had.

"It was formed as a passive intelligence group, not an active one," he said firmly, his voice gaining authority with each word. "The various labels it has used have been more for accounting convenience than a guide to its function—it goes under Research and Development at the moment, but its true relation with the conventional intelligence arms is broadly analogous with pure research departments in a university and the applied research departments in major commercial companies."

"What the Americans call a 'Think Tank'," observed the General helpfully, watching Villari.

"Broadly speaking, yes," Boselli nodded. "But there was a considerable spin-off in foreward intelligence."

"They forecasted international trends."

"And trouble spots, sir. And likely reactions. They appear to have done this rather well. The only drawback was that they couldn't do it to order. Clinton just let them follow their inclination, and then passed on what he thought might prove of value to the active departments and the appropriate ministries."

He risked a surreptitious glance at Villari and was gratified to observe that the mask of aristocratic boredom had descended again. If the fool was stupid enough to show his disdain before the General—disdain of a briefing ordered by the General—then so much the better: the General always noticed things like that.

"Yes . . . that about sums it up. Sir Frederick Clinton is an uncommonly astute and persuasive man," the General murmured, the last words half to himself as though he fancied the idea of a private Think Tank at his own finger-tips.

"Quite so, sir," said Boselli quickly, hastily evaluating the note of envy in his master's voice and thoroughly disapprov-ing it. Such a group of intellectual outsiders would tend to devalue his own importance more likely than not. "But there is a disadvantage in his system—a disadvantage and a temptation. And this man Audley exemplifies each of them."

"Indeed?"

"These men—" Boselli martialled his thoughts very care-fully, "—they are difficult to control. There is a—a rogue factor in them. They pursue truth rather than policy."

"I see . . ." The General nodded thoughtfully. "And if the truth gets out, you mean—?"

"Exactly, sir!" It was an addictive pleasure to talk to a man who always grasped the exact meaning of one's words. "This man Audley specialised in the Middle East. And he was good—he was very good. He was too good."

"He was unpopular in some quarters, that's true."

Boselli nodded back. "He became committed to what he saw as the right course. Clinton had to get him out before there was a big scandal." He paused, seeing the pitfall ahead just in time : the General evidently knew all about the Arab-Israeli report, and he disliked being told what he already knew—and what the Clothes-horse did not need to know even if he could grasp its significance.

"And that exposed Clinton to the temptation to use him in a different way—to deal with specific assignments, the sort of awkward thing that would interest him."

The General started to speak and then cocked an eye at Villari, who seemed half-asleep now.

"Would you say that was a temptation, Armando?"

Villari stretched. "Hardly. I rather think—Signor Boselli is making something out of nothing. Clinton uses the fellow as a troubleshooter, that's all. Nothing strange about that, nothing at all."

Boselli watched the General's almost imperceptible bob of agreement with dismay. He had failed to make his point, even though he felt in his bones he was right; it could only be that he had been a shade too quick to attack the Think Tank idea and the General had seen through him. He retired bitterly into his shell.

Villari seemed to sense that the initiative was going begging again. He stirred languidly.

"And just what has this so very terrifying Englishman to do with me, General?"

The hatred inside Boselli was so absolute now that he could feel it as a lump in his chest, choking him. That adjective had been as much an insult directed at him as would have been an actual blow on the face.

"He is here in Rome at this moment," said the General.

"Doing what?"

"Doing nothing—so far." The General paused. "He arrived on the night flight from London early this morning." He paused again. "With his wife, his child and his German *au pair* girl."

"His—?" Villari gave a short, incredulous laugh.

Boselli lifted his eyes to the General's face, the leaden lump of hatred instantly dispersed by his renewed interest.

"His wife, his child and his *au pair*?" Villari repeated the words as though he doubted his ears.

Fool, thought Boselli briefly. Fool not to wait for the additional facts which must lie beneath this one like vipers in a bed of flowers.

"We weren't watching the flight, and he was on the passenger list anyway. It was an ordinary scheduled flight and a routine entry. Purpose of visit—holiday."

Boselli waited patiently for the viper.

"But as luck would have it we did have a man there."

"He was met?" Villari was trying to sound interested.

"Audley? No, he was not met," the General shook his head, "not in the sense you mean, anyway. But there was someone there waiting for him all the same. Someone who didn't want to be seen by him. Someone who followed him when he drove off in his Hertz car."

Someone we know, thought Boselli.

The General looked at him. "George Ruelle—does that name ring any bells with you, Boselli? It's possible the bastard was before your time."

George Ruelle. The curious thing was that the General had used the English form of the given name, *George*.

George Ruelle.

Before his time. But his time here had been almost exactly continuous with the General's—they had both been new boys at the same time, albeit one at the bottom and the other at the top.

And that left one strong possibility at least.

"A partisan, General?"

"Good thinking." The General's smile was heartwarming. "Or should I say 'good guessing'?"

"It was a guess, sir," Boselli admitted.

"But a good one. Yes—Ruelle led a group in the next valley to mine. Group Stalingrad."

Group Stalingrad. Now, that rang a bell, or the faint echo of one—a memory of ancient and better-forgotten beastliness: of war to the knife with the Germans, when no prisoners were taken and no questions asked, and when reprisal brought bestial counter-reprisal.

It had passed the studious young Boselli by, but it had not left him unscarred.

Group Stalingrad. That had been one of the merciless ones—and wasn't there also a tale of British PoWs (or were they American?) who had escaped in the confusion of 1943 only to be cold-heartedly sacrificed—by George Ruelle?

If that was the man he must be quite old by now—and frighteningly young to have been the leader of a partisan group in those far-off, unhappy days . . .

"This Ruelle followed Audley?" Villari's voice cut through the memory.

"We think so. He was there at the airport, waiting in his car. He didn't collect anyone, he went off directly after Audley's car. He doesn't live in Rome and as far as we know he hasn't any business here."

"Where did they go?"

"That's the problem. Our man wasn't in a position to follow them himself. We know where Audley's staying, of course. But for the rest—" The General's shoulders lifted eloquently.

It was pretty slim. In fact it was really far too slim to act on if that was all there was to it, thought Boselli, still watching the General intently. A viper there certainly was; in fact it was patently because of that viper—Ruelle—that the General had become interested in Audley's arrival in the first place, not because of Audley.

He re-ran the General's voice in his head : there had been a tightness about it when it supplied its minimal information about Ruelle, "a group in the valley next to mine. Group Stalingrad." There could very well have been bad blood—if not actual blood—between the two partisan leaders, both young and ruthless, but one a Communist (only a Red would have named his group like that) and the other a blue-blooded army officer. Indeed, the more one thought about it, the more certain it seemed.

But there was precious little in reality to connect Ruelle and Audley beyond the fact that they had left the airport one after another.

"Is Ruelle active?" asked Villari.

Boselli looked at him quickly, annoyed with himself for not asking the same question. The Clothes-horse's mind must be labouring along roughly the same track as his own, but its very slowness had enabled it to see something he had overlooked : tailing people was a young man's game, not an old man's one.

The General considered the question. "If he is, then this is the first we've heard about it," he said slowly. "In fact, if he is then it will be—disturbing."

"Why so?"

Once again there was an uncharacteristic delay before the General answered. "There was a time—it's a long time ago now—but there was a time when George Ruelle was considered to be a coming man, and a very dangerous one, too."

He looked from one to another of them. "That was after the war, when things were . . . very different from now. Tito hadn't shown his hand then, and Albania was Red, and it was touch and go in Greece. Those were the days when the bastard used to visit Moscow two or three times a year." The General smiled suddenly and frostily. "I rather think that if things had gone his way, then he might have been sitting at this desk. And I would have been very dead, that's certain."

The frosty smile faded. "But they didn't go his way. And when Stalin died, that was the end of him. They didn't want to know him any more."

Villari frowned. "But there's still a Stalinist Wing here— I saw Brusati in the Senate as large as life when I went to see my uncle there in the spring—"

"True, boy!" The General nodded. "But Stalinism is one thing and Stalin's crimes are another. There are some things even the hardliners don't want to be reminded of, and that's what George Ruelle does to them : he reminds them of the dirty things they've done. So they've disciplined him and pensioned him off—and told him to keep the hell out of their way and ours. And so he did, until we spotted him again at the airport."

So it was even slimmer still. If Ruelle was a has-been, his presence in the car park at the time of Audley's arrival was probably no more than coincidence.

And as for Audley—*Purpose of visit—holiday* might well be the fact of it. The whole business was simply not worth following up, and the sooner the General was advised to that effect, the better.

"Well—" he began neutrally (the General liked to be shown at least two sides of any problem, no matter how many or how few sides there were), "—in my view—"

"Nothing to it," Villari steamrollered over his words. "If we acted on every chance meeting like this we'd never have time for real work. Ruelle obviously doesn't count any more —the Russians are working towards a detente at the moment, anyway, to take more of the stuffing out of NATO, so they wouldn't use his sort anyway. And—Jesus Christ!—the Englishman's got his family with him! It just adds up to a big zero." He turned at last towards Boselli, but with offensive courtesy. "Of course, Signor Boselli may have other ideas, I've no doubt . . ."

The lump of hatred came back so fiercely, so suddenly, that Boselli felt the sweat start on his forehead in spite of the air conditioning.

"As a matter of fact, I have," he heard himself say in the far-off distance.

There was a ringing silence in the room, as though even the distant hum of the city had been stilled by his words.

But what ideas? he thought wildly.

Only that the bullying swine had pinched his words, just as he had stolen his information, and that he couldn't—*wouldn't*—agree with him under any circumstances!

But he couldn't say that.

The General was looking at him expectantly, though: he had to say something.

And something which made sense!

"It's hot in here," he said involuntarily, wiping his forehead with the silk handkerchief.

"Is that an idea?" asked Villari.

An idea?

"Yes, it is," said Boselli suddenly, plucking his line of argument out of space. "This is always the hottest time of year—and the newspapers said yesterday that this is the hottest end of July we've had since 1794."

"That's right," the General nodded at him, interested curiosity written in his frown. "I read that too."

"He's well off, Audley is," Boselli felt his earlier panic subsiding as he drew on the facts—and that financial fact was always a prime one in any dossier. "At least, he's got enough money of his own not to have to worry too much. So he can afford to pick and choose where he goes on holiday—and when."

"I fail to see—"

But this time it was Villari who was interrupted, and by the General.

"You mean, only a fool would holiday in Rome at this time of year?" The General stared thoughtfully out of the big window at the midday glare. The sound of the city was hushed not only by the heat and the *mezzogiorno*, but because it was half empty: as many of the Romans as could abandon it had already done so, as they always did at this time of year.

"Mad dogs and Englishmen," murmured Villari. "It's a song of theirs."

Boselli ignored him. "Only a fool, or a beginner, or someone who had no other holiday time. And he's none of those. Or someone who had a job to do, a job that wouldn't wait."

"With his family in tow—and his *au pair*?" Villari sneered.

Trust him to remember the *au pair*. But this time Boselli was ready to meet him sneer for sneer. "The best cover in the world. It's still fooling you, anyway."

He sensed Villari's hackles rising—the barnyard rooster insulted by a worm just out of its reach; or would the rooster become so incensed as to injure itself in a bid for vengeance?

But the man's instinct hadn't altogether deserted him—or it held him back for a moment, anyway, and in the next moment the General saved him.

"Go on, Boselli, go on! I'm listening."

He saved Boselli too, by reminding him of the priority. Convincing the General was the important thing, and he could see now that there was one advantage he had which was even greater than his own eloquence: quite simply, the General wanted to be convinced.

It had nothing to do with the Englishman, who was no more than a means to an end. And the end must be the settling of some unfinished score with Ruelle.

"You said that the man Ruelle was dangerous once?"

"Very dangerous."

"And could still be?"

"Men like that don't change."

Boselli nodded. "And I say that this Englishman is dangerous too. Not as Ruelle would have been—he is not an assassin or a thug. But he goes where there is trouble, and where he goes there is more trouble, one way or another."

He had no need of explanation, because the General would not have passed him on unread files. Yet he needed to silence Villari finally.

"You only have to read his dossier to see it—it's spotted with accidental deaths. There was some shopkeeper in '69— just about the time the KGB boss, Panin, was in England. Then there were those two Egyptian officials who were drowned in the Solent—their bodies were never found. And even while he was at the University of—of—" he floundered momentarily, knowing that it was useless to open the file, which was in total disorder now.

"Cumbria," said the General, his eyes bright.

"Cumbria," Boselli nodded, the sweet tightness of success in his brain. "Two more accidents: the professor and the student—that was only a few months ago."

"A trail of accidents," the General murmured. "He does seem to make people . . . accident-prone."

With a great effort Boselli held his tongue and assumed his mask of intelligent humility, knowing how his master's mind worked and his own role in its working. He had seen too many overstated cases fail before this, as much because the General disliked having his mind made up for him as for any internal weakness of their own. His only worry now was that he had used his ingenuity in a decidedly doubtful cause. But he could always plead caution, which was more a virtue than a failing in this work, and to see Villari's holiday spoilt by an unprofitable assignment in Rome would be worth a few harsh words from the General.

And already the Clothes-horse appeared to be most gratifyingly chastened, sitting in silence staring at his elegant hand-made shoes while the General decided his fate.

Boselli had to work doubly hard to maintain his expression as his thoughts diverged from it. It was quite beautiful really: Villari would have to read the Audley files—the gorgeously disarranged Audley files—and then the Ruelle dossier. And after that he would probably have to follow Audley, and Audley's wife and Audley's baby and Audley's *au pair*, through the stifling streets of Rome—or maybe tail Ruelle in some unspeakable suburban housing estate—all to no useful purpose.

It was so beautiful that he felt like singing—Cavaradossi's aria "Vittoria" rose like a hymn of triumph within him.

38

"Very good!" The General looked from one to the other of them. "Boselli has read the files, Armando, and you haven't had the chance yet—if you had I think you might very well have agreed with him." He leant forward towards them with his elbows on the table, the knuckles of his clenched fists coming together with an audible crack. "When two potentially troublesome men like Audley and Ruelle come together then we cannot afford to ignore them. I'm inclined to believe that either the British or the Russians are up to something. With the progress of the Common Market negotiation they are both taking a hard line towards each other at the moment. The Russians don't want the British to sign the Treaty of Rome, and the British know it. And as *we* know, they're both prepared to play dirty to get what they want."

Boselli's jaw dropped in surprise. It wasn't like the General to justify his decisions, least of all with aspects of high policy —and with mention of the Treaty of Rome he was lifting this non-starter into the realms of very high policy indeed.

"In any case," the General went on harshly, "I do not intend them to create a scandal in Italy."

"You mean—we send Audley packing?" There was a sudden hopeful note in Villari's voice. "And there are plenty of ways of shutting up Ruelle—"

"That is exactly what I do *not* mean. You should know better than that, boy! We would simply be swapping men we know for others we might not." The General gave Villari a pitying look and turned towards Boselli. "First I need to know why Audley is here, and why Ruelle is interested in him. And for that—" he paused, and in that moment's pause Boselli saw an awful unthinkable possibility bearing down on him, "I'm putting you both to work."

Villari and Boselli stared at him speechlessly.

"Together," said the General.

III

IT DIDN'T NEED a ruddy genius to guess that some-one had dropped their drawers, or wetted 'em—or even lost the little darlings; not when they'd pulled him out of Dublin at ten minutes' notice and bundled him on the first available flight, and all after they'd just turned down his transfer application flat.

It could be that the rumoured offensive against the Russian industrial espionage *apparat* was on at last; all they needed was an excuse, and the way the Moujiks had been chancing their arm recently, there ought to be one by now.

But Richardson knew enough now not to waste deep thought on infinite possibilities, which could vary from the sublime to the ridiculous. Better to conduct a requiem in his mind for the Guinness, which would be a ruddy sight dearer now, and for little Bernadette, who might worry for a day or two about the sudden disappearance of her passionate Italian boyfriend. She'd probably blame the British, as she always did, and just this once she'd be dead right.

Then he saw the familiar signpost.

It was like the poet said—Chapman's Homer and stout what's-'is-name silent on his peak in Darien: Upper Horley meant Steeple Horley, and Steeple Horley meant David Audley, and David Audley meant something one hundred per cent better than pissing around Dublin pubs on wet evenings.

He hadn't asked the driver because it was bad form as well as agin' the rules to ask. But now he didn't need to pop the question: *it was David*.

David was a shit, and maybe you couldn't trust him much.

And there were times when he was more than a bit of a bore, when he started theorising and moralising and soul-searching.

But David was also nobody's yes-man. He didn't give one damn for the bosses—he had proved that when the crunch came. And—this above all—David always got the really interesting jobs which nobody else dared touch. At least, he always got 'em in the end.

He grinned to himself and stretched for sheer joy—and caught the driver beside him grinning too. So the man had noticed his reaction to the signpost, and understood it and even shared it. And that was interesting in itself, if not a brand new piece of information: it was the people below David who liked him, for his courtesy if for nothing else, while the people alongside and just above him disliked him in what was probably an inverse ratio to how much they needed him.

Good old David! There were inverted chevrons on his coat-of-arms, which was carved over the door of the Old House, but there ought to have been two fingers, raised and improper.

The shock came when they were half-way up the drive to the house, when the rain-caped policeman materialised out of a gap in the hedge to stop the car.

The driver clicked the door lock and wound down the window the regulation half-inch.

"We're expected," he said casually, before the policeman could speak. "Bennett and Captain Richardson."

"Would you please show me your identification, sir?"

"After I've seen your warrant card."

Face immobile, the policeman felt under his cape for the folder and then posted it through the gap. Behind him Richardson could see a civilian and another uniformed man. He caught a glimpse of sergeant's stripes on the arm that was lifted to take back the warrant card and collect their own folders.

They'd got a sergeant on the gate, checking the visitors—a sergeant in the rain, doing the job while his underlings looked on. Christ! It shook him almost as much as the first sight of the high blue helmet : first the discretion—no police cars parked in view anywhere so far—and then this too-high-ranking gate-man, two sure signs of the worst sort of trouble.

The car crawled up the last few yards of drive slowly, and the house was still standing at least. But neither David's new grey Austin nor Faith's white Mini were among the half dozen cars parked in the forecourt. He scanned them for one he could identify, but without success.

"Captain Richardson?"

Another policeman had come out to intercept them. The place was crawling with them.

"Would you like to go straight in, sir?"

Inside the front door there was another policeman. And there was also Oliver St John Latimer.

Richardson and Oliver St John Latimer regarded each other with concealed distaste. Ordinarily he would not have worried Richardson in the least, because although he was considerably senior and brainier, he was also in Richardson's carefully considered opinion a pompous, arse-licking time-server—you couldn't throw a snowball at Sir Frederick Clinton's backside without hitting Fatso in the back of the neck.

But he was also an enemy of David's, and here he was walking about David's house as though he owned it, with an insufferably smug smile on his chops. So it was necessary to tread a little carefully.

"Where's David?" Richardson smiled sweetly. "And where's Faith, come to that? What's up?"

Latimer returned the smile with a smirk. "You'd better ask Brigadier Stocker, old boy."

"I'll do just that when I know where he is—or is that a secret too?"

"Just follow me, old boy."

Fighting off the temptation to kick the fat backside undulating just ahead of him, Richardson followed Latimer to the long, low-beamed sitting room.

"Ah, Peter!" Stocker took the pipe from his mouth and held out his other hand in welcome—a friendly gesture which somehow seemed as insincere as a whore's smile, at least in this setting; Stocker was another one with not so much breeding as brains, or he wouldn't have tried to welcome one man at another man's hearth. Nevertheless, there was a good, tough peasant streak under this ersatz behaviour, which made him a man to reckon with, as well as an acceptable boss.

"Hullo, sir." Richardson decided to keep things as casual as possible, if only to give Oliver St John Latimer less gratification. But the cold question was unavoidable. "Where's David and his missus?"

"As far as I know, they're both in Rome at this moment," replied Stocker, eyeing him unblinkingly.

"Oh..." He couldn't quite keep the relief out of his breath. "... then what are all the bluebottles for? I was beginning to think there'd been a death in the family."

"There's been a death right enough. A burglar was shot dead here last night."

Richardson stared at him, his brain adjusting to the information and amending it. Not a burglar, that was for sure—not a burglar. For whatever Brigadier Thomas Stocker and Master Oliver St John Latimer were interested in, it wasn't dead burglars.

"Who was he?"

"The burglar? We don't know."

43

It hardly needed amplifying : the sort of person who broke into David Audley's home and interested Stocker and Latimer wouldn't be carrying his home address and next-of-kin.

"We're working on it though," continued Stocker. "We don't have his—a—face to go on, but his prints are un-damaged."

"He got it in the face?"

Stocker nodded.

"From whom? Who shot him?"

"David's handyman or gardener, I'm not quite sure which he is."

"Old Charlie?"

"That's right. Charles Clark. It seems he thought some young hooligans had broken in—they seem to have been causing trouble round here—at least that's what his wife said at first. But we haven't been able to get a coherent word out of him so far."

Charlie was big and slow—slow in mind and body. Yet he was also slow to anger, not the sort to shoot first and ask second.

"You're quite sure it was Charlie?"

"Not the least doubt about it. His wife had gone to fetch the village policeman—they found him sitting at the foot of the stairs crying his heart out, with his shotgun across his knees. And on the top of the landing there was this chap with half his head blown off."

He paused, chewing at his pipe, but Richardson waited : there had to be more to it than this.

Stocker shrugged. "Actually we're pretty sure it was pure self-defence. The fellow on the landing shot at Clark—cut his ear with the bullet. There's a bullet-hole in the newel-post, which would have been just by his head. And of course we found the chap's gun at the bottom of the stairs near

Clark. It must have fallen there, because he hadn't touched it. American army Colt, standard issue—one round fired.

Richardson frowned. That figured well enough : Charlie had reacted instinctively, though faster obviously than any-one who knew him would have expected. But that wasn't of any real interest. What mattered was that David's home had been raided by someone quite prepared to shoot it out with anyone who disturbed him, and that ruled out both the pro burglars and the juvenile scum. Steeple Horley was still light years away from New York in that, as in other things.

Also, it wasn't the first time that David had had uninvited visitors, he remembered suddenly : in fact that MVD chappie—Guriev?—had been given the bum's rush from Britain for that, among several other incivilities.

And that, in turn, might account for Stocker's speedy arrival, for the Old House must by now be in the special Red Book the police had of people and places whose well-being was of interest and importance to security. A gunfight and a dead man in a Red Book house would set all the wires humming to Whitehall.

"Do we have any idea what he was after? Had David got something juicy locked up in that safe of his?"

"Dr Audley had no classified material at home," Latimer murmured in a plummy, self-satisfied voice. "He wasn't working on a classified sector."

Richardson flicked a contemptuous look at Latimer. "I seem to remember David has a way of catching sharks other people let through the safety nets," he said coolly. "What does David have to say about it, anyway?"

There was a second's silence—a silence prolonged just one cold fraction longer than natural, so that it sank down through every layer of Richardson's consciousness until it came to rest in the pit of his stomach.

Too many policemen. Too many policemen and not a

word in the morning paper he had read in the plane, or on the radio news. And now Stocker looking solemn and Oliver St John Latimer looking smug enough to make a chap throw up his Aer Lingus breakfast on to the nearest Persian rug. And neither of them looking at each other—both of them looking at him . . .

"Christ—bloody no!" Richardson expelled the words as though they were poison. "I don't believe it. Anyone else— but not David."

And yet it sounded feeble in his own ears : too much like an appeal, too little like an affirmation—too much like those other first moments of disbelief.

Not Guy—not Guy *and* Donald!

Surely not Kim, of all people!

George? You don't mean George Blake?

But Philip is the last man—

David?

He needed time to think.

"Probably not," agreed Stocker. "On the whole I think I would agree with you. But we have to be sure—and at the moment we simply don't know."

"Just what do we know, exactly?"

Stocker nodded towards Latimer.

"Dr Audley has been behaving—" Latimer made a show of pausing judicially, "—eccentrically of late."

"Hell's teeth—he always behaves like that. I've never known him act any other way."

"Eccentric isn't quite *le mot juste*," said Latimer hurriedly. "I didn't wish to sound offensive—I still don't wish to—but to be quite frank he seemed to me to have delusions of infallibility. And when one questioned his conclusions he's been extremely disagreeable, to say the very least."

46

"Oh, come on!" Richardson cut in derisively.

It was the sound of those clichés that suddenly gave him strength : it was precisely that habit of Latimer's of denying that he intended to be offensive just before he delivered his worst insults, and of proclaiming his frankness when he was about to be less than frank, that drove David Audley farthest up the wall.

"There's more to it than that, naturally."

"There'd bloody better be, hadn't there?"

"There is," said Stocker bleakly.

Richardson felt his new-found confidence shrivel up as quickly as it had inflated, like a child's balloon. If Latimer was quite capable of mounting a palace revolution against a rival, the brigadier was too cautious a man either to join such a plot or to be easily taken in by one.

"It could be that David has simply been very foolish, but the fact is that he's gone to Rome with his family, bag and baggage, without any sort of clearance from the department whatsoever. In fact he didn't tell a soul where he was going —except his cleaning woman, Mrs Clark. If it wasn't for her we wouldn't have the faintest idea where he was."

He paused to let the enormity of the security breach sink in. "He slunk off on the cheap night flight. And if we didn't have this dead man on our hands we'd never have checked up on him either, because he's supposed to be on ten days' leave that was due to him."

Foolish! By damn, it was that right enough, thought Richardson bitterly. And more than that : it was almost the classic pattern for a defection, neither too elaborate nor too simple, but just enough to delay precipitate action under normal circumstances.

Only a dead man had blown it sky-high—it hadn't even required any malice of Latimer's to stir things after that. No bloody wonder they were all in a muck sweat.

But he still needed time to think—time, and a lot more information.

"Mrs Clark," he exclaimed suddenly. Almost the classic pattern, but not quite : Mrs Clark was the odd thread in the design. She was a lot more than David's cleaning woman, he knew that : she had been an integral part of the landscape of the Old House for over half a century. As a young girl she had mothered the lonely boy after his real mother's death, had been his confidant in the step-mother era and had naturally graduated to the post of house-keeper when he had come into his kingdom. Indeed, during one long drunken evening on that last assignment in the north David had as good as hinted that it had only been with her approval that he had married Faith. So it was not in the least surprising that she alone knew where he had gone. But if he hadn't intended to come back he would have sworn her to secrecy, and she would have kept the secret over a regiment of bodies.

"What about her?" Stocker watched him narrowly.

"What does she say?"

Stocker grimaced. "Nothing—that's the trouble."

"Nothing? But she told you David's Rome address?"

"She told us that, yes. And she told us that someone shot at her husband. But beyond that she won't say a word. She won't even admit that her husband shot back, even though they found him with the shotgun still in his hands."

"What does Charlie say?"

Stocker stared at him, frowning. "He won't say anything either. Apparently she told him to keep quiet, and that's just what he's done. The police can't get a word out of either of them."

He could well believe the news of Charlie's silence, because Charlie was taciturn by nature as well as obedient to his wife by long-established custom. But Mrs Clark's closed mouth was another matter, and a much more suspicious one too. In an unnaturally garrulous moment her husband had once observed that she talked enough for two, and it was the plain truth: she had a tongue like a teenager's transistor.

"I'd like to have a go at her then," said Richardson. "She doesn't know you, but she does know me and I think I'd stand a better chance with her than most anyone else."

"I'm relieved to hear that you think so," said Stocker, with the ghost of a calculating smile. "Because that, Peter, is one of the chief reasons why you are here."

There was a large man in thorn-proof tweeds talking to another man in a rain-darkened trenchcoat outside the door to the dining room. At second glance Trenchcoat was maybe an inch taller than Tweeds, but Tweeds carried a weight of confidence and authority which gave him extra inches, the boss-man's eternal unfair advantage.

When they turned towards Stocker, however, their faces bore exactly the same guarded expression in which deference and hostility exactly cancelled each other out. Richardson had seen that look before, and understood it only too well. He even felt a twinge of sympathy: on its own this was a nasty little affair, involving firearms—which the British police violently disliked—and a shooting match between civilians—which mortally offended them. But at least it was clear enough what had happened, or so it must have seemed at first glance.

But now they faced the added and appallingly tricky dimension of national security, the cloak under which crimes were not only committed but sometimes allowed to go unpunished. So now these guardians of the peace could feel the solid ground of the law shifting under their feet; at the best they might be required to turn a blind eye, which they hated doing, and at the worst they might be forced to connive at felony—that was what they feared most now.

"Ah—Superintendent!" The clipped tone of Stocker's voice left nobody in doubt as to who was the senior officer present. "This is the—ah—officer from the Ministry I briefed you about—Captain Richardson."

The Superintendent appraised Richardson briefly, then nodded.

"You think you can make Mrs Clark tell her husband to talk to us, Captain?"

Richardson could not help grinning. The difference between them was that the police only wanted old Charlie to admit he'd pulled the trigger, whereas Stocker wanted to know how Audley had taken it into his head to disappear. But obviously both of them were surprised and galled to come up against a pair of old countryfolk who were not overawed by the combined sight of the police and the Ministry of Defence.

David would have enjoyed that!

He shrugged. "It's possible, but I wouldn't bet on it. Just how much have you got so far?"

"Not much." The Superintendent admitted, turning towards his subordinate. "You tell him, John."

"Not much indeed." Trenchcoat grinned back wryly at Richardson, as one journeyman to another. "And most of it comes from the constable here, Yates."

He paused. "Mrs Clark woke him up about half-past one this morning. Said someone had broken in here, they'd seen a torch flashing, and Charlie had gone up—that's Mr Clark —to stop 'em getting away. Yates came on straight up here with Mrs Clark—she wouldn't stay behind. They found Clark sitting at the bottom of the stairs, and this other fella up on the landing. Charlie had stopped *him* right enough."

"But Charlie said something?"

"Aye. Not that it makes much sense. He said—at least Yates thinks he said—"Bloody Germans—shot at me." And then his wife said "Hold your tongue, Charlie. And not a word we've had out of him since."

"Germans?"

"That's what Yates thought he said, but the old man was in quite a state so he may have misheard."

"On the contrary," Richardson shook his head. "I'd guess that was exactly what Charlie said."

"Indeed?" Trenchcoat looked interested. "He was in the war then?"

"He was in the army for about a year—he was invalided out after Dunkirk. From what David's told me I think he had a bad time during the retreat, but it wasn't a subject you could get him to talk about—not that you could ever get him to talk about anything really. Only he certainly had it in for the Germans. . . . And is that all you got out of them?"

"The woman gave us Dr Audley's address without us asking for it—she had it written on a piece of paper. She just said she wanted to talk to this solicitor of hers and she wouldn't talk to us."

A look of irritation passed across the Superintendent's face. Glancing sidelong at Stocker, Richardson was rewarded with a similar expression. So that was the size of it: the shrewd old body had not just simply closed up on them—she had claimed her rights with the speed of an old lag! Small wonder the big shots were vexed as well as suspicious.

It occurred to him suddenly that some of that annoyance had been directed at Trenchcoat as well. That Stocker had not been wholly open with him was no surprise, of course; the detail about the solicitor merely confirmed what could be taken for granted. But obviously no one had thought to warn Trenchcoat. So—

"I was going to tell you about that, Peter," Stocker said. "You can see what it means."

"Yes, I can see how important it is to stop her blabbing to a solicitor," Richardson replied helpfully. He turned back quickly to Trenchcoat before anyone could change the action. "What about the rest of it?"

"You mean the other man?"

"The other man—" Richardson held his gaze to the exclusion of anyone else's warning expression. "—Yes. The other man."

Trenchcoat shrugged. "Apart from the imprint of his shoes in the flowerbed at the back where he jumped out of the window, we haven't got a thing on him. He must have beat it fast after Clark shot his mate, but he didn't leave his calling card anywhere."

So there'd been two of them, and the news—whatever the news was—was out. Two of them, and they hadn't bothered to tell him: his role was simply to soften up Mrs Clark and then return to the joys of Dublin.

"Of course, we haven't asked round the village yet—" Trenchcoat stopped abruptly, as though someone had pressed his switch.

"I think—" Stocker filled the break smoothly "—we'd better find out first whether you can open up Mrs Clark before we tie up the loose ends for you, Peter."

"Right." Richardson spread an innocent glance around him; Stocker was playing it deadpan still, although Trenchcoat could not quite conceal his confusion any more than the Superintendent bothered to hide a suggestion of contempt at this turn of events. It was Oliver St John Latimer's expression of suspicion which decided him on his course of action: the man was a slob, but not a foolish slob to be taken in by false innocence. The moment he got Stocker alone he would make one thing clear: that Richardson was a disciple of Audley's, and therefore not to be trusted. And Stocker would believe him—now.

So there was nothing more to be gained by being a good little boy!

"Right," he repeated. "So what sort of deal do I make with her?"

"Deal?" The Superintendent frowned. "What do you mean—deal?"

"Just that. She's not going to talk to me because I've got a kind face—she'll talk because when I offer her a bargain she'll know she can trust me to keep my side of it. And don't tell me you haven't tried that already."

"What sort of deal have you in mind, Captain Richardson?" said the Superintendent cautiously.

"There's only one that'd do: let old Charlie off the hook."

"We'll promise to go easy on him."

"Easy on him? Christ—the poor old bastard hasn't committed a crime!"

"He's killed a man, Captain."

"In self-defence—and if he hadn't he'd be dead."

"It doesn't alter the case." The Superintendent shook his head. "But we'll go in and bat for him—that's the most I can do."

"Well, it's no damn good. It's the court appearance that'd break Charlie. But you aren't offering him anything he hasn't got already—there isn't a judge or a jury on God's earth that'll touch him, and she knows that even if you don't. But the damage'll be done all the same—she knows that too."

"Then what exactly do you suggest?"

"We fake it up. The man fell down stairs and blew his own head off. I believe it's called 'misadventure'."

The Superintendent shook his head. "It can't be done, Captain."

"It's been done before."

"Not by us, it hasn't." The Superintendent looked hard at Stocker. "And we aren't starting now, that's final."

And that, also, was a mistake, thought Richardson happily: it was exactly the sort of challenge Stocker could not afford to overlook.

"Final?" Stocker's tone was deceptively gentle. "I wouldn't quite say that, Superintendent. It seems to me that we might manage something along those lines, you know."

"Indeed, sir?" The Superintendent said heavily. "Well, I'm afraid I can't agree with you there. You're asking me to break the law."

"To bend it, certainly. But not to pervert it. After all, since you've already agreed to—ah—bat for Clark the case would be little more than a formality, wouldn't it?"

"The law is the law, sir," the Superintendent intoned the ancient lie obstinately.

"I'm well aware of the law."

The danger signal was lost on the Superintendent. "Of course, you can promise the woman anything you like, sir. As far as I'm concerned you're free to do whatever suits you."

Richardson opened his mouth to protest—the double-crossing sod!—and then closed it instantly as he saw the light in Stocker's eye. The Superintendent had made his final error.

"You are exactly right there," said Stocker icily. "I can promise her anything I like and I am free to do what suits me—you are exactly right."

The Brigadier had come to the Department from a missile command, but before that he had been an artilleryman: the words were like ranging shots bracketing the Superintendent's position.

On target!

"And it suits me now to remind you that I am in charge here—"

Shoot!

"—and you are absolutely free to telephone your Chief Constable if you have any doubts about that."

The two men stared across the hall at each other.

"You make yourself very clear, sir."

Target destroyed! No doubt about that, anyway: it was there in the droop of the tweed shoulders and the immobile facial muscles.

"It's better that we understand each other."

The Superintendent nodded slowly. "I take it you will be putting this in writing—that you have assumed responsibility?"

"Naturally," Stocker nodded back equally slowly. Then he turned towards Richardson. "You can go ahead and make your deal, Peter."

"Right—" In the instant before Richardson's gaze shifted from the Superintendent to the Brigadier he glimpsed a fleeting change of expression, a change so brief that it should have passed unnoticed "—sir."

It was a look of profound satisfaction though, not defeat. . . .

So that was the way of it after all: that target had been a false one, no more than an incitement of Stocker to take all the responsibility, and to take it over a formal protest and in black and white. . . . Except for that momentary twitch of triumph it had been neatly done, too.

Not that it would worry the Brigadier, who was as accustomed to carrying the can as he was to breathing. It was simply a reminder that for him the Clarks and their victim were of very little significance.

What mattered was David Audley.

IV

"Hullo, Clarkie!"

"Mr Richardson!" Surprise, relief and then suspicion chased each other across Mrs Clark's face in quick succession. "Well I never!"

"Never what, Clarkie?" It pained him to see that shrewd, good-natured face so changed : the good nature had been driven out by fatigue, the pink cheeks were pale and the shrewdness had been sharpened into wariness. Standing up to the Superintendent and the Brigadier had not taken the stuffing out of her, but it had pushed her hard nevertheless.

"I never expected to see you, Mr Richardson, sir. Not just now."

"Never expected to be here, and that's a fact." He turned to the uniformed policeman who stood like a monstrous statue beside the grandfather clock, out of place and out of proportion among the shining brass and polished oak of the dining room. "Very good, officer—you can leave us."

The policeman stared at him doubtfully.

"Out!" commanded Richardson, irritation suddenly welling up inside him. "Go on with you!"

But as the door closed behind the policeman he pinned down the spasm of anger for what it was and took warning from it : either way this thing was hateful, but it was not that which was fraying his nerves. It was that caution and instinct were pulling him in opposite directions.

Something of this must have shown on his face, because there was regret in Mrs Clark's voice when she spoke.

"I'm sorry, sir, but I still can't say anything to you. Not unless Sir Laurie Deacon says I can."

"Sir Laurie Deacon?"

"That's right, sir—Sir Laurie Deacon."

Laurie Deacon! Richardson felt laughter—God! It was almost hysteria—rising up where anger had been seconds earlier. No wonder they were wetting their pants out there in the hall! No wonder Stocker had dragged him all the way from Dublin, expense no object, and was quite prepared to twist the law into knots—and no wonder the Superintendent was only too happy to crawl away into a place of safety!

Deacon—Sir Laurie Deacon, baronet—was not only a barrister of vast experience and a Tory MP of even vaster influence and notorious independence of mind, but also a veteran campaigner on behalf of underdogs all the way from Crichel Down to Cublington.

So they'd leaned on this poor old countrywoman without a penny in her purse, and if she'd summoned up the Archangel Gabriel and all the hosts of Heaven she couldn't have frightened 'em more with the name she'd given 'em back.

"Clarkie—how on earth do you come to know Sir Laurie Deacon?" He couldn't keep the admiration out of his voice and he didn't try to. "You really do know him?"

"I do, sir. But I'm not saying more than that."

Richardson stared at her for a moment, then rose from his chair and began carefully and ostentatiously to examine the room. First the flower vases, then under the table and chairs, behind the ornaments, in the fireplace. When Mrs Clark stared at him in surprise he put a finger to his lips and continued the search wordlessly until he was satisfied that there was nothing to be found. Then he listened silently at the door, bending even to peer through the keyhole, and as a final obvious precaution craned his neck quickly through the open window.

"I think we're clear," he murmured conspiratorially, pulling up one of the chairs from under the table until it was directly opposite where she was sitting.

"Clarkie, you're bloody marvellous. . . . Now, you don't need to say anything if you don't want to. You've got 'em all beaten anyway, I tell you—but I just want you to listen to what I've got to say, and listen carefully."

She watched him intently.

"You're worried about Charlie, aren't you? About what it'd do to him—all the police and the newspapermen and so on, never mind what might be said in court. I know that and I understand it."

Mrs Clark's lower lip trembled and Richardson reached out and patted her knee.

"Well, don't you worry about that, Clarkie. I can fix that —I give you my word I can fix that, even without calling up Sir Laurie Deacon. He's your second line—I'm your front line. Because I can fix it so Charlie never has to go to court. If you'll trust me—and if you'll both promise never to talk about what happened last night—then they're willing to tell everyone it was an accident. Charlie needn't come into it at all. You just heard the shot and went and called Constable —what's his name—Yates."

She was frowning at him now, but frowning in evident disbelief. But why should she disbelieve him?

"Don't you believe me, Clarkie?"

That frown had deepened at the mention of Yates, the Constable—the village copper. Richardson tried to project himself into her mind to pinpoint the line in it where trust ended and distrust began.

The village copper . . . could it be as simple as that? Could it be that in a world of fallen idols she still believed that some still stood, neither to be bribed nor bullied? That the law really was the law, though the heavens fell?

Or was it even more simply that his word was not enough and she needed to know why he was able to make a mockery of law and truth so easily?

"I'll tell you why you've got to believe me, Clarkie. You

see this—business—is a lot more complicated than it seems. It doesn't involve just you and Charlie. It involves Dr Audley."

"I don't see as how it can do that, sir."

So David and Charlie ranked equally, each to be protected from outrage, the need to speak up for the one cancelling the need to keep silent for the other.

"Because he isn't here?" The wrong word now would spoil everything.

She nodded cautiously. She was still with him.

"That's just it, Clarkie. He really ought to be here." This, he judged, had to be the moment: the risk had to be taken now whether he liked it or not. "You know that some of the work Dr Audley does is very important—" if she didn't know it she would be pleased nevertheless at the importance of her Mr David "—and very secret. So secret that I'm not allowed to tell you about it."

He paused. "But when you do that sort of work, Clarkie— when you do it as well as he does—you make enemies. Like people who don't agree with you, or even people who want your job. You know the sort of people." He nodded towards the closed door. "Like the fat one out there—he's been waiting a long time for David—for Dr Audley—to make a mistake—"

"But he's only gone off on holiday, Mr Richardson, sir," Mrs Clark protested. "They haven't been away together, not for a proper holiday anyway, since little Charlotte was born. And they both needed a holiday, 'specially Mr David. He's been like a bear with a sore head just recently, he has."

Richardson's heart sank: in her own innocence she was only confirming Oliver St John Latimer.

"And they'd planned this for a long time, had they?"

"Lord—no, sir! Mr David only decided just a few days ago. And he was that excited—he hadn't been like that since

59

the baby came, sir—he had us running to get everything ready. He was like a boy with a new bicycle, sir!"

"Excited?" Richardson grabbed at the word like an exhausted swimmer reaching for a lifebelt. "You mean *happy*?"

"Happy as a sandboy, sir—and so was Mrs Audley to see him like it. He'd been that grumpy with us both, and then suddenly he was laughing and joking—"

"Because of the holiday?"

"Well, I suppose so, sir. But it was the night of the dinner-party he first brightened up."

"The dinner-party," Richardson grinned at her. He mustn't spoil it now, letting elation outrun discretion—there was much more to come still if he played his cards in the right order. "You mean it was one of your apple pies that put him in a good mood?"

The dinner party. . . . He mustn't probe too quickly into that, or too obviously. She was staring at him now as though she sensed the lightening of his mood, but the slackening of tension was bringing her closer to tears.

He leaned forward and patted her knee again. "It's okay, Clarkie—I really am on your side—on your side and on Charlie's and on David's. And between us I reckon we've got 'em where we want 'em—the other side."

She drew a long breath. "You mean you can do that— what you said you could—for him?"

"I can and I will. But they couldn't do anything to him anyway, you know—not when it was self-defence and he'd got Laurie Deacon speaking up for him." He smiled. "You never really had anything to worry about."

She shook her head. "You don't know, sir. Charlie's quiet and he seems slow-like, but he's got a terrible temper when he's roused. When we were children he near killed another boy once—he'd been teasing Charlie, you see. And there was that business during the war."

"What business was that? He's never talked about it."

"He wouldn't, no. But it's still there in his mind after all this time, I know, because he has nightmares about it. Not often, he doesn't, now. But he used to have them regular as clockwork."

"About the war?"

"About this farmhouse in France, sir." She stared at him doubtfully, then at the edge of the table. "I never told anyone about it before exactly, not even Mr David. . . . But there was this farmhouse. . . . Charlie hadn't done any fighting, because he was in the pioneers and they were retreating. And they were bombed a lot by those aeroplanes that made a screaming noise—"

"Dive-bombers."

"He didn't call them that—Stinkers he called them."

"Stukas."

"That's it, sir. All the way back until they were near Dunkirk. And the Germans were right behind them then, almost mixed up with them, you might say. And they sent Charlie and some other soldiers to find out if they was in this farmhouse. At night it was—that was really why it was. They couldn't really see what they were doing, you see—"

She was staring at the table edge as if it fascinated her.

"And there was Germans in it. One of them shot at Charlie on the stairway, and Charlie killed him. And then he went up and there was another, and he killed him too. And then he heard this door open, and he went at it with his bayonet, sir—it was dark, and everyone was shouting and shootin'—"

She raised her eyes to his at last. "It was the farmer's wife, sir. But he couldn't *see*, that was the trouble—it was so dark. And when she screamed out, then the farmer came for him, tryin' to stop him I suppose, and he—he—he didn't know—"

She was pleading with him now.

"It's all right, Clarkie. Of course he couldn't know. No

one could have known—it could have happened to anyone. He shouldn't blame himself."

"That's just it, sir. He doesn't even remember it, or he doesn't seem to remember it clearly, like it was mixed up with the nightmares in his mind."

"But he's told you about it."

"No, sir. That was what the army doctor told me in the hospital when he came back, when he wasn't himself like. He'd got it all written down, the doctor had. That's why—" She stopped, staring at him.

That's why.

Richardson stared back, seeing at last, fully and clearly, right through the pathetic tangle.

He could see her fear now, the reason that had shut her mouth: taken by itself, what Charlie had done was no more than pure self-defence, a reflex action. But if this old horror had been resurrected—the big, simple soldier, more likely wilder with fright than with anger, slaughtering a couple of innocent civilians in the dark and by accident, and then cracking up when he'd found out what he'd done—!

He ought to have realised that Clarkie's fear was a practical one, not an emotional response: she might guess what it would do to old Charlie to have that night raked up in court, that memory he'd locked away self-defensively in his subconscious mind. But what she feared was the doctor's record, the dusty proof not only of Charlie's mental instability but also that once before he had killed first and questioned afterwards.

"And it was my fault, Mr Richardson, sir—I forgot clean about it when I saw the light up here. I made him come, he didn't want to."

So it wasn't for David's sake, to cover his disappearance, that she had kept quiet, that at least was certain; David had simply become the victim of her concern for Charlie.

But David was no defector, that was certain too: the

traitor who came to the end of his tether and was forced to abandon his home and his fortune and his country would never have made his getaway happy as a sandboy, excited as a boy with a new bicycle!

He nodded reassuringly at her. "Don't you fret, Clarkie—it's going to be all right, I promise you. I'll see that Charlie's in the clear, don't you worry."

But equally David would not have swanned off so happily without any by-your-leave—not when he'd been acting the way he had—unless he'd been up to something, that too had to be faced.

David was no defector, certainly. But unlike old Charlie, David was still in trouble.

"But first I'd like to know a bit more about that dinner of yours, Clarkie," said Richardson.

V

BOSELLI WAS A long way out of line and he knew it; it was this knowledge rather than the first heat of the day which now raised the prickle of perspiration on his back.

He had never stepped out of line like this before, at least not so dangerously. But this, he admitted candidly to himself, was partly because his work rarely exposed him to such temptations, Indeed, it had been one of his little tasks to watch for signs of such curiosity in others—what the General described as the itch to know a little too much for their own good—and he had become adept at spotting them. Only now he was beginning for the first time to sympathise with the deviationists.

He looked up and down the narrow street suspiciously. The prospect of the General's discovery that he was being surreptitiously investigated by one of his own staff didn't really bear thinking about; it made him shiver at the same time as he perspired, which in turn made him remember inconsequentially that his wife had said only yesterday that she had gone "all hot and cold" after nearly being run over by some foreign driver who'd tried to change his mind in the Via Labicana. He'd been on the point of telling her that such a contradictory physical condition was unlikely, and here he was experiencing it himself.

He paused at a street fountain and drank greedily from it. It seemed to have a bitter flavour, but he knew that it was not the water, only the taste already in his mouth.

He splashed his face and wiped it with his silk handkerchief, glancing again up and down the street, It was the General's fault, anyway, even if that was one excuse he would never dare to advance openly. The Ruelle File started—or appeared to start—with impossible abruptness in 1944, as though George Ruelle had sprung from the ground full-grown into the middle management ranks of the newly-respectable Italian Communist Party. From nowhere usually meant from Moscow, but that clearly didn't apply in Ruelle's case; he had been fighting in the south in '43, if not earlier, and his first Moscow trip had not been until '46—there was no mystery about those dates. Indeed, there wasn't even any mystery as to just where that missing pre-1944 section of the dossier was: it was reposing safely in the General's own safe —no betting man, Boselli would happily have bet his last *lire* on that, at hundred to one odds.

Under cover of folding the handkerchief Boselli took a final look at the street. Nothing, as far as he could see, had changed and no one was watching him. Which left him with the reassuring but galling probability that there was no one on his tail and that the General had given him this task because he was the least likely of all men to scratch that dangerous itch.

Half a dozen hurried steps carried him across the pavement and into the alleyway—well, for once the great General hadn't been as clever as he thought he'd been.

Frugoni's apartment—it was a ridiculous exaggeration to call two crummy little rooms an apartment—was predictably jammed under the eaves, without any access to the roof, a rathole fit for a rat.

And that was good, thought Boselli as he knocked sharply on the scarred door: the worse off Frugoni was (and with any luck he would have gone considerably farther downhill since he had last come round bumming for a handout), the cheaper his tongue would be to loosen. There ought to be some juicy expenses in this work, but Frugoni's name could

65

never be listed in the accounting so there was no question of generosity, real or fabricated, in his case.

"Who is it?"

That was the voice, the hoarse whine rather.

"Boselli—Pietro Boselli."

"Who? Pietro who?" The whine was suspicious, as though its owner was accustomed to bad news knocking at his door. "I don't know any Pietro."

"Pietro Boselli—General Montuori's personal assistant." Boselli paused to let the names sink into the man's befuddled mind. "I've got something for you, Signor Frugoni."

"Something for me?"

"That's right. Open up."

There was a rattle as Frugoni feverishly attempted to open his own door, only to discover that he had bolted it top and bottom as well as securing it with what sounded like an old-fashioned padlock. It took him a full two minutes of clumsy grappling with the lock and alcoholic puffing and blowing with the bolts to relax its defences. And even then it caught on the uneven floor and shuddered so violently that it was a toss-up whether it wouldn't fall to pieces before it was finally opened.

Frugoni peered at him uneasily in the greenish light from the unwashed landing window.

"You remember me, Signor Frugoni," said Boselli patiently. "We last met when you—ah—consulted the General two or three years ago. About your pension."

"My pension?" Frugoni looked at him stupidly.

"Your war wound, I believe—or a war disability of some sort," Boselli prompted him with helpful vagueness. "The General didn't tell me the exact details, but I gathered that you and he were old comrades. Once comrades, always comrades—that's what he said."

Frugoni blinked and screwed up his face with the unexpected mental effort needed to resolve the enormous gap between what he must remember had actually happened when he tried to touch the General for a sucker's handout, and the rose-tinted pack of lies he had just heard.

In fact no one knew the extent of that gap better than Boselli himself. It had devolved on him to check up on the man's tear-jerking tale of a veteran fallen on unmerited hard times, and he had very soon found the General's suspicions to be well-founded: Frugoni had fallen not so much on hard times as through the skylight of the restaurant he had been robbing—his "war wound" had been the compound fracture of the leg and the mild concussion which had resulted from this descent.

Central criminal records had also revealed that in addition to being an inveterate and unsuccessful petty thief, Frugoni was a quarrelsome boozer who had abandoned his wife and children—it had been that last detail, rather than the man's actual misdemeanours, which had finally directed the General's charity—

"Put the woman on my list then, Boselli—she's probably better off without him anyway."

"What about the man, sir?"

"Leave him to me. It'll be a pleasure to kick his backside again after all these years. . . ."

"My wound—of course!" Frugoni twitched into full consciousness. "You must pardon me, Signor Boselli—naturally I remember you—but my health, you understand. . . ." He heaved a gallant sigh ". . . at my age things are hard."

Boselli nodded sympathetically.

"Not that I am grumbling, you understand," Frugoni added hastily, uncertain of the most profitable role open to him until he could establish just how much Boselli knew. "But let us not speak of such things. You said—I believe you said—?"

"That I have something for you. That is correct. But

something in turn for something, Signor Frugoni. Perhaps I might step inside for a moment, yes?"

Frugoni regarded him in complete bewilderment; the possibility that he possessed something—anything—which was likely to be saleable, but of which he was totally unaware, seemed to have knocked away what little balance he could muster so early in the day.

"I—but of course, Signor Boselli—"

The moment he entered the attic room it was Boselli in his turn who was knocked off balance, however. The smell on the dingy landing had been unpleasant enough, combined as it was of all the different aromas of cooking and concentrated humanity which had risen up the stairway from the warrens below. But in Frugoni's room this smell graduated to the rank of stench, in which stale wine and the sweet-sour mustiness of old unwashed linen united into a miasma.

Boselli dragged out his damp silk handkerchief and held it across the lower part of his face, fighting his sickness.

"Signor Boselli—?" Frugoni was looking at him solicitously, oblivious of the foulness.

"A moment's giddiness—no, please do not bother—" Frugoni was removing some unmentionable garments from a rickety-looking chair "—I'd prefer to stand, if you don't mind. It will pass."

"A cup of—" Frugoni looked uneasily towards what must be his kitchen "—coffee?"

"No. . . . thank you." The thought of consuming anything—of even touching anything—coming from these rooms made his stomach turn.

"How can I serve you, then?"

Boselli took a firm grip of his senses. It was always better to offer types like this something in exchange for something if one was not relying on good old-fashioned blackmail. He would have preferred the latter method, and he had no doubt that with very little digging he could have uncovered the right lever. But digging took time, which he didn't have—and digging would also involve exposing his actions to others, which multiplied the danger of the General coming to hear of it.

But if unsolicited charity would have roused Frugoni's suspicions, or at least his curiosity, the chance of doing some sort of deal would arouse his trading instinct, and that must be squashed quickly.

"It is nothing of great importance—nothing you will find in the least taxing, my dear Frugoni," he began heartily. "You are simply one among a number of veterans I am consulting for your wartime recollections, you see—for a work of history a colleague of mine is undertaking."

Frugoni's expression sagged with disappointment.

"It will be a scholarly work—a work of reference primarily, so I fear there will be little profit in it for anyone—" Boselli nodded regretfully "—but remembering that you had served with the General in the mountains I knew I could rely on your strong sense of patriotism—" Frugoni looked as if he was about to burst into tears; it was time to dust the pill with a trace of sugar "—and naturally your name would be mentioned in the acknowledgements in addition to the modest honorarium we are making to some contributors."

"Honorari—?" Frugoni abandoned the attempt.

"Payment," said Boselli briskly. "Small, of course. More a gesture than a payment. But in deserving cases like yourself we do the best we can . . . if the information supplied is of use, of course."

"Of use?"

"Of interest. I'm sure you saw a great deal of action when you were in the mountains immediately after the Armistice of 1943."

"When we threw in the sponge, you mean?" Frugoni gave a short, bitter laugh. "Jesus Christ! You can say that again—

more than I wanted to, that's how much action I saw. But I wasn't in the mountains, Signor Boselli, not at first, anyway."

"Indeed?" Boselli wasn't interested in anything Frugoni had done before he reached the mountains, but it wouldn't do to seem too eager to reveal that fact.

"No—we were in billets just outside Salerno—good billets, too. Then the bloody Germans turfed us out—turfed us all out, and disarmed us too. Shot two of the officers right in front of our billet when they wouldn't play ball, they did— they knew what was in the wind right enough, the Germans did. What they called *Panzergrenadiers*—trigger-happy sods, they were. We reckoned afterwards that someone had told 'em the Yanks and the English were going to land there— which they did, of course. . . ."

"But you stayed and fought?"

"Without our guns?" Frugoni started to laugh again, and then stopped as though he had remembered the more heroic role he had to sustain now. "No—'cause we *wanted* to, but without our guns, see, an' with the place crawling with German tanks—well, this mate of mine and me thought we'd have more chance up Naples way—"

More chance of getting home, more likely. In a word, Frugoni had deserted at the first opportunity.

"More chance of resisting the enemy?"

"That's right, sir. But when we got to Naples things were real bad there, I can tell you—they'd been fighting the Germans in the streets there, the people had. Even the little kids —they're bloodthirsty—and everywhere they'd blocked the streets with trams and lorries so the Germans were shooting everyone on sight, practically." He shook his head unbelievingly at the memory. "The main roads were jammed with supply columns heading south—there was no chance of gettin' through 'em—gettin' through to join up with some proper unit, I mean."

Frugoni had jumped out of the frying pan into a very

hot fire: he had escaped formal captivity with his regiment only to find himself in the midst of a popular insurrection. Even Boselli could remember the tales of Neapolitan carnage which percolated northwards as the enraged inhabitants of that dangerous city had turned on the Germans with medieval fury . . . tales of stranded tank crews parboiled and houses full of women and children put to the torch. It had been from such horrors that men like George Ruelle had risen.

"So you headed for the hills?"

"It was the only thing to do, seein' as how things were, you see—"

"And met the General."

"Yes." For one second Frugoni failed to keep the bitterness out of his voice. "That was a bit of—luck—for us, of course."

Of course! Twice the wretched man had fled from his duty, though each time in circumstances which would have daunted better men and for which Boselli could not in his heart wholly blame him. And all in order to fall into the clutches of the one man who would make very sure that he had no third opportunity of escaping! Fate had surely played a cat and mouse game with Private Frugoni.

"Number One on the Breda, I was for the General, Signor Boselli, sir." All the whine and pretence had gone from the voice now; this at least was genuine. "An' that's a rotten bad gun, too—the Breda 30—a proper swine to clean, with that oil pump in it. An' it's got no carrying handle, either: I'd like to make the silly fucker that designed it carry it up the mountainsides that I had to, carrying it like a bleedin' baby—"

"That would be a responsible job, I'm sure," Boselli cut through the old soldier's complaint. "The General must have trusted you, then."

"The General. . . ." The memory half strangled the words

and then re-injected the old mendacious note. "A major, 'e was then, major in the Bersaglieri—'e made us jump, Christ 'e did, an' no mistake. We blocked the road from Campobasso for nearly a week—took a regiment of their Alpine troops, what they call Jaegers, to shift us. An' they wouldn't have done it then if the bastard hadn't let us down."

It was odd, but under the hate which lay like a half-hidden substratum beneath the pretence of soldierly pride there was a thin vein of genuine admiration. It was probably true that—

The bastard?

That was the word which had been lodged in his mind like a tiny thorn under the skin : the General had used it yesterday—had used it twice in one short space of time. And yet under ordinary circumstances his language was always notably free of such words—beyond an occasional "for the love of God" in moments of exceptional stress the General's vocabulary was as disciplined as a priest's.

Boselli's own mind had been fully extended at the time, yet those two "bastards" had pricked nevertheless; and more, there had been something curious about the sound of them— the emphasis had been too evenly distributed, just as it had been in Frugoni's tone : too even and lacking in vehemence. . . .

And then he had it : it had quite simply been a name and not an epithet—not "the bastard" but more precisely "The Bastard" !

He examined his fingernails. "You mean Ruelle?" he said casually.

"Ah—I guess you've heard a thing or two about The Bastard, eh?" Frugoni leered at him. "You'll 'ave to be careful puttin' 'im in your book alongside of the General, you will—'e won't like that, I can tell you, not at all. Come to that, The Bastard won't neither, if the swine's still around. There wasn't no love lost between them two, there wasn't."

"Yes, so I've heard," murmured Boselli, stifling the rising sense of excitement he felt at so easily getting to the one question he had feared to ask directly.

"I could tell you a thing or two about them," Frugoni confided maliciously. "I bet you ain't 'eard the 'alf of it, not the 'alf of it!"

"I expect I've heard it all before, my dear fellow," said Boselli, controlling the level of disinterest in his voice with scientific exactness. "But do go on all the same."

It was going to be a good day after all.

VI

COMING OUT OF the midday sunlight into the cafe's shadow, for a moment he could see very little. Then, as he peered round the supporting trellis-work of the vine-covered roof, his gaze was directed by the admiring eyes of two young girls towards the corner in which Armando Villari had arranged himself.

Not that their admiration was going to do them any good. They weren't in the Clothes-horse's income group for one thing, and the Clothes-horse was on duty anyway (although that was probably the least important consideration). But above all the swine was far too busy admiring his own profile in the mirror on his left—Boselli didn't know which offended his sense of decency the more, the girls' sickening bitch-on-heat look or Villari's narcissism. Almost it made him want to quit the job cold, except that the General's parting words and his own recent discoveries made the situation painfully clear : he had to work with Villari or risk not working at all, and for a man with hungry relatives and no cushion of private savings that was no choice.

But at least that certainty firmed his own meagre reserve of courage. At the time of the General's pronouncement he had been ready to accept the assignment as a test for them both—a proof that they could sink their personal antipathies in the state's service. He still admired his boss enough to hope that that had played a part in the whole design, but he no longer believed that it played the only part. Because the General was a fair man he would accept honest failure—but because of his personal involvement he would be in no mood to put up with tantrums from either of them.

Villari gave no indication that he had noticed him except to put on the dark glasses which had lain beside his glass, a simple action which he contrived somehow to render affected.

So it was going to be unpleasant. . . .

Boselli smiled politely. "I do not think I am late, but I am sorry if you have been kept waiting. Is anything happening yet?"

The dark circles considered him briefly. "If anything was happening I would not be here. And then you would have been late."

So it was going to be difficult too, thought Boselli. But he had expected nothing less ever since the fellow had walked out of the meeting without so much as one word to him. And since then he had obviously not bothered to work out any of the implications of the situation.

He sighed as he sat down. The difficulty was all the less bearable for being unnecessary, because the simplest of those implications was that he, Boselli, would be less afraid of offending Villari than of risking General Montuori's anger, but Villari was too stupid to understand that fact.

He stared directly into the dark glasses. "Signor Villari, I will be plain with you—" an eyebrow lifted above one of the gold frames "—I have been ordered to work with you and that is what I must do if it is at all possible. I do not care for you and you do not care for me—"

"I don't really think that much about you either way, frankly, *Signor* Boselli."

"—But it seems that you clearly do not intend to work with me. Consequently it is not possible for me to work with you."

Villari's lip curled. "Little man—you do tie yourself into knots when you talk! I tell you again, it's of no consequence to me what you do. I can handle this man Audley perfectly well without you farting about beside me."

"And George Ruelle? Can you handle him as well?"

The lip straightened. "Him also, if I have to."

"And General Montuori too?"

"General—?" Villari cut the name off quickly, but could not stop the question forming.

"What's General Montuori got to do with this? Apart from setting it up?" Boselli nodded with a confidence he did not feel. He had to gauge this bit exactly: he had to put just a touch of fear into Villari, but it mustn't seem a deliberate act—the man must scare himself, which might not be a quick process in one so lacking in imagination, never mind sense. But it had to be attempted none the less.

"Tell me, signore—tell me this one thing—" he forced humility into his tone "—why do you think the General has ordered you to work with me?"

He paused only momentarily, because he did not expect any answer—Villari would never admit that he could not think of one. But he must, he surely must, have at least formulated that question in his mind all the same.

"I will tell you then, because the General never does anything without his reasons. . . . It is first because in this instance we complement each other. You have all the proven executive skills in the field—the daring and the resourcefulness when there is danger—" (Was he laying it on too thick? No! One glance at the arrogant lift of the chin confirmed that!) "—the quickness of mind and body, the firmness. . . ." That was enough—and in another second the words would choke in his throat, anyway.

"And in addition you are not known so well here in Rome —at least not to the agents of the British and those who might associate with Ruelle."

He paused again, opening his hands in a gesture of self-deprecation. "Whereas I—I too am not well known— though for a different reason, of course—and I have some specialist knowledge of—of present political considerations and personalities" (Villari would scorn such knowledge, so he could fairly safely claim it himself).

But this was all window-dressing: now he was coming to the real merchandise hidden in the back room!

"And it is because I have that knowledge that I am frightened, signore—because I have just a little more of it than even the General himself suspects. Enough to frighten me."

He had the man's attention now; even though not so much as a muscle moved in Villari's face Boselli was sure of it. Whatever scorn the pig might affect, he would be uneasy at the thought of Boselli digging like a termite beneath him.

"You see—first, signore—I happen to know now who it was who saw Ruelle and Audley at the airport. I know also that it was not Audley he recognised—it was Ruelle. It was Ruelle that interested him, too. And now I know *why* he was so interested in the man. . . ."

He allowed the sentence to tail off mysteriously.

"Who was it, then?"

As Villari spoke at last a shadow fell across the table between them.

"What—?" Boselli began irritably, only to catch the absence of surprise or irritation on Villari's face.

Much more surprising was that Villari turned back towards him briefly with what was for him a remarkable gesture of courtesy.

"One moment—" the dark glasses tilted upwards again—"Well?"

"The man and the woman have left the house—they've taken the car."

"In which direction?"

"Towards the Porta San Paolo, signore. Unless he's taken the wrong direction they're heading out of the city."

Villari stared at the speaker, a compact, youngish man unknown to Boselli. Then he shook his head.

"No. He knows Rome well enough not to do that."

"Then it could be the EUR—there are some big museums there. Or maybe the beach at Ostia. It's going to be hot today."

It was damned hot already, thought Boselli. What it would be like later didn't bear thinking about.

"Very good. Depretis is following them, then. I—we—will follow him. You go back and relieve Piccione at the house."

Boselli watched the man out of sight with a twinge of uneasiness. Depretis and Piccione were also names he was unable to place.

"Who is he—and the others?"

"One of the police special squads. The General must have borrowed them—he's had them watching Audley from the beginning, not our own men." Villari watched him, head cocked slightly to one side. "Would you have any thoughts about that, too?"

Boselli rubbed his chin reflectively. The Clothes-horse had changed his tune quickly enough, so perhaps he had some sense after all.

"I might."

"But in the meantime you have a name for me."

Boselli nodded. "Yesterday I took some reports to leave with Signorina Calcagano. She was giving the General's driver the evening off; she said the General would take the car to the airport himself. It slipped my mind until after our meeting. Then I checked up on it."

He nodded again. "It was the General who spotted Ruelle."

"You're sure of that?"

"I'm sure. Because General Montuori has wanted George Ruelle dead these twenty-eight years. Only he's had to leave well alone."

"Until now, eh?"

Boselli shrugged. "Maybe . . . but I rather think he's still keeping clear. I'd guess he's hoping the English will do his work for him this time."

"We—shall we have trouble catching them up, then?" Boselli spoke breathlessly, because Villari's legs were each a full fifteen centimetres longer than his and their pace was forcing him into an undignified half-trot behind him down the pavement. After the cool of the cafe he could already feel the sweat running down his body again.

"Eh?"

"If he is already—close to Porta San Paolo—he has—a long start on us—the man Audley. That is—if we are—going to follow him—wherever he is—going."

"Follow him?" Villari replied casually over his shoulder. "We shall let the police follow him. That's what they're paid to do."

"Then what—shall we do?"

Villari stopped suddenly beside a monstrous sports car parked in defiance of the sign above it. Boselli's spirits sank at the sight of it. It was so exactly the sort of car he would have imagined for this sort of man that it did not surprise him, yet its shocking disregard of common prudence was dismaying nevertheless—a tank or an armoured carrier would have been hardly less ostentatious.

His reaction must have been evidently headlined across his face, for Villari grinned at him mischievously across the blinding roof—at least the prospect of physical (as opposed to mental) activity appeared to purge his bullying streak and dissolve his petulance, anyway. When he spoke there was almost no cutting edge in his voice.

"Don't panic, little Boselli—this is the easy part. The Englishman drives like an old woman on the way to Sunday Mass—I could catch him if he was already halfway to the coast. But it isn't necessary. The police will follow him in their car, and we will follow them in ours, if I can make myself drive slowly enough. So stop worrying and get in."

Boselli clambered awkwardly into the low-slung black leather bucket seat, first overawed and then abruptly slammed back into the padding by the Ferrari's explosive acceleration.

Then, as he gathered his wits, all thought of the problems and difficulties ahead was submerged in the heady pleasures of speed and power and opulence : this—the snarl of horse-power and the wide bonnet stretching ahead of him away into the distance—was the very stuff of his own private dreams. If success and promotion ever came, if patience and application were ever rewarded, if merit and intelligence were recognised, it would be *thus* and with *this* that it would be celebrated, not with the petty family aspirations of his wife and her crow of a mother and that rapacious crew of nonentities from Viterbo who had pinned their hopes of comfortable old age on the clever civil servant their only sister had married . . .

"Chase has joined the Via del Mare—Chase has joined the Via del Mare—Over."

The crackling voice jerked him back to reality, and a reality in which there could be no more day-dreaming if he was to pass the tests ahead.

Villari threw a small switch. "Acknowledge—over and out." He threw the switch again and smiled almost con-spiratorially at Boselli. "You see? Nothing at all to worry about. Nothing to do but talk."

The Tiber sparkled momentarily in a gap on his left and then was gone as the accompanying traffic fell away from them, unwilling to match their insolent speed. That boast at least had substance—and substance which aroused Boselli's reluctant admiration : whatever the Clothes-horse's defects, he used the road like a prince in his own territory, disdainful of laws made for lesser men.

But a prince who was going out of his way to be affable to one lesser man now: patently Villari had at last recognised the need to work with him—or at least to tap that "special knowledge" he had hinted at. Only the working would be on Villari's terms, with Villari leading and getting the credit. The nuance of command had been clear in those last words—"nothing to do but talk" meant that he must now spill all his hard-won information on pain of displeasure.

"It rather looks like the Lido, then," he began cautiously. "There is nowhere else to go from the autostrada unless they are heading for the airport. And as they have left the baby and the *au pair*, I would think—"

But Villari was not prepared to accept this conversational gambit.

"And I would think," he interrupted, "that you have not quite finished telling me why the General wants this man Ruelle dead."

Boselli gestured vaguely. "They are old enemies, signore. From the war. . . ."

Villari looked at him quickly, unsmiling now. "Don't start playing your little games with me again—I know they were in the war together, and I know the General doesn't love Reds. Answer the question."

Boselli pretended to give in obsequiously. "No, of course —I beg your pardon, signore! It was in 1943, just at the beginning of the—period of co-belligerency, at the time the Anglo-Americans landed at Salerno, that this thing happened. There was a German column crossing the Appennines from Foggia, and the General and Ruelle joined their forces to block the road . . . or they were supposed to join, that is."

"Go on!"

"Well, I do not know the full details of it, but Ruelle double-crossed him, that is what it amounts to . . . and he did it cleverly, so that it looked like a misunderstanding. Half the

General's men were cut off without a chance—and the Germans did not take any prisoners, either."

Villari grunted. "Typical Red trick—the scum!"

The Clothes-horse was probably summing it up more accurately than he knew, Boselli reflected. Ruelle had undoubtedly fought the Germans in his own savage way; but at that stage in the war he was already looking ahead to the struggle for power in post-war Italy, and he had merely used the Germans to weaken his future political opponents, who would be needing men like the fire-eating Bersaglieri major he had betrayed.

"Yes," he nodded, "and the General guessed as much, but there wasn't anything he could do at the time."

"And afterwards? He let the scum get away with it? That doesn't sound like our Raffaele!"

It was typical of Villari that he understood nothing of the realities of the post-war period.

"He had even less chance then, actually. After the war, you remember, signore, the Government sent him with the negotiators to London—he had fought beside the Anglo-Americans and they had given him one of their medals. And then he went with the arms commission to Washington. By the time he returned it was too late to settle such a score without causing great scandal." He shrugged. "The Bastard was too important in the Party hierarchy by then—that's what they call him, by the way: The Bastard."

"That makes two of them—our Raffaele's something of a bastard too when the fit takes him."

"Ah—but Ruelle really is one. I mean, he was born out of wedlock. The story is that his father was one of the English soldiers who fought alongside our army on the Piave in the Great War. Apparently he left Ruelle's mother in the lurch, or maybe he was killed in the Vittorio Veneto offensive—no one knows for sure. But Ruelle was born in Treviso in 1919, anyway, and his mother called him George, after the Englishman. And that's all his father left him, just the name. Perhaps that's why he doesn't like the English."

"He doesn't like 'em?"

"He hates them."

"And yet he calls himself 'George'?"

"Yes, he does." It was curious how Villari was echoing the same questions he had put to Frugoni; and in default of that missing section of the Ruelle dossier he could only advance Frugoni's replies. "Maybe it helps him to keep on hating—a constant reminder. He was a good hater in the old days, so it seems, anyway. . . . Perhaps this other Englishman had better look to his back." Boselli watched the handsome face carefully. "Unless we are busy making something out of nothing, of course. . . ."

But there was no hint of change in the aristocratic blankness of Villari's expression, nor any suggestion that he intended to give anything back in return for all the information he had received. He was not simply ignoring Boselli, but even more simply Boselli had ceased to exist for him while he digested what he had been told.

Boselli turned back towards the shimmering highway ahead. They were out of the city now, almost magically— he had been too busy answering carefully, playing his answers one by one as frugally as he knew how, to notice how fast they had been travelling. Now they were eating up the kilometres to the sea even more rapidly, rushing to whatever rendezvous lay ahead.

For this was not square one again, that at least he knew without Villari having to let slip one helpful word. It had been there from the start, even in the man's assumed non-chalance in the cafe: if there had really been nothing to report it would have been scorn, or sarcasm, or even anger waiting for him there, or certainly something very different from that first guarded hostility. Whereas when he had revealed that he had something to offer, Villari had been

83

eager to take it—eager enough to affect that sickening contemptuous jocularity. . . .

So one thing was sure: they had staked out Audley's apartment on the Aventine and against all reasonable expectation it had quietly paid off. He had been right—it no longer mattered for what ridiculous reason; nobody knew about that anyway and looking back on it he felt that in fairness to himself it had been logic and instinct as much as any other consideration which had prompted him to suspect that the English were up to something.

He had been *right*. He hugged the knowledge to himself triumphantly. And Villari had been *wrong*: that was almost as satisfying.

And he had been right against the odds and in the very presence of the General: that was the sort of thing he needed to establish himself, exactly the sort of thing! He had shown his quality in a way which would be noted: not a man of facts and figures, little more than a clerk, but a man of decision and discernment. . . .

"*Chase is turning off main highway*," the crackling voice on the radio took him unawares again. "*Turning right— sign reads . . . Ostia Antica—do you read me?—Ostia Antica.*"

"Check—Ostia Antica." Villari flicked the switch and frowned at Boselli. "What is there at Ostia Antica?"

"The excavations."

"Excavations?"

"It was the port of ancient Rome, signore," said Boselli patiently. The Clothes-horse was clearly pig-ignorant of everything that did not concern him, but that was only to be expected. "It was the imperial port until the river-course changed. I suppose it silted up first. And there would have been the malaria from the marshes too—"

"I didn't ask for a history lesson. I know what the place

was," Villari snapped. "But what are the excavations like?"

Boselli scratched his head. The truth was he had never visited Ostia Antica, although he did not care to admit it just now.

"Just ruins." He shrugged. That was safe enough: the past was always in ruins, and one ruin was much like another. "Just ruins. You can see them alongside the road to the Lido—I'm sure you must have seen them sometime."

"I do not go to the Lido." Villari contemptuously relegated the city's beaches to the city's rabble. "Do the tourists go there?"

"To the Lido?" Boselli gazed at him stupidly.

"To the ruins, you fool—are they crawling with foreign tourists?"

"I—I suppose so," Boselli floundered, irritated with himself for having misunderstood the question and also for not having admitted from the start that he knew nothing about the Ostian excavations. But far more irritating was the realisation that Villari had some idea of why the Englishman was making this trip and that he was sitting on his suspicions out of sheer bloody-mindedness.

Crawling with tourists? He stifled his annoyance and concentrated on the vision the phrase conjured up: of the Trevi submerged and the Forum overrun by hordes of sun-beaten Americans and English and Germans, their cameras endlessly clicking and their dog-eared Blue Guides clutched in sweaty hands.

So Audley had come to meet someone or to be met under cover of such crowds; an old trick, but one not much to Villari's taste evidently.

"Yes," he smiled at the Clothes-horse maliciously, "I'm sure it will be crawling with foreigners, signore."

VII

BUT OSTIA ANTICA was not crawling with tourists, native or foreign. It was not crawling with anything at all, except heat and solitude.

Boselli stood miserably in the shadow of an umbrella pine just beyond the entrance building, fanning himself uselessly with the official guide-book, waiting for Villari to finish with the policeman who had stayed behind on the end of the radio. Presumably his partner had gone in after the Englishman and his wife, though there was no sign of them down the tree-lined avenue which led to the ruins.

There was, indeed, no sign of anyone : either it was too hot, or perhaps because of the heat the nearby sea had proved an irresistible counter-attraction for all those sight-seers who would otherwise have made their pilgrimage to the forgotten port of Rome. But whatever the reason, he could not have been more wrong in his forecast.

In fact he had been so wrong that Villari had not bothered to rub it in; he had merely grunted derisively at the two cars in the parking lot and had ordered Boselli to purchase the guide-book and wait for him inside, and although Boselli would have dearly loved to hear what the policeman in the car had to say he had been glad to scuttle off with his tail between his legs, away from the danger of further humiliation and the hot asphalt of the car park under his thin-soled city shoes.

He knew that he ought now to be using these precious moments to familiarise himself with the town's layout, but for the life of him he couldn't, for the place overawed and disquieted him in a way he had not expected.

For he had been wrong also about the nature and extent of the remains. Those few hurried glances from his own driver's seat on the family excursions to the Lido had not prepared him for the actuality : there was much more above ground here than could be glimpsed from the roadside, which must have been merely outlying structures far beyond the town's perimeter.

Not just above ground—he flicked quickly through the illustrations in the back of the little book—but high above ground. There was an absolute labyrinth of buildings standing to the first and even to the second storey here. The problem of tracking down anyone, and of doing so in this emptiness without making themselves obvious, would be formidable.

Clearly, this must have been the shrewd Englishman's idea in coming to such a place. The streets of Rome provided cover for enemies as well as friends; here it would be possible to accept or decline a contact with far greater certainty of having done the wiser thing.

It was not the Englishman's cunning that disturbed him— the man was enough of a professional to be wary and amateur enough to be unconventional at the same time in his choice of a rendezvous. It was just pure bad luck that he had fixed a place which aroused the deepest feeling of unease in Boselli's soul.

Ordinarily he was not subject to such odd notions. He was a city-dweller born and bred, with a natural contempt and suspicion for the peasant countryside—he knew those gut-reactions of old, and allowed for them. But this place was neither city nor country; nor, without the colourful crowds of tourists and the surrounding noise and bustle of a busy city, was it like the antiquities he was used to back in Rome. It was much more like a bombed and plague-emptied town, something which had been alive yesterday and was newly-dead—a corpse unburied, rather than an old skeleton disinterred . . . an obscenity.

No sooner had he formulated that thought than he was overtaken by embarrassment with it: it was the sort of mental absurdity he would never have dared admit to his colleagues and for which his wife invariably prescribed a laxative. Even the unshockable Father Patrick, his favourite Dominican, had warned him against it: *too much imagination, Pietro—a good measure of it is a great blessing, but too much is a weakness. . . .*

"Give me the guide, then—wake up!"

Villari whipped the book out of his hand, flipped it open, ripped out the folded map from it and thumped it back into his possession before he knew what was happening.

"Hmm. . . ." Villari scanned the map, frowning at its complexity. Then he turned to the second policeman, who had accompanied him through the entrance, running a slender finger over the paper. "You go ahead along the main street—the Decumano Massimo here—until you spot Depretis. Then you wipe your face with your handkerchief— I assume you've got a handkerchief?"

A muscle twitched in the detective's cheek, high up and very briefly, as he nodded. He was careful not to look at Boselli, who knew nevertheless with certainty that the Clothes-horse, running true to form, had made another life-long enemy in the last five minutes. It might not be wholly deliberate now—it might have started as a defence designed to keep inferiors in their place and become second nature over the last few years—but without doubt Villari had perfected the art of being offensive.

"Very well. You will go on past the theatre—there—" the finger stabbed the map "—and wait for me to catch up if the theatre is a high building and there is a stairway on it. If there is then I shall climb it and you will wait until I have seen what there is to see—is that understood?"

Again the detective nodded.

"Then you will continue down the Decumano Massimo—
that is, unless I wipe *my* face—as far as the Porta Marina."

"And if I do not see him by then, signore?" the detective
inquired neutrally.

Villari stared at him for a moment, as though slightly
surprised by the question. "Then you will come back, and
I will tell you what to do," he said coolly. "But the important
thing for you to remember now is that you are no longer
interested in the Englishman—you and Depretis. It is his
contact you are interested in : who he is and where he goes—
do you understand? Once Depretis is spotted, then you
come back here and cover the entrance. When the contact
comes out Depretis will be following him, and then it's up
to you both not to lose him. Now—move!"

The detective took one last glance at the map, and then
turned away down the avenue without a word. As he went
he slipped off his jacket and loosened his tie; he did not,
thought Boselli, look very much like a student of antique
remains, but neither did he look like a policeman, although
there was a shiny, threadbare air surrounding him which
proclaimed the minor and underpaid government function-
ary—a guide employed by the Ministry of Public Instruction,
maybe, nosing the excavations in search of gratuities.

He watched the thick-set figure dwindle among the pines,
then faced Villari. "And what do you wish me to do,
signore?"

"Watch him," Villari nodded down the avenue. "And
keep from under my feet if anything happens."

"Something will happen, then?"

Villari shrugged.

"But you know that Audley is meeting someone here?"

Villari shrugged again.

"But—" Boselli persisted desperately "—you know something is going on?"

The Clothes-horse shifted his glance from Boselli to the detective and then, lazily, returned it. "The Englishman is being watched."

Boselli frowned at him, perplexed.

"Not just by us, idiot—by others."

"By whom?"

"We are not sure."

Not sure, Boselli digested the tiny fragments of information, trying to make a meal of them.

By others. Logically, Ruelle would be continuing his surveillance, but they were quite properly more concerned with Audley at this point—and with his contact—than with Ruelle, so they hadn't risked trying to find out who was watching on the Aventine for fear of blowing the whole thing, for the contact himself might be keeping an eye on Audley too. That "others" implied as much, anyway, though the English themselves might also be maintaining a protective watch on their man if he was as important to them as the file suggested.

Boselli shivered in the heat at the memory of that file, with its cold little facts and hot little theories. He knew so little about what was going on, but he also knew too much for his own peace of mind. Audley and Ruelle, and above them Sir Frederick Clinton and General Raffaele Montuori —they all had one thing in common: they were dangerous men. He thought nostalgically of his little airless room back in the city: by now it would be almost as hot as Ostia Antica, but it would be much safer.

As they advanced down the Decumano Massimo he began to grasp the principle on which Villari was searching the excavations. He was using the two detectives as hunting-dogs—what were they called, pointers?—Depretis to cover the minor streets which ran at right angles to the main thoroughfare, and the threadbare man to watch for him. So long as Depretis kept sight of Audley and remained in sight of the Decumano Massimo at the same time he would serve as a moving signpost to the Englishman.

The trouble was that not all the side streets were absolutely straight, and there were lateral alleys branching off them, so that they needed luck as well as logic. In fact the farther they progressed the more unlikely it seemed to Boselli that they would see anyone at all, certainly anyone who didn't want to be seen, in that maze of walls. The Clothes-horse had delivered his briefing decisively and confidently, but the frown of concentration on his forehead indicated that his self-esteem was drying up fast.

Still, he had been right about the theatre: it was a substantial—or substantially restored—building, with a series of arcades facing the street and a stair leading up to the seating on the other side. But when Boselli made to follow Villari up the stairs, the Clothes-horse gestured angrily down the street towards the detective, who was now loitering fifty metres ahead of them.

"You watch *him*—can't you remember a simple order?" Villari hissed.

Chastened, Boselli made for the shadow of the arcade, reaching in his pocket for his handkerchief, and then remembering just in time that the one thing he mustn't do was to mop his genuinely sweaty face with it. He must make do with his equally sweaty palm.

"It's hot, eh?"

Boselli jerked as if stung, and then relaxed, his heart still thumping: one of the arcades had been turned into a refreshment room, and the serving man in it was standing in the shadow just inside the doorway, watching him hopefully.

"Yes," he muttered.

"And it will get maybe just a little hotter." The man squinted up at the sky. "You want a cool drink, eh?"

Boselli was about to refuse when it occurred to him that so sharp an eye for custom might have intercepted earlier prospects.

He pretended to consider the question. "Pretty quiet today."

The man nodded. "It is the mezzogiorno, though."

"I reckon we must be the only ones here," Boselli surveyed the scene with a dissatisfied sniff, as though it didn't surprise him now that it was no tourist attraction. "Except for him, at least," he nodded towards the detective in the distance.

The conflict in the refreshment man's expression suggested that he was torn between loyalty to Ostia Antica and the proposition that the customer—especially the would-be customer—was always right.

In the end he compromised, as Boselli had hoped he would. "Almost the only ones, signore," he said.

"You mean there are others here?" That was just the right note of not-quite-polite disbelief: "I haven't seen anyone."

"Oh, yes—" the refreshment man was on his honour now. He stepped out into the sunlight and stared down the Decumano Massimo —"just a few minutes ago there was a foreign couple—a big bull of a man and a woman in a big hat, slender like a model-girl—"

"Well, they seem to have disappeared," murmured Boselli. "Perhaps they knew where to go—where the best things to see are, eh?"

"But there is much to see, signore!" The refreshment man spread his hands. "Behind here there is the Piazzale delle Corporazioni—they come from all over the world to see the mosaics there—and—" He stopped suddenly as though it had dawned on him that only a barbarian could have come so far and remained unmoved by his surroundings.

"Where did they go, then, the foreigners," persisted Boselli, like a man who has had what he believes to be a sharp idea which he intends to pursue to the exclusion of better advice.

The man shrugged, disillusioned. "I think maybe they turned off to the right, to the House of Diana or maybe the Temple of Livia. Or they may have gone to the Museum— but it is closed now."

Boselli acknowledged the information with a nod as he heard Villari's footfall on the stair.

But the man was a trier. Even as Boselli turned away from him he called out: "You want for me to get you that drink now, signore?"

Boselli raised a negative hand. He wanted a cool drink it was true, but it would only make him want to urinate more than he did already—it was that damned drink he had had back at the fountain in the city which was already beginning to discomfort him. Nevertheless—he had made progress, and a good deal more of it than had Villari, who appeared round the corner of the theatre with a face like thunder.

"They went—"

Villari cut him off. "I heard. Come on."

He strode off, bristling. Not a word of approbation, thought Boselli hotly, panting after him—not even an encouraging look could he manage. It was childish, even allowing for the fact that Villari had always worked alone in the past, but more than that it might soon become positively dangerous and he could not afford to allow it to go on much longer.

A few metres farther on Villari stopped to examine the map again. But this time Boselli closed up on him and craned over his shoulder.

"The House of Diana—which is that?" he asked. The map was crudely drawn, and although the streets were named the buildings along them were numbered according to a key which was under Villari's thumb on the far side. "And the Temple of Livia—"

Villari refolded the map just as Boselli had managed to identify a *Via di Diana*, which seemed to run parallel to the main thoroughfare. There was no way of telling from the numbers where any of the actual buildings were.

"Signor Villari, this is ridiculous—" he began.

"Be quiet!"

It was not the order that stopped Boselli, but the fact that Villari had embarked on a curious sequence of hand signals to the detective ahead of them. But curious or not, the detective seemed to understand what he was trying to convey, for he bobbed his head before starting off again.

"Now—" Villari turned back to him "—what the devil is the matter?"

Boselli swallowed, then nerved himself. "I cannot—Signor Villari—I cannot continue like this, not knowing what is happening. You do not tell me anything—and you do not show me anything—" the words foamed out as though a dam had broken "—you ignore me, you treat me like a child! I must insist—"

"Insist?" Villari showed his teeth.

"Yes, signore—insist!" Boselli was desperate now. "If things go wrong—General Montuori spoke to both of us—if things go wrong then I shall be held responsible just as much as you—"

He paused, aware that his voice was rising towards a plaintive squeak.

"If there is nothing for me to do here, then I will return to the city," he said firmly. "And I will report to the General that you have no use for me."

As a final statement of intent that was not wholly without dignity, he decided. From the spreading smile on Villari's face, however, it seemed to lack something as an ultimate threat, though under the face-concealing glasses it was difficult to make out what species of smile it was.

"Then you have a long walk ahead of you," said Villari equably. "But I have never said I had no use for you—you must have patience, little Boselli. This is a game of patience you know, is it not?"

"What use am I, then?" Perversely Boselli found the Clothes-horse's amiability as off-putting as his insolence : it made him wonder whether his real usefulness was not in truth simply as someone to carry half the responsibility for failure. Perhaps he had underrated the man after all. . . .

"You can put names to faces for me, I'm told. And that's what we need at the moment, a few more names to add to this Englishman's. Then we can really get started." Villari sounded almost friendly now. "Does that answer your question?"

Boselli stared at him wordlessly, conscious once more of the insistent pressure on his bladder.

"Is there anything else you'd like?" asked Villari.

"I—I—you must excuse me for one moment," Boselli muttered. "The call of nature—"

He stumbled down the nearest alleyway until he was just out of sight of the main street, fumbling as he went for the zip-fastener on his fly. It was partly nerves, of course, as well as nature, but it was also hugely humiliating. Why did people like Villari never, *never* need to do it, though?

He sighed with relief at the little lizard staring at him with bright eyes from a crack in the wall just above his head. To his right he had a part-view of a little courtyard with a faded black and white geometric mosaic pavement already half covered by modern detritus. Around it were splintered columns like a line of tree stumps felled by inexpert foresters.

A little hysterically, physical and mental relief at two distracting jobs done restoring his spirit, he thought : this is the moment when the Englishman and his contact come strolling round the corner, or if not them then the Englishman's model-girl wife in her wide hat, catching him in the unstoppable moment of mid-flow.

The thought made him rise on tip-toe and peer round him, and then back away from the spattered wall as he pulled up the zip, still searching the alleyway for prying eyes—

There was a man leaning in a ruined opening halfway down the alley—a man with a bright red cravat like a stain running down his white shirtfront—

As he stared, hypnotised, the man raised a red hand to adjust the cravat, turning slightly away from him as he did so, totally ignoring him.

Boselli's mouth opened—he felt it open as though his lower jaw was falling away from the upper one, its muscles severed—and a meaningless sound rose out of it.

The bright blood rippled over the fingers suddenly and the head sank against the wall as though the man was overcome by weariness. In ghastly slow motion he sank on to his knees, head and shoulder scraping down the stone work; for one instant he remained balanced, then he began to fold forward until he was bent double, the top of his head resting on the ground—

The sound inside Boselli became coherent.

"Villari!" he wailed.

As though released at last by the sound, the kneeling man pitched over suddenly on to his side, his back towards Boselli. His left leg straightened and kicked convulsively at the stone doorstep on which he had been standing.

"Villari!" This time the wail was much louder, more like a scream.

There was a low, bubbling rattle ahead of him and the sound of running footsteps behind, but both were lost in the tide of sickness which swept over Boselli: he vomited helplessly and painfully into the dust at his feet, the tears starting from his eyes as he did so.

"What the—" Villari stopped dead beside him. "*Jesu!*"

"He was standing in the—" Boselli choked on the lump in his throat. "He—just fell down."

Villari moved forward, but cautiously now, staring all around him and stooping. As he moved he reached back inside his coat with his right hand, towards his hip. Boselli blinked the tears out of his eyes, fascinated even though fear was now flooding inside him to replace the sickness: it was like watching a cream-fed tom-cat transformed into a tiger hunting in the territory of its enemies.

When he reached the opening out of which the man had fallen Villari paused, setting his back against the wall for a moment. Then, with his automatic pistol held at the ready across his chest, its muzzle level with his left breast, he peered into the courtyard over his left shoulder. The movement was smooth and continuous: the right shoulder swung away from the wall and Villari pivoted across the gap, facing it squarely for an instant with the pistol now extended to cover the interior, stepping over the legs of the man in the alley without looking down and ending up with his back against the wall on the other side in exactly the same stance as he had started. He looked up and down the alley, shifting his pistol from his right to his left hand as he did so, and then sank down on one knee beside the body, reaching with his free hand for the pulse at the neck.

It was unnecessary, thought Boselli, the memory of the man's collapse still horrific in his mind. But it was also enormously reassuring: this was an altogether different Villari from the languid, aristocratic brute of a few minutes ago. A brute still, no doubt—but one with all the necessary jungle qualities and skills.

He recalled with a pang of surprise that he had said as much to Villari in the cafe an hour earlier, ascribing it to the General without believing in it himself. Once more he saw that his instinct had been sound, although he had allowed his personal feelings to confuse it and to doubt the wisdom of the General's design. He should have known better than that.

Villari rose from his knee and beckoned to him.

For a moment Boselli stared at him uncertainly. Irrationally, he felt that so long as he stood where he was then he was somehow safer, and that unseen eyes would disregard him as an innocent passer-by who had stumbled by accident on something in which he had no part and sought none. But the first step forward—if his legs didn't buckle under him—would bring him into the front line, however.

"And keep your head down," Villari mouthed at him.

There was no way out or backwards or anywhere except forward. He hunched his shoulders and lurched forward in what he knew was a parody of the other's cat-like wariness.

"Stop there!" Villari hissed.

But Boselli had already stopped on the safe side of the ruined doorway. Nothing short of danger from behind, he felt, would induce him to cross that hundred-mile gap out of which death had come.

"I want you to go back and get Porro," Villari whispered across the opening.

"Go back—?" Boselli's squeak was cut off by the registration of the second part of the command. "Who's Porro?"

He blinked with embarrassment as Villari's lips tightened with contempt. "The policeman?"

Villari nodded. "Tell him to come here, to the Temple of Livia," he whispered patiently, as one explaining a simple game to a dull child. "And tell him that Depretis is dead."

"Depretis!" Boselli's voice rose in shocked surprise.

"Who the hell did you think it was?"

"I—I didn't think—" Boselli looked down at the body between them and then looked up again quickly. At this distance and from this angle he could see more clearly how Depretis had died and he didn't like what he saw. He felt the lump in his throat rising again sickeningly.

"You didn't think policemen get killed?" Villari spoke softly, almost soothingly. "Little clerk—it happens, and now you know it happens."

"But—" Boselli did not feel at all soothed. Policemen did get killed, and in this line of duty not only policemen, as he had good reason to know from his files. But it only happened when someone became desperate—

He looked pleadingly at Villari, struck hopeless by the recollection of his own forecast once more. It was all happening as he had forecast, *but it was happening to him*!

"Now, Signor Boselli, just don't panic—just do as I tell you—" the gentleness of Villari's voice was hideously counter-productive: it impressed the gravity of the situation on Boselli more convincingly than urgency or anger could ever have done "—walk, don't run. But don't stop, keep moving—and tell him—"

Villari never finished the sentence: it was lost in the change in Boselli's eyes looking over his shoulder past him down the alley, the fish-like *NO* forming on his lips and the contraction of his body against the stone wall in a vain attempt to disappear into it.

Boselli was staring into his own death.

His death was a black finger, a finger which was long at first and then foreshortened as it came up to point directly at him: a shocking extension of the hand of the man who had appeared out of nowhere at the end of the alley.

Ever afterwards, when he relived that instant through the light of his candle burning before the altar, it was with a prayer to the Virgin of Miracles for his deliverance from that finger steadying on his heart. But there was no prayer in his mind or on his lips in the instant itself, only blank horror and disbelief, mindless and soundless; and to his private shame he did not even see the manner of that deliverance. His eyes were already closed when Villari moved. . . .

He heard a *thump*—more like a blow than a true sound —and a much louder *crack* of Villari's pistol, which almost blotted out the second *thump*, shattering the silence of the alley.

Then he was alive again, with the wall still at his back and the hot sun beating down on his head.

The sunlight was white, but not too blinding to conceal the miracle from him: the end of the alley was empty, wonderfully empty!

But his exhilaration was even briefer than his despair—it was quenched by a grunt of agony.

Somehow, during those seconds of darkness, Villari had catapulted himself right across the alley—across it, and back down it, and into the shadow of the wall opposite. He was sitting in the dust, his weight on his left hand, his right hand pressed tightly against his ribs. His hair was ruffled and his dark glasses had fallen off on to the ground in front of him— without them his face seemed naked and pale.

As Boselli gazed at him in mute horror he raised his head slowly and grimaced back.

"Don't—just stand there—man!" The words came out slowly but surprisingly clearly. "My gun—I've dropped it—"

Reality came cold into Boselli's brain, rousing him out of confusion: the other man had gone, but it had been Villari who had been hit—it must have been his sudden movement which had changed the target at the last moment from himself—so that any second the killer might appear round the corner again to finish the job on them.

He looked around wildly for the weapon, not finding it in the first sweep, and then, as his legs came to life at last, spotting it in the shadow beyond Villari's foot.

"Give it to me—*argh*!" Villari clapped the blood-stained palm back against his side.

It was amazingly heavy for so little a thing. During his military service he had had a rifle, though mercifully for only a short while because he had been no sort of combat soldier and they had soon realised that he was deadlier with his pen and his brain. But this was altogether different from the big, clumsy rifle : its contradictory weight and size, even the snug way it fitted into his hand, inspired a sudden confidence in him that resolved the quandary into which he had felt himself falling.

He had wanted to run away, ostensibly to get help, and then he had realised that this would mean leaving Villari wounded and helpless, a sitting target literally. But he himself had been equally helpless, a target also.

Now he was no longer helpless!

"Boselli—you idiot!" Villari coughed painfully. "Don't try it—"

But Boselli was no longer listening.

He felt disembodied as he started down the narrow street, like a camera swinging this way and that to record images of decay and emptiness. Gaps opened up first on the right, and then on the left : another courtyard, another black and white mosaic half covered with drifting sand, a broken stair ending in a blank wall. Hot sunshine and cool shadow as he zig-zagged from one gap to the next. Nothing moving and nothing alien—in this stillness movement itself was the only enemy.

Then he was at the intersection.

This, he fully understood, was the moment of greatest danger, for if the assassin was still bent on finishing them off it would be round one of these corners that he would be waiting. Yet if this was the case he knew he was doing the best thing and the only thing left for him to do, for he had no illusions about his ability to hit anything with Villari's pistol at any range other than point-blank. Given a fair chance perhaps Villari might have managed it from where he lay back there—and the killer himself had proved that a marksman could do it. But he knew that he could *not*—even with his old army rifle he had never harmed a target.

So this way the odds were shortened : it was what the General would have called "good thinking" and Father Patrick "a little of God's good sense." But neither the General nor the Irish Father were here now to stop his knees shaking and his hands trembling as he leaned against the last safe piece of wall, contemplating that bright patch of no-man's-land just ahead of him. For God's good sense also warned him that the odds were still too long and that his best was likely to fall ridiculously short of what was needed out there.

If only Villari were here beside him—or better still ahead of him : he would have known what to do and how to do it. And the General would have known too—and the big Englishman would have known and so would the bastard half-Englishman, Ruelle. . . .

But only he, little useless Boselli, was here, up against the wall—God damn them all to Hell !

The blasphemy served to release him from the paralysis which had threatened to set in, but he couldn't bring himself to leave the wall altogether : he bent down and poked his head awkwardly round the corner.

The movement was so clumsy—it was as though his body was unwilling to risk obeying a self-endangering order—that he had already started to lose his balance before he saw what lay ahead of him. And what he actually found was so unexpected that pure surprise completed the loss of co-ordination, twisting his left foot behind his right ankle to pitch him head first into the open.

Yet this unplanned and unorthodox appearance also possibly saved his life, though he was never conscious of any bullet's passage near him but only heard the sound of the shot as he rolled over in the dusty street. The noise was itself more than enough to keep him rolling in a confusion of knees and elbows until he fetched up flat, breathless and half-concealed behind the body of the man Villari had killed stone-dead with his own single snap-shot.

Miraculously he did not lose his pistol in the fall—rather, he held on to it so convulsively that it began to buck furiously in his hand of its own accord as he thrust it out ahead of him over the body. Where the shots went he had not the least idea; by the time he had begun to gather his wits enough to see what lay ahead the street was the usual empty expanse of brick and stone and parched summer grass, broken only by a dark clump of cypresses far down it. As he focused on the cypresses he had a vague feeling that he had maybe seen something moving against them, or in them, in the split second before he had started to fall. The feeling ran out of his brain, down his arm to the pistol: he closed one eye, aimed the short barrel at the clump and pressed the trigger.

To his dismay the first bullet struck sparks from the paving stones ten metres ahead of him, and as the little gun jumped the second lost itself in the blue sky. Then, with one final metallic click, it went dead in his hand.

Boselli cowered down behind the body, fumbling desperately to cock the gun. Again there was a click—it came just as he realised that he was pointing it in the direction of his own foot.

He lay flat against the smooth sun-hot pavement, trying to think. But his thoughts were only a jumble of disjointed cries for help inside his mind. There was a little puddle of blood, bright red, just beyond his fingers: a large ant emerged from a hole in the crevice between the stones just beside it, halted as if bewildered at the edge of the puddle, and then set off purposefully into the shadow under the dead man's outflung arm. Beyond the arm, almost in the centre of the street, lay the long-barrelled weapon down which he had stared so recently—he saw now that the long barrel was actually the black tube of a silencer. At least, he supposed that was what it was now he was so close to it: the classic accessory of the assassin.

Another ant emerged from the hole. Like its predecessor it scurried directly to the blood, as though there was some invisible ant-path in that direction, paused in exactly the same way, and then set off in the footsteps of the first ant. Did these tiny creatures leave a spoor just like the larger wild beasts, then?

The coherence of the question roused Boselli: there ought to be more bullets in the killer's gun and it was there almost within his reach. But even as he lifted his hand to stretch out for it he heard a tiny scraping sound behind him which turned the movement to stone instantly.

"Signore!"

The voice was almost as startled as he was, but it was not an enemy's voice. With a sigh of relief Boselli relaxed in exhaustion against the paving stones.

"Signore—are you all right?"

Boselli raised his head suddenly as he remembered the hidden marksman: his rescuer must be in plain view behind him. He turned on his elbow just as Porro bent over him.

"There's—" his own voice cracked hoarsely, "—there's someone down the street with a gun. . . . By the bushes, I think—"

The concern vanished from Porro's face immediately as his eyes followed Boselli's nod. But after he had studied the empty street for five seconds he shook his head and sank on to one knee beside Boselli.

"I think he's gone, Signore. . . . There was a car just now —somewhere beyond the trees on the upper road, beside the museum—did you not hear it?"

Boselli shook his head. He had heard nothing and Porro sounded decidedly relieved that the enemy had retreated;

certainly under his tan he was almost as pale as Villari had been when—

Villari!

"Where are you hit? Can you walk?"

"Hit—?" Boselli frowned.

"There's blood on your face," Porro spoke slowly. "Are you wounded?"

Boselli instinctively raised his right hand to search for the injury. There was a stickiness on his temple, and what might be the beginning of a bump.

"I don't know—I don't think so." He stared at his fingers: there was blood on them, but only a little. "I must have grazed myself when I—when he fired at me I threw myself down in the street. I'm not hurt."

"And you got the murdering swine!" There was grim satisfaction in Porro's voice and admiration—undoubted admiration—as his glance shifted briefly to the body and then returned to Boselli. For a moment Boselli was confused both by the tone and the look. Then he saw Porro's error and the circumstantial reasons for it.

"I didn't—" he began, embarrassed, "I didn't mean—"

Porro patted him on the shoulder reassuringly. "That's all right, signore. This is one they won't blame you for—it was him or you and no time for questions." He stood up. "I must get back to the car, signore—we can't get the other swine, but at least we can pick up the Englishman double-quick. And I can call up an ambulance for your friend."

"He's alive?"

"Your friend's alive—he was a minute ago, anyway," said Porro heavily. "Sergeant Depretis is dead."

"Wait!" Boselli scrambled to his feet. His clothes were covered with dust and there was a tear in his trousers at the knee—his best office trousers. He brushed at himself ineffectually. Alive or dead, Villari was out of it now, and the immediate decisions were up to him.

"We'll lose 'em both, signore—if I stay here."

Boselli screwed up his brain.

"Don't pick the Englishman up. Phone General Montuori's office. Tell him what has happened—get through to the General himself, not some—some underling. Don't touch the Englishman unless he says so. That's an order."

Porro stared at him.

Boselli took a deep breath. He felt appallingly tired—drained. With the last shred of his will he met Porro's stare.

"That's an order," he repeated.

After Porro had gone he stood in a dream, thinking of nothing. Then he stumbled the few paces to the junction of the streets. It was remarkable, he thought, how his immediate surroundings had contracted: Villari and the dead police sergeant lay only a very short distance up the alley on his left and the killer just those two or three steps behind him. Yet the distances had seemed immense only a few minutes ago.

How many minutes? Maybe it was no more than a matter of seconds, during which time as well as distance had somehow been elongated.

The effort of thinking was beyond him. There were probably other things he should have done, or should be doing. But he knew so pathetically little about what was going on. He looked up the alley again: the place was like a battlefield with himself the sole unlikely survivor on it—and he didn't even know why he was fighting. Or who.

But he ought to do something for Villari, anyway.

It was up to the General now.

He had done his best.

VIII

The Elgin Marbles gallery wasn't difficult to find, which was just as well in view of the time shortage; and although it was by no means empty a merciful providence had just cleared it of chattering schoolchildren.

It seemed to Richardson that the British Museum itself hadn't changed much in fifteen years: the foyer was still jammed with the little monsters. That last and only time he had been inside the hallowed portals he had been one of the monsters himself, but unlike the present crop he had been a monster regimented and controlled into silence. The crowds through which he had just passed had obviously been just as bored as he had been (the BM probably ranked a poor third to the Imperial War Museum and the Science Museum now, as then) but they were as belligerent as a football crowd.

"Professor Freisler."

There was no doubt about the identification, even though he had only seen the old man once before: the huge close-shaven head was unmistakable—it might have served as a model for those old Punch cartoons of square-headed Prussians stamping on the bleeding body of Gallant Little Belgium.

The head froze, and then began to revolve on its jowls until Freisler was facing him.

"Sir?" A hairy hand adjusted the spectacles. Then the little piggy eyes brightened with recognition.

"It is—it is Captain Richardson—is it not?"

"Plain 'Mister' nowadays, Professor."

"*Mister* Richardson—I beg your pardon!" The old man

flashed a hideous steel-toothed smile. "Mr Richardson—so!"

Richardson returned the smile.

"There was a notice on your door saying you were here. I hope I'm not disturbing you in the middle of something important?"

Freisler dismissed the notion with a wave of his hand. "There is no disturbance. The notice—it is for my students. They come to me when it suits them, and I come here when it suits me. Then they come here and we talk just as well, perhaps better."

"You come here often, then?"

Freisler nodded. "Indeed so! To live so close to all this beauty and not live with it, I think that would be foolishness, eh? And who knows—one day you British may decide to give it all back to the Greeks. That would be an even greater foolishness of course, but these are foolish days I am thinking, are they not?"

The eyes bored into Richardson. Thinking—he was thinking right enough, but not about the marbles and their ultimate fate. That was merely what he was talking about while he took stock of the situation.

Richardson stared round the gallery, pretending to consider the question for a moment.

"I reckon they're safe enough for the time being, you know—no one even wants to give the present lot in Greece the time of day." He grinned at Freisler. "Not that I'm any sort of judge of such things."

"No, of course." The old man nodded seriously. "It is not your field of interest—of business. And you have come to—see me, not the marbles, is that not so?"

"That's right, Professor."

"About your—business?"

"In a way, yes. But not officially." Richardson dropped his voice. "I need your help and I need it quickly."

"My help?" The eyes were expressionless now, as blank

as pebbles. "And in what way can I help you, Mr Richardson?"

"You're a friend of David Audley's."

"I have that honour, yes." The tone as well as the words had a curious old-fashioned formality about them, and the guttural quality was suddenly more pronounced—the "have" had an explosive, Teutonic sound which had been hitherto absent.

"And so have I, Professor. That's why I'm here."

No reply. *Prove it, Mr Richardson, prove it.*

"David's put up a big black, Professor—"

"A big black?" Freisler frowned. "A big black what? That is an idiom with which I am not familiar, no."

"Hell—a black mark. A *faux pas.*"

"Now I am with you. An error of judgement, yes?"

"That's it. And somehow I've got to get him off the hook."

"I understand. That is to say I am able to guess your meaning, Mr Richardson. But I beg you to stop using these unfamiliar figures of speech, or I shall not be able to help you quickly. . . . Now, what was this error he made?"

"He went abroad without telling anyone."

"That does not seem to me so very—erroneous."

"In our—business—there are rules, Professor."

"Rules?" Freisler shook his head quickly. "For a man like David Audley rules are made for other men. I would say— yes, I would say that half his value lies in that alone. Do you not trust your friend then, eh?"

"Damn it—it's because I trust David to hell and back that I'm here now, sticking my little neck out!" Richardson paused. "What I mean—"

Freisler raised his hand. "No. That I do understand. To stick the neck out is a very ancient gesture of trust and submission in the animal kingdom. You have no need to explain it for me. You trust David, but there are others who do not— or they wish to make trouble for him—that I can well appreciate. He is not a man who would be popular everywhere, I would think."

"You're dead right there!"

"Of course I am right. But there is more to it than that I am thinking, eh?"

"How do you mean—more?"

"My good young man—" Freisler adjusted his glasses "—I am not in your business and I would not be if my life depended upon it—no! Only for David I have answered small questions from time to time. And on occasion I have asked questions for him in certain places back in my fatherland, where I am not yet wholly without influence—all out of friendship, you understand, and maybe a little out of gratitude for my quiet life here."

"Professor. I—"

"Please to hear me out, Mr Richardson. I am not in your business, but I am not stupid and I have studied for fifty years the way men think and act ... causality, Mr Richardson, causality!"

Richardson blinked. "You're losing me now."

"Then listen. You say David makes a big black mark, breaking a little rule that is no rule to him. And I say that I believe you—that David is in trouble. But not for the breaking of any *kleinliche* rule. He is in trouble because he is ripe for it—he has been ripe for it for months, ever since he settled the Zoshchenko affair of yours."

Maybe not in the business, thought Richardson, carefully concealing his surprise, but too goddamn well-informed for comfort if he had had a finger in that pie. Indeed, if the Professor had aimed to impress him he could hardly have chosen a better name to do it with: the late comrade Zoshchenko was not buried under it, and the name he had used was not buried in the Dead Files either, but even deeper in the top secret Closed Active files of the department, like a bit of lethal radioactive waste. . . .

He thrust the memory into the back of his mind; there were more pressing matters now.

"Then you know what David's up to?" he murmured. "Thank the Lord somebody does!"

The bullet-head shook in violent disagreement. "No, Mr Richardson—I indicated that it is no surprise to me that he is causing trouble. As to what kind of trouble, there I cannot help you."

Richardson stared at him for a moment thoughtfully. "I think maybe you can, you know, Professor."

Freisler frowned, his eyes almost lost in the overhanging folds of skin; it was, thought Richardson, a face of absolutely outstanding ugliness, brutality even. And yet everything the man said, and the aura he threw off, contradicted his appearance: so might the Beast in the fairy tale have aged if no Beauty had ever arrived to turn him back into his true princely shape, lonely and gentle—and dangerous only when someone imputed his honour, as he had seemed to do now.

"I don't mean you're holding out on me," he said hurriedly. "But tell me one thing first: what makes you think David's in trouble?"

The frown dissolved. "Not in trouble—I did not say that —but *ready* for it, Mr Richardson. You see, I know the symptoms of his condition."

"His condition?"

"It is not infectious—do not fear!" There was the merest suggestion of a glint behind the glasses. "At least, not to such a person as yourself. It is the scholar's sickness—the good teacher's too. Are you not familiar with *accidie*?"

"Acc—?" Richardson goggled. "Accidie?"

"Accidie. It is the fourth cardinal sin."

"You're joking!"

"I never joke, Mr Richardson," Freisler shook his head seriously. "It is regrettable, but I have no sense of humour.

So I do not joke and I am not joking now. So—you do not know of accidie?"

"You can say that again."

"Again? I—Ach! Another of your little sayings! But I am being stupid. You are not an historian, as David is—or as he should have been. *He* knew!"

"You told him, then?"

"But of course! Friendship is for truth telling or it is nothing. I told him of his sin and he agreed that I was right."

"So—" Richardson bottled his impatience with an effort: this was one hard lesson he had learnt these last three years, not to let the seconds stampede him when time was pressing "—just what is this sin of his?"

Freisler beamed at him. "Sloth, Mr Richardson. Sloth and sluggishness. It was a peculiarly monastic sin in the Middle Ages—it is I think a medieval word, accidie, and I do not know the true modern word for it in English."

"But David isn't slothful, Professor. He works like a ruddy beaver with his files and his reports. He eats 'em up by the dozen."

The old man's face fell. "No, then I have missed the right word . . . *dégoût*, the French would call it, perhaps. . . . It is when one loses the interest in—and the desire to do—those things which one does habitually and does well. When some men do well it is for them fulfilment, but for others it is dust and ashes—and David is such a man."

"He's bored with his job, you mean?"

"So! Except that 'bored' is too little a word."

"And when did you tell him all this?"

Freisler looked at him questioningly. "Pardon?"

"When did you tell him he'd got this—accidie?" Richardson pushed forward gently. "Was it when you had dinner down at his place?"

"Dinner?" For a moment Freisler seemed confused. "It was—yes—it was then. . . . But you know about it?"

"Not enough. Not nearly enough. And not the right things yet—I know you had roast beef and apple pie to follow."

The piggy eyes brightened again momentarily at the memory. So far all Richardson knew of the crucial meal was a cook's view of it: the roast beef had been for the old German himself—a fine big sirloin, with fiery-hot home-made horse-radish sauce and Yorkshire pudding and roast potatoes and three vegetables, because it was heavy eating that he loved; and the apple pie with thick Devonshire cream was for Sir Laurie Deacon, because he had a famous sweet tooth and Mrs Clark's apple pies had taken prizes in shows from Steeple Horley to Guildford for twenty years; and the very Englishness of both dishes made them right for the oilman Ian Howard, just back from a year of tinned food and Arab delicacies in Saudi Arabia.

But that cook's view had not been unprofitable. For David Audley loved these apple pies as much as any man—and this one had been good enough to make Sir Laurie promise his services free to Clarkie if she ever needed them, to the subsequent utter confusion and discomfort of the authorities. Yet to Clarkie's chagrin David had left his pie to congeal while he listened with rapt attention to what was being said—an event so unlooked-for that sharp-eared Clarkie was too disconcerted to eavesdrop into the actual conversation.

That had been the moment, though: something had happened between the cutting of the pie and the serving of the cheese to turn David from a taciturn sorehead into the schoolboy who kissed his wife publicly and outrageously in the middle of the kitchen and pinched Clarkie's backside as she bent over the washing-up.

Whatever it was it had been a cure for accidie, anyway.

And whatever it was Richardson was betting it had already brought one man to his death.

"Not the right things?" The Professor was staring at him

now, alert. "You are meaning that I know of those right things, eh?"

"I hope so, yes." Richardson nodded. "What did you talk about over dinner?"

Freisler thought for a few seconds, then spread his hands. "But—so many things we talked of. . . . The food, the European Community—which you insist on calling the Common Market, the Industrial Relations Act—"

"What did David have to say?"

"He did not say much. That is, at first he did not say much—it was for that that I finally chided him."

"Go on."

"But I have told you. I spoke of his sin and he agreed. He said he was—" The wide brow crinkled with concentration "—confined and—'cribbed' I think was the word he used. It must have a meaning other than that my students attribute to it, though."

"It does. 'Cabin'd, cribb'd and confin'd'—"

"Ach! A quotation. I see."

"From *Macbeth*, Act Three," murmured Richardson, gratified at the surprised lift of Freisler's eyebrows, which decided him not to add that he had once been conscripted into the play at school and knew every line of that act, in which he had featured prominently in ghastly pale green make-up as Banquo's Ghost. "I'm not just a pretty face, you know—but please go on."

"What more do you want?"

Richardson considered the question. "Well, just when did David say this—during the beef or the apple pie?"

"Is that important?" Freisler's forehead crinkled again. "But obviously it is. . . . Well, I will try to recall. . . . It was, I think, before the pie, Mr Richardson."

"Very good, Professor. Now—what happened next?"

"Next?" Freisler paused, his face heavy with concentra-

tion. He was beginning to take the game in earnest at last.
"Next it was Mr Howard who spoke."

"The oilman."

"He is in the oil business, yes."

Richardson nodded encouragingly. There was nothing odd
about David entertaining oilmen; in his Middle Eastern days
he had been as thick as thieves with some of them and he was
not a man to jettison good contacts. In fact it was agreed in
the Department that half the secret of his success lay in his
ability to hold on to them.

"What did he have to say?"

"He disagreed with me. He said—"

"Confined? Don't you believe it, man—you're just plain
old-fashioned unpopular. You've been right too many times,
and you've said 'I told you so' afterwards. People don't love
you for that, David—not in any business."

"Yes. And then?"

"David just grunted. And Lady Deacon asked him how
he had won his reputation for foretelling the future so accurately—a silly question, but he couldn't very well grunt at
her—"

"All I do is extrapolate on the past and the present, Helen.
It isn't too difficult if you have enough accurate information.
The trouble is we seldom have enough to do the job properly,
so most of the time I'm just guessing like everyone else.
Nobody sees into the future. I'm not an astrologer."

"How unromantic!"

"There was a little silence then—what you call an awkward silence, I think. So I took the liberty of pointing out
that Adolf Hitler had his astrologer who had not done him
very much good. But then Sir Laurie Deacon reminded us

that the astrologer Theogenes foretold that young Octavius would succeed Julius Caesar—Octavius went to see him incognito and Theogenes threw himself at his feet—and what had David and I to say to that?"

"And what did you reply to that?"

"I said that Theogenes was no fool and that he would have made it his business to know who Caesar's heir was. And David said—"

"I agree with Theodore—there's always an unromantic reason somewhere. I remember how the news of the blowing up of the King David Hotel in Jerusalem by the Irgun back in '46 came in to London two hours before it happened. One of the big agencies got a flash, and then an hour later it was cancelled. And then an hour later the place was blown apart. But it wasn't a case of second sight. It was simply that the agency's man was an undercover agent for the Irgun and he knew what was going to happen. Only his friends postponed the job and they forgot to tell him. And the moral of *that* is that we very seldom know what's actually going on under our noses in the present, never mind the future."

"Jolly good, Professor. And what happened next?"

"Ach! Next. . . . Is it you are wanting what we ate now, or what we were saying?"

"Both, for choice."

"So! Well—we ate and we talked . . . after David tells his story of the King David Hotel—yes—comes the housekeeper from the kitchen—"

"Mrs Clark."

"Mrs Clark, that is right. She comes with the pudding in a deep dish and the thick cream, and as David's wife serves it she says to Sir Laurie Deacon, 'This is specially for you, Laurie, although it is David's favourite too.' It is made with apples—" Freisler wrinkled his nose in disgust "—and cloves, which spoil the apples for me . . . and then the oilman Howard says—"

"I know a character who's got his own private line into the future."

David said : "I take it you mean your boss, Narva."

"Oh—you can laugh, David. But Eugenio Narva is one hell of a smooth operator. And then some."

"I never doubted it. He has remarkable flair for doing the right thing—and not doing the wrong one."

Deacon said : "You mean, like pulling out of Libya when he did? That certainly was nicely judged—remarkable is the right word for it. I wish we had done the same."

Faith Audley said : "He got out just before Colonel Gaddafi's coup?"

"Not just before, my dear. *Well* before would be more accurate, eh Howard?"

"He pulled out sure enough. But that isn't what I meant by the future—I think Gaddafi was as much of a surprise to him as it was to everyone else—"

David Audley said : "Not to me it wasn't."

"Okay—not to you, David. But he didn't have you on his payroll. What I mean is that he got out of Libya because he wanted his ready money for something else."

"The North Sea."

"Right—you're on the button, David. The North Sea . . . which is a long, long way from the sands of the desert, I can tell you."

Faith Audley said : "I didn't know there were any Italian companies drilling in the North Sea."

"There aren't. Narva didn't go into the exploitation business, he went into the equipment side. He pulled me out of the desert because I cut my teeth on off-shore work, I suppose, and I knew roughly what he wanted."

"And what did he want?"

"A middle-man's finger in all the pies that were going—rigs—he ordered two of them straight off—and all the paraphernalia that went with 'em. And manpower too—he put all the best men he could lay his hands on under the longest contracts they'd put their crosses on. Technical whizz kids, divers, the lot. What he could get he got. I know, because I spent his money like water."

"And there's profit in this?"

"Faith honey, that's where the money is at the moment. Or where it's going, anyway. You only have to compare the development and production costs. . . . I guess it takes a production investment of $100 per barrel a day in the Middle East. But in the North Sea it's going to work out at anything from twenty to seventy times as much—it takes a million pounds just for one exploration well, and that's if the weather's nice and kind. Which it darn well isn't most of the times I've seen it."

Deacon said : "What you're saying, Howard, is that at the moment more money is going into the North Sea than is coming out of it. But that's common knowledge—everyone knew it was going to be a devil to develop. If it wasn't for the political stability of the area compared with the Middle East there'd be a good deal less enthusiasm than there is now, I tell you."

"Sure—everyone knew it was going to be tough. What they didn't know was whether it'ud be profitable."

"Oil exploration's always a gamble. But ever since the Groningen strike—"

"That's just it : Groningen was a gas field, apart from being safe on land. That's where most of the hopes were—in the gas."

"But they knew oil could be there."

"Hell, of course they did. The gas comes from the carbon-iferous layers under the sandstone in the Permian rock—

sorry, Faith, I'm going technological now, damn it, aren't I!"

"Geological, anyway. But do carry on, Ian. We're all fascinated."

"So says every good hostess! But I will go on all the same. You see, you do get oil in the older carboniferous layers on-shore, but precious little of it, and drilling in the southern sector early on seemed to bear that out—in the end there was plenty of gas, but precious little oil."

"But they went on looking for it all the same."

"That's because they're oilmen. A good oilman's rather like a gold miner—the next hole's bound to be the end of the rainbow, he always thinks. And yet look at the timing: Groningen was in '58. It wasn't until '65 that Phillips and Shell-Esso and one or two others got the courage to take out licences in Scottish waters.

"Then Phillips found the Cod condensate field in the Norwegian sector in '68. But even that only proved there were hydrocarbon reservoirs—it didn't ring the till commercially. There were some damn cold feet about before that, I can tell you. It was only when Phillips brought in Ekofisk and Xenophon found the Freya field, that the balloon went up. And then it really went up. But that was only a year or so ago, remember."

Audley said: "But just what has this to do with Eugenio Narva's being able to see into the future?"

"Timing, David—it's all in the timing. Groningen in '58, just a smell of it in '68 at Cod and bingo at Ekofisk and Freya in '70. But I was buying for Narva in a big way *before* Cod."

"So he made a good guess. He's a shrewd fellow."

"David, it wasn't a guess. He knew."

Deacon said: "But on your own evidence he couldn't have known. He could only have gambled."

"I tell you—he knew. He was making a bomb in Libya

and he pulled out and made another bomb in the North Sea."

Deacon said: "Let's get this straight, Ian—stop being oracular for a moment. You know he wasn't gambling because you asked him and he told you."

"Naturally. He's a straight-shooter and I've put in a lot of sweat for him over the years, and what I was doing was giving me the shivers—I knew what the finance boys in the big companies were saying about the North Sea at the time. They said it was only good for the fish."

"So you asked him what he was up to."

"Right. I flew all the way from Oslo to Naples—to his place near Positano—just to ask him whether he'd flipped his lid. And he hadn't."

"What did he say?"

"He said we were on a sure thing."

Lady Deacon said: "And did he have his astrologer with him, Mr. Howard?"

"Not with him, ma'am. His astrologer was in Moscow."

"Moscow?" exclaimed Richardson.

"That is what he said, Mr Richardson."

"Those were his exact words?"

"Exact words?" Freisler nodded at him knowingly. "Now that is precisely what David wished to be told. Only it was the words of this Signor Narva he desired—"

"Why surely—he said a little bird whispered in his ear. A little bird from East Berlin who had it on the highest authority in Moscow."

Deacon said: "Well . . . that's uncommonly interesting. But it's just as David says—there's always an unromantic reason somewhere."

Lady Deacon said: "What do you mean, dear?"

Deacon said: "The Russians simply had one or two of

their own men on the Phillips and the Xenophon rigs, that's all. It's not in the least surprising. Three-quarters of the men they have over here are more concerned with industrial espionage than political and military spying . . . and North Sea oil would overlap both of those spheres anyway. But full marks to Narva for listening in on them—that was rather bright of him."

Ian Howard said: "It was more than bright. It was a goddam miracle!"

David said: "How was it a miracle, Ian?"

"Well, maybe the Russians had their chaps on those rigs, I don't know. But it doesn't matter, because I was on the job long before they were. I was on it weeks before they struck at Cod—before the Freya rig even cleared harbour. And if you can tell me how Narva's little bird in Moscow smelt oil before the guys on the spot in the North Sea did—man, I'll sign the cheques for you and you can fill the figures in yourself—"

IX

"I DON'T SUPPOSE—" Sir Frederick Clinton regarded Richardson with a faintly jaundiced eye "—you are acquainted with William Pitt's Guildhall speech after Trafalgar."

Richardson shook his head. The temperature was perhaps slightly less arctic now he had said his piece, but that was no sure sign that a second and more uncomfortable ice age was not about to set in. He had feared the worst from the moment he had been passed straight along the line, like some carrier of a loathsome disease whom no on else dared to handle; this was certainly not the moment to attempt to cap the *bon mot* which was assuredly coming.

"I was almost resolved to cast you back into the Irish darkness." Sir Frederick lifted a hand towards the intercom. "You arrive late here, after having contrived to offend everyone in sight, including Brigadier Stocker, who has the patience of Job. . . . Mrs Harlin, would you be so good as to ask Neville Macready to come up here at once. And will you have the dossiers on Eugenio Narva and Richard von Hotzendorff—Hotzendorff—sent up to me, *quam celerrime*. Thank you. . . . And I rather think, Peter, that you have done all this out of a certain intuitive regard—I won't say loyalty—for David Audley. Who would be the first, incidentally, to warn you against such instincts."

Almost resolved! Richardson sighed inwardly with relief at the benison contained in that "almost": he was in the clear.

"You have committed us to covering up a clear case of homicide, however justifiable. You have leaked heaven only

knows what information to an outsider—a foreigner at that
—however trustworthy."

"I didn't tell Prof. Freisler anything he didn't already
know, sir," said Richardson.

"Except now he knows that he knows it. Did it not occur
to you that Sir Laurie Deacon might be a more discreet
contact from a security point of view?"

"I understood he was in Paris, lobbying the Frogs on behalf of the pro-Market boys, sir," lied Richardson hopefully.
"In any case, David once told me Freisler has a memory like
an elephant. And I rather gathered he'd helped us before."

"Not us—just David. And under the present circumstances
that is something I'd prefer not to remember. One David is
enough for any organisation. . . . Indeed, the view has been
canvassed that even one David is too great an extravagance."

"I—"

"Nevertheless, Peter, like William Pitt's England you
appear to have saved yourself by your exertions. I only hope
you can save David by your example."

"He is in the clear, sir. I'm certain of that."

"He is not in the clear. He is never in the clear. He has not
defected, if that's what you mean," Sir Frederick indicated
a long white envelope on his desk. "I received a letter from
him by the midday delivery—a somewhat delayed letter—
explaining that he intended to take a few days of his leave
in Rome."

Richardson risked a quick glance at the envelope. It had
been sent by second-class post and the postmark was no more
than a tired blur across the stamp. It was more than likely,
though unprovable, that David had the aged postmistress at
the Steeple Horley village shop trained to his needs in such
matters.

"Ah! So that accounts for it!" he murmured wisely.

Sir Frederick stared at him silently for a moment which
lasted just too long for comfort. Belatedly Richardson

reminded himself that the man had known David far longer than he himself had.

"You do well not to smile, Peter. Because amusing as David Audley's little stratagems may seem to you, I think this may not turn out to be a smiling matter—either for him or us."

"I wasn't smiling."

"Good. Because it looks as though David has raised the devil again. But this time he's done it off his own bat, for reasons best known to himself. And what is worse he may very well not be aware of what he's stirred up."

"You mean he doesn't know about—last night?"

"He doesn't." Sir Frederick frowned. "The moment you obtained his address Brigadier Stocker alerted our Rome people, but by the time they got there the place was already under surveillance. And not just by the police, young Cable thinks—so he thought it advisable not to rush in. It'll be no use phoning, either, because it'll be bugged for certain."

"Christ!"

It didn't need to be spelt out, thought Richardson, watching the frown: David was oozing with brains and inside information, and decisive with it, sometimes to the point of arrogance. But he was strictly a headquarters man by training, and despite his massive physique and rugger-playing youth he probably wouldn't know his arse from his elbow if the opposition turned ugly.

"What complicates it is that he has his wife with him too. Which means he's not expecting trouble."

Richardson nodded. Faith's presence in Rome was conclusive proof that David was convinced what he was doing was safe; during his last assignment in the north of England he had angrily refused to allow her to visit him, even with the department's blessing.

"It couldn't be that this really is just a holiday?" he said tentatively.

"Do you think it possible?"

Excited as a boy with a new bicycle.

"No," said Richardson.

"Neither do I. In fact, after what you've told me—which knowing David I find all too plausible—I'm absolutely sure it isn't." Sir Frederick glanced down at the intercom unit and then reached forward again towards it. "Yes, Mrs Harlin?"

"Mr Macready is on his way, Sir Frederick."

"Very good. And the dossiers?"

"I have the Narva dossier, Sir Frederick. The documents relating to Hotzendorff are in the Dead Filing Section, and there seems to be some hold-up there just at the moment."

"I see. Then give Macready the one you've obtained and please hurry the other one up. Otherwise I don't want to be disturbed on any account."

"Yes, sir—" The voice was guillotined by the slender finger. Sir Frederick's eyes lifted to Richardson's. "You know Macready?"

"He briefed me before I went to Dublin."

"On the Belgian–Czech arms deal—of course!" The eyes flickered. "But you know his regular field?"

"Industrial intelligence."

"Correct. And he knows his stuff, so the Narva file is probably superfluous—it's more than likely that he wrote it himself."

"And the Kraut? Hotzen-what's-it?"

"Little Bird? Maybe that too. . . . We'll have to see."

Neville Macready was still wearing the preoccupied look he had affected whenever he wasn't talking himself during the Irish briefing, so presumably it was a habit rather than an affectation.

Another screwball, thought Richardson, with half-amused resignation. But then nearly all of Sir Frederick's Permanent

Advisers were mad as hatters in at least one quadrant of their behaviour, like the recruits of some intellectual Foreign Legion. Even David Audley, the nearest thing to a human being among them, was decidedly odd—which of course was why this whole thing had blown up.

But at least the screwball was no respecter of persons, like David and unlike Fatso Latimer: his knock and entrance were simultaneous, and his demeanour was that of someone accustomed to losing his way and finding himself in the wrong room, if not the wrong building, and no longer disconcerted by it.

"Neville!" Sir Frederick said affably, as though equally accustomed to such behaviour.

Macready's gaze passed over Richardson with a slight frown and cleared as it settled on Sir Frederick.

"Ah, Fred—Mrs—Thing—said you wanted a word with me about—she didn't seem to know what it was about."

"Yes, I do. . . . You've met Peter Richardson, I believe?"

"Richardson?" Macready repeated the name vaguely to himself, and then swung round suddenly towards its owner.

"You were going to Dublin." He turned back to Sir Frederick before Richardson could say a word. "Something gone wrong there?"

"Not as far as I know. This is about something quite different, Neville. North Sea oil."

"Huh!" Macready snorted derisively.

"Why 'huh'?"

"We've made a dog's breakfast of that all right."

"Neville—"

"This bloody crew of nitwits—that's half the reason why I got to hell out of the Board. God knows I'm not a socialist, but if Norway and Holland can get their taxpayers a fair cut and still attract capital it oughtn't to be beyond the bounds of reason for us to do it too—"

"Neville—"

126

"Even Spain, *even Spain*, knows enough to get their exploitation on the right lines. Whereas all we do is piss around trying to make quick profits while the foreigners are making the real money. It isn't even as though our own major companies are going to fork out—they pay damn little over here because of what they have screwed out of them overseas. And I told them—"

"Neville, it isn't a rundown on Government policy I want."

"Well, it should be. Auctioning blocks indeed! With the access to the geological information we've got now we can pick and choose the best bits just like that. But will we?" Macready waved a podgy finger. "Will we hell! We'll sell the hottest national asset since the coal mines in the nineteenth century for a mess of pottage. And the Lord have mercy on our souls!"

Richardson listened fascinated. If half the reason for Macready's flight from the Board—the Board of Trade?—had been the nitwits in Government, the other fifty per cent had been the marvellous intemperance of his opinions. As David had once observed, most of the best Civil Servants were unsuitable for their jobs, but Neville Macready was beyond anything he had yet encountered.

Yet Sir Frederick was equanimity itself; if anything he seemed pleased with the tirade, as though it reassured him that no one else would be tempted to steal Macready's formidable brains from him.

"Eugenio Narva, Neville," he said equably.

"What?"

"Tell us about Eugenio Narva."

Macready rubbed the end of his nose, frowning. Then he abruptly dumped a file he had been carrying tucked under his arm on Sir Frederick's desk.

"There's the Narva file. Mrs—what's-it—Harlin had it, so I took it. It's all in there. And he's a case in point, too."

"A case in point?"

"Yes. I don't mind him being part of the Italian economic miracle, but I'm damned if I see why he should also be part of the British one."

"Indeed?"

"Not that he's the worst of 'em. Narva's an honest man as well as a smart one, which is rare—apart from his Norwegian interests he's got himself well spread in British firms now, so we'll get some of his gravy."

"What firms?"

"Well, he's got a rig of his own now, but he's also on the board of Singer and Bailey. And he provided the capital for the Enfield Alloys expansion. Last time I read the reports he was dickering with the French consortium ETPM, which has a connection with Laing in Britain, and I shouldn't be surprised to see him turn up on Wimpey's one of these days. He's built a platform yard of his own at Hartlepool, and of course he's got a big chunk of Xenophon now—he bought in low and now it must be worth a packet. But that's in the oil business itself. Most of his money's in equipment and sub-contracting. But he'll be in the bidding when the next allocation of licences comes up in March, mark my words." Macready nodded wisely. "But I suppose you know all that by now."

"Why should I know it?"

"Well I've already told all this to David Audley. I thought he—" Macready stopped with embarrassing suddenness and began to rub his nose again.

"I haven't been able to see David yet," said Sir Frederick smoothly. "He's on leave and I don't want to disturb him. Just tell me what you told him. For a start."

Macready stared around him vaguely, quickly looking away when he met Richardson's eyes.

"This was a day or two ago, you spoke to David, wasn't it?" Sir Frederick prodded gently. "On the phone?"

"No. I mean yes, it was two or three days ago," said Macready guardedly. "I was down in the Reading Room—they'd just got in the American Economic Quarterly. David was down there."

The Reading Room was next to the Dead Files Section, Richardson remembered. In fact you had to go through the Reading Room to get to the section, a claustrophobic, windowless box, with a table and chair which nobody used, partly because those in the Reading Room were much more comfortable and partly because the weight of the decaying past contained in the surrounding metal cabinets was oppressive. It would be easy to check up on whether David had used it, however, because although the dead files had a low classification they still rated as secret and could only be consulted after signing for the Archivist's key.

"Yes?" said Sir Frederick patiently.

"Eh?" Macready looked at his watch nervously, as though trying to remember some more pressing and congenial engagement. "Oh—well, he just wanted the rundown on Narva. Actually, he seemed to know most of it already—" he gestured towards the desk "—it's in the file, and he'd read it."

"Yes, but of course David wanted to know about the very beginning, didn't he?"

Smooth. Very smooth.

"So he did. But that was before my time here. And it's all conjectural, anyway—even though David had got one of his bees in the bonnet about it."

"Conjectural—yes. But it's interesting all the same, the way Narva moved into the North Sea so early, don't you think?"

Macready looked up at the high ceiling above him morosely without replying. It was almost as though he was no longer interested himself in the possibilities of further conversation.

"What do you think put him on to it in the first place, Neville?"

Richardson looked from one to the other with intense curiosity. By any normal standard Macready's silence was at the least rude, bordering on offensive; and Sir Frederick's restraint was remarkable, bordering on surprising, since there was no indication that the screwball was inclined to save himself by his exertions, like William Pitt's England. Yet instead of annihilating him Sir Frederick was damn near pleading with him. If this was how screwballs were treated there was obviously a percentage in the role.

Macready sighed. "Frankly, Fred, I haven't the faintest idea. And that's what I told David. It's not merely inexplicable . . . it's irrational."

There was an undercurrent of irritation in Macready's tone, as though Narva had been needling him personally. And that, thought Richardson with a sudden flash of insight, might very well be close to the truth after all. He had assumed initially that Macready had been unwilling to shop David, but it now seemed more likely that David had merely asked a question—the very question that Sir Frederick was now remorselessly pursuing—which had been bugging Macready for a long time without any satisfactory answer.

"Yes, that's very much the way we felt about it," said Sir Frederick. "The—ah—the *timing* of it."

"That's exactly it!" Macready swung his arms and started to pace away from the desk towards the window in an oddly disjointed fashion. "He ducked out of the Italian miracle— but everyone knew that was going to slow down sooner or later, apart from the political mess . . . and Libya . . .

"But the North Sea—" he swung round towards Sir Frederick "—you know what it's like? It's a sod of a sea, the weather and the waves. And until three years ago they really didn't know how to drill in water deeper than 300 feet anyway.

"And they didn't know enough about the geological structures either. I wouldn't have put any of my money in looking for hydrocarbons in the younger Tertiary sequences, maybe not even after Phillips found that gas condensate field."

Young Tertiary—? Richardson didn't dare look at Sir Frederick.

But Macready was fairly launched now on a submarine voyage far below those treacherous winds and waves. "Even now no one knows for sure whether the block next to where someone's struck it rich is going to show anything. The salt dome structures—"

He paused momentarily and Sir Frederick moved into the hiatus quickly.

"Narva took a big risk, certainly."

"That's what David suggested—" Macready shook his head vehemently "—but it's just not on at all. Narva didn't make his stake by taking risks, and men like Narva don't change overnight."

Richardson gave up trying to place younger Tertiary sequences and salt domes and grabbed at what sounded like much more relevant information.

"What sort of chap is this Narva, then?"

Macready missed his step, glancing up at Richardson as though taken aback by the dumb half of his audience suddenly exhibiting the power of speech.

"What sort?" He raised his eyes to a point above Richardson's head. "He's a man who believes that making money is a science, not an art—that's what sort of man. He never has played outsiders. Or he didn't until he went into the North Sea, anyway."

So that was it straight from the horse's mouth: Macready the hard-headed economist and Howard the hard-headed oilman confirmed each other's mystification, and in so doing justified David Audley's excitement. For if David knew no more than any well-informed layman about the oil business (and for all Richardson knew he might be a great deal better informed than most) he would assuredly know all about Eugenio Narva from his days in the Middle Eastern section.

This time he couldn't resist catching Sir Frederick's eye, but before he could speak Macready gave a derisive snort.

"And now you're going to suggest that he had some sort of inside information!"

Sir Frederick looked at him innocently. "What makes you think that, Neville?"

"Because that's what David believed. He practically suggested that the Russians had given Narva the green light."

"Which is nonsense?"

Macready squared up decisively in front of the desk.

"Fred—I simply don't believe it was possible for anyone —not the Russians, not us, not anyone—to forecast the presence of oil in commercial quantities. Small amounts, yes —everyone knew there might be some there. After all, it's got the same rock sequences as the major producing basins in the Middle East and the States. But when Narva moved nobody—and I mean *nobody*—could have known what was there."

Sir Frederick did not attempt to reply; he merely watched Macready with a curiously deferential intentness, almost as though he was the junior partner in the exchange, waiting for enlightenment. Indeed, from the moment Macready had blundered into the room like a fugitive from *Alice in Wonderland* he had said remarkably little except to spark the economist on from one burst of exasperation to the next. It was, thought Richardson with a small twinge of bitterness, a very different technique from that which had been applied in his own case : it was like David himself had once observed after a tough session—there were some you led, and some you drove, and some you ran behind, hoping to keep up with.

"But suppose—" Macready turned away from the desk

and started to walk the carpet, following its pattern like a child on the cracks of a pavement. "That's what you want me to do, just like David did—suppose . . . suppose, suppose, suppose. . . ."

He stared into space, his brow furrowed.

"Well, they wouldn't help Narva, the Russians wouldn't for a start. He's right wing Christian Democrat—not neo-fascist, but the MSI have certainly made a play for him. And I can't think of any reason why they might want to tempt him out of Italy either, and certainly not into North Sea investment—it wasn't in their interests to encourage that at all. Quite the opposite, in fact."

"Could his movement of capital have had that sort of effect?" asked Sir Frederick encouragingly.

Macready thought for a moment, still moving like a robot over the carpet. "It's hard to gauge exactly. He's nowhere near in the big league even now, and the companies were pretty well committed by then. . . . But he damn well boosted their morale—and he certainly gave Xenophon a shot in the arm just when they needed it. . . . Except that all militates against the Russians giving him anything, even if they had it—"

He swung round and set off again "—because that's the real objection—the technology. . . . Offshore operations are the coming thing all right; they're maybe budgeting for four, five hundred millions on underwater exploration next year, world-wide, the companies are. . . . But Houston is where the action is, not Baku—and if anyone comes up with a way of finding oil without drilling for it then it'll be someone from the Capitalist Republic of Texas, not the Azerbaidjan Soviet Socialist Republic, take my word for it. And so far no one has—you can take my word for *that*, too!"

"Hmm!" Sir Frederick looked down at his virgin blotter, straightened it, and then examined his fingernails. "I rather think Lockheed's are involved in underwater oil technology these days, aren't they?"

Macready jerked to a halt.

"And of course they would have obtained their underwater experience from working with the American navy on submarine rescue systems, since one thing has a way of leading to another in such fields—eh?" Sir Frederick smiled at Macready, who was now at last giving him the appearance of undivided attention.

"Now, it does occur to me—" continued Sir Frederick smoothly, "—that ever since they have been operating a nuclear submarine force the Russians have also been working very hard on the problems of ultra deep-sea systems. In fact they performed quite creditably in recovering the wreckage of one of their Far East boats off Sakhalin Island last year. So I'm wondering—and I'd be obliged if you would wonder also, Neville—if one thing might have led to another with them too."

Macready continued to stare at Sir Frederick, though now with an air of calculation.

"I was pretty sure David had something more than hypothesis to work on," he murmured, nodding to himself as if satisfied that both Audley and Sir Frederick could not be really as foolish as their questions. "Just what is it you've got, Fred?"

"What about the Russians?" Sir Frederick's tone hardened for the first time.

Macready shrugged. "I wouldn't have thought anyone is able to operate on the seabed yet without surface supporting vessels, certainly not far from their home base. And as far as I'm aware they haven't had any vessels keeping station in the North Sea." He paused, evidently grappling at close quarters with the possibility of something he had been categorically denying a few moments earlier. "But if they can—Fred, just what is it you've got?"

"Nothing concrete, I'm afraid, Neville. But it does look as though Narva managed to tap a leak in Moscow."

"A leak—not a tip-off?"

"I don't know which. But I agree with you that this isn't the sort of thing they'd give away, and certainly not to Narva. Only in any case it seems that it was one of our own men who passed on the information." He reached forward to the intercom. "I don't suppose you remember Little Bird? —Mrs Harlin, where the devil is that file on Hotzendorff?"

The intercom was silent.

"Mrs Harlin—are you there?" snapped Sir Frederick.

The intercom cleared its throat.

"I beg your pardon, Sir Frederick." Miss Harlin did not sound flustered, but she did not sound quite like herself. "The Hotzendorff Dossier has just arrived. The Archivist has brought it himself."

Sir Frederick frowned at the machine.

"Yes?"

"He wishes to see you." The sudden tightness of Mrs Harlin's voice completed the story: Sir Frederick had not wished to be disturbed and in her opinion the Archivist had constituted a disturbance she reckoned she could handle; but he had evidently turned out tougher than she had expected.

"For God's sake, woman—" another voice, distant but sharp with anger, crackled from the intercom.

"Superintendent Cox is with him, Sir Frederick," Mrs Harlin said quickly. "He will not state his business."

Oh God, thought Richardson, when the Special Branch wouldn't state its business except to the top man, then something unpleasant was invariably about to happen. And he had a premonition that it would happen to him.

X

"MR BENBOW — SUPERINTENDENT — ?" Sir Frederick acknowledged the unlikely deputation neutrally.

"Sir!" Cox halted two yards from the desk, noted the presence of Macready and Richardson with two photographic blinks of the eye, and stood at ease with the calm resignation of a veteran bearer of evil tidings.

Benbow murmured something unintelligible and came to a stop alongside him. Then, almost as an afterthought, he took two more nervous steps forward, deposited a grey file on the edge of the desk and retreated again.

"Thank you, Mr Benbow," Sir Frederick nodded graciously. "Is there something I can do for you?"

"I asked Mr Benbow to come here with me, sir," said Cox calmly. "I think we may have an emergency on our hands."

"You think?"

"I think." Cox looked at Sir Frederick steadily. "The Librarian didn't report for work this morning."

"The—Librarian."

"Mr Hemingway, Sir Frederick," said the Archivist. "He is in charge of the non-classified printed material—newspapers, periodicals and journals."

Richardson tried to place Hemingway. A surprising amount of interesting and useful information emerged from routine publications, but it usually reached him in digested form after having been carried from its original source by some Argus-eyes expert like Macready or Fatso Latimer— or David. He had hardly ever penetrated to the bowels of the building himself, where the Reading Room—

The Reading Room!

"The Duty Officer carried out the routine check at ten-hundred." The neutrality of Cox's voice matched Sir Frederick's. "His wife was in a state—he went out last night and didn't come home. Didn't use his own car. Said he might be back latish. None of the hospitals within a radius of a hundred miles has admitted him. None of the Police Forces in the area have anyone answering to his description in custody." Cox paused. "But . . . the Chief Constable for Mid-Wessex advised me to have a word with Brigadier Stocker." He paused again. "Just that—a word. Only the Brigadier isn't available at the moment, and I thought it best to have the word with you first, sir."

Sir Frederick turned to Richardson.

"Well?" he said heavily.

"What's the description?"

"Grey-brown hair, moustache, blue eyes, prominent—"

"Not the face."

Cox didn't bat an eyelid. "Aged fifty, height five feet ten inches, weight 168 pounds. A photograph won't help then?"

"It won't." Richardson tried not to imagine the face of Charlie Clark's victim. They had been ready to let him see it, but he had managed not to have time to take up their offer. He had already seen one face like that in his career, and he didn't want to seem greedy.

"Dark grey suit, white shirt, maroon tie, brown suede shoes." Cox was watching him intently. "Well, we've got Hemingway's prints on file. That is, if—" he slowed down judiciously, "if you can provide anything for comparison."

He was almost there, thought Richardson, looking questioningly at his master.

Sir Frederick nodded. "Go on, Peter."

Richardson met the Special Branch man's gaze. "It could be. The general description's about right—height, age and so on. And the clothes are about right. It could very well be."

Cox relaxed. "I take it you have a body?"

"That's right."

One lost and one found. At least the books balanced.

"Suicide or foul play?"

"The verdict will be misadventure, Superintendent," said Sir Frederick. "As it happens that is not far short of the truth. But officially we shall fail to establish an identity. It will be an unknown intruder for the public record."

"Might I ask where he was intruding, sir?"

"Dr Audley's place down in Hampshire."

Cox's face went blank—the books had unbalanced themselves again—and then clouded with surprise.

The change in expression was not lost on Sir Frederick. "Audley had nothing to do with it, Superintendent—at least not directly. He's . . . on holiday with his family."

"I'm relieved to hear it."

"Relieved?"

"Yes, sir." Cox was feeling his way circumspectly now; he hadn't yet been warned off, but he recognised the signs. "I understood he was not a violent man. Off the rugger field, at least. He's never had a weapon booked out to him." He paused. "But we do have a security problem now, sir."

"If the body is Hemingway's, we do—I agree," Sir Frederick's eyes shifted to the Archivist. "What was his security category?"

"Hemingway, sir?" The Archivist looked startled.

"Yes, Mr Benbow."

"Grade Four, sir."

It was Sir Frederick's turn to look surprised: Grade Four was hardly a security category at all. If the man who delivered the morning milk to the building had needed a category, that would have been it.

"I didn't know we had any Grade Fours here."

"He didn't handle anything requiring a higher clearance, sir. And he wasn't authorised to go above the ground floor."

Benbow was now pink with embarrassment. "His appointment was quite in order."

"I'm sure it was. But who the devil agreed to it?"

The Archivist braced himself visibly. "You did, Sir Frederick," he said.

"I did—did I?" Sir Frederick scowled reflectively.

Neville Macready, who had drifted away from the group to continue his examination of the carpet's pattern, gave an irreverent snort.

"So I did, so I did!" Sir Frederick muttered at last. "I remember now: you wanted a Grade Two Deputy and I wouldn't let you have him. You're quite right, Mr Benbow —I apologise."

"It was a matter of finance, sir, as I recall."

"Quite so. . . . Hmm! Then where did we get the man from, Superintendent?"

"From the Army, sir. He'd just taken early retirement from the RASC—warrant officer class two. He was in War Department records, so he had the right qualifications. It was a perfectly proper appointment."

"Perfectly proper stupidity, you mean!" Sir Frederick shook his head regretfully. "And he had no access to classified material?"

"None at all," said Benbow emphatically.

"What about the Dead Files? Weren't they next door to the Reading Room?"

"They're properly secured, sir. There's an electronic lock and the key has to be signed for."

"Of course," Sir Frederick nodded. "And you were satisfied with Hemingway?"

"He was competent."

"Competent?" The renewed question probed Benbow's slight hesitation. "No more than that?"

"There was no scope in his grade for more than that, Sir

Frederick." The probe was rewarded with a suggestion of distaste.

"But you didn't like him, Mr Benbow?"

"I can't say I cared for him. He was—he tried to be friendly, I suppose. He was always talking about what he saw on television—he had a colour set."

The Archivist made television sound like a physical handicap not spoken of in polite society, the coloured version being a particularly unfortunate manifestation of it.

"I didn't know him very well, Sir Frederick," Benbow concluded rather defensively.

"Very good." Sir Frederick stood up. "Thank you for your help, Mr Benbow. If this body of ours does turn out to be Hemingway, you are certainly not responsible in any way for what has occurred. But even if it doesn't we shall get rid of him. And you shall have a Grade Two deputy for the Reading Room, I promise you . . ."

"Well?"

Richardson waited for Cox to speak first.

"He could have been got at, sir," said Cox. "It would be worth their while to have someone in this building, even in the Reading Room. He could report on comings and goings at the least. And on the things that interested us. A foot in the door's better than nothing."

"Richardson?"

"He overheard David talk to Macready here. That's what set him off, I'll bet."

"Neville—was Hemingway there when you met David?"

Macready stopped pacing, shrugged. "He could have been. We were there—he's just part of the furniture as far as I'm concerned."

"Could he have seen the file?"

"What file?"

"The one David was looking at," said Sir Frederick with well-controlled patience.

Macready frowned. "I didn't see any file."

"David was looking at that file," Sir Frederick pointed to the desk.

"Not when he talked to me," said Macready.

"It is important, Neville," Sir Frederick said softly, but with an iceberg tip of firmness showing.

Macready stared at him. "Oh—come on, Fred! I went down there to look at the new AEQ. I was just going to sit down and David came up—we walked around a bit as we talked. I didn't look under the bloody table for spies—"

As he trailed off in vague irritation Richardson found himself once more searching for emotion in the faces of the other two men, and finding very little. He felt he was learning something useful about man-management, but he wasn't at all sure yet what it was. But they'd got what they wanted, anyway, even if it was not exactly reassuring: while Macready and David had communed with each other on their own esoteric intellectual plane Hemingway could probably have learnt the file's contents by heart without disturbing them.

"What's in it that's so special, for God's sake?" said Macready suddenly, lurching towards the desk and scooping up the file. Without another word he split it open with a well-chewed thumbnail and plunged into it, oblivious of his surroundings.

"Superintendent—" Sir Frederick's equanimity was undented by this raid on his desk: he simply ignored it. "I think you'd better get after the Hemingway angle."

"I'll do that, sir," said Cox. For the first time there was a hint of eagerness in his voice. Or was it gratitude?—it sounded quite remarkably like gratitude.

"Captain Richardson—" as the Special Branch man

nodded towards him Richardson detected a flicker of sympathy, "—good luck to you."

It *was* gratitude.

The speed of Cox's retreat took Richardson by surprise. And then, even before the door had clicked shut, its implications presented themselves to him like the figures on a bill run up by someone else which was about to be passed to him for payment.

Since Macready's arrival, and even more since Cox's, he had seemed to be no more than a spectator of a game in which he had already played his part. But Cox had been sent about his business at this point not simply because internal security was his job, but because Sir Frederick did not intend to involve him in its wider aspect. And he, Richardson, had remained—and was still uncomfortably remaining—because that too was part of the design.

Not for the first time he had the sense of being manipulated—of having only partial freewill: not a bus, not a train, but a tram. . . .

He had not been pulled out of Ireland because he was the only man who could make Mrs Clark talk: Hugh Roskill was also one of Clarkie's favourites, and Hugh was still convalescing from his last operation and would therefore have been much more easily usable. So it had all along been planned that if the case developed the assignment would be his, and that most obviously because of his special fitness for Italian operations.

But for once the thought of his second homeland aroused no light in his soul, for it was overshadowed by the realisation of what had really happened at Steeple Horley. What had seemed like a daring display of independence had in fact been nothing of the kind: he had not outfaced anyone with his demand to go straight to the top on David Audley's behalf—he had merely anticipated his own orders.

"You don't look happy, Peter," said Sir Frederick.

Well, it still might all be conjecture, because it was no good kidding himself that he was up to calculating all their angles yet. But one thing wasn't conjecture, and it ruddy well cooled his ardour now: Superintendent Cox had seized his dismissal like a thirty-year prisoner snatching a Royal Pardon, without asking questions or waiting for answers. And it wasn't just because Cox preferred the safe routine of checking on a dead Hemingway to the mind-bending frustrations of handling live Macreadys and Audleys, but because he knew enough not to want to know more.

"Should I be, then?" Richardson grinned insecurely. It was just like David had once said, the time to worry was when other people looked sorry for you as they said goodbye.

"You don't fancy a trip to Italy?"

Ten out of ten for Answer Number One.

"To bring David back in chains? Not especially, no."

"Not in chains. . . . Would you rather go back to Dublin?"

"You must be joking!" Richardson shuddered.

"Then what's so awful about Italy?"

"Nothing—about Italy." Richardson hardened his voice. "But there are too many loose ends in England."

"For example?"

"Hemingway, for a start. If he's the man old Charlie shot —their inside man here on an outside job—it doesn't damn well make sense—"

"And neither does *that*." Macready tossed the file on to the table irritably.

"Why not, Neville?"

"Because the idea of Hotzendorff bringing a plum out of Russia verges on the ridiculous, that's why."

"He didn't bring it out. He sent it. And he didn't send it to us, so it seems." Sir Frederick paused. "And it rather looks as though he died for it."

"He died of a heart attack—" Macready frowned suddenly. "You know what's in the file, then?"

"I read it when the news of his death finally reached us. And then there was the—ah—question of the widow's pension to be settled."

There was a half-second of awkwardness, lost on Macready, whose pension and life expectancy were matters of black and white actuarial certainty, but not lost on Richardson.

"You see, Peter—" Sir Frederick ignored Macready, "—Hotzendorff worked for us for fifteen years as a courier in Russia."

"A sort of postman," amended Macready.

"But useful enough. He travelled for an East German farm machinery company—he was our main source for the Virgin Lands scheme for example."

"In North Kazakhstan, which happens to be about 3,000 miles from the North Sea," said Macready, "and has no oil."

"He covered a great deal of territory elsewhere. And he was always very careful—and they trusted him."

"So did we."

"With very much better reason. You don't have to play the devil's advocate, Neville."

"I'm not trying to. It's simply that he wasn't the sort of man to pick up this sort of information. He was just a delivery agent for second-class mail."

"He put in his own reports too."

"Most of which he could have copied from the magazines and papers he bought in the streets. For the sort of thing we've been talking about he just didn't have the background —and he certainly didn't have the contacts, Fred."

Sir Frederick sighed, then shook his head. "You can say what you like, Neville. But at the end of the day the only clue we've got points to him. And—" he tapped the file, "there's circumstantial evidence in here that backs it up, too."

Richardson grasped thankfully at last at the answer to the question which had been nagging him increasingly: "What clue?"

Sir Frederick half smiled. "The one you brought to us, Peter—the one Narva gave to David's friend, and he gave to David, and Professor Freisler handed on to you: the Little Bird from East Berlin."

"The little dickey bird?"

"He started as Dickey Bird, curiously enough, short for Richard von Hotzendorff. He was rechristened Little Bird in '61. Born in Königsberg, which is now Kaliningrad, in 1914. David would have recognised him straight away, naturally—"

"David's signature is on the authorisation transferring the file from active to dead," said Macready. "His and Latimer's. July 1970—that would be the yearly clear-out."

"So he'd have remembered the circumstantial evidence too, then," Sir Frederick nodded.

Richardson looked at him expectantly.

"Nothing to do with oil, I'm afraid, Peter—Neville's right there. There isn't a smell of it."

"What is there a smell of?"

"The warm South—Italy. Three smells of it, too: Hotzendorff was there first with the German army in '42 and '43. The second time was twenty-five years later."

"Twenty-five?" The addition rolled in Richardson's brain like a jackpot number. "1968."

"Early in that year. He was dead before the end of it."

"And Narva was buying into the North Sea."

"Exactly."

"The Italian trip isn't in the file." Macready's tone was aggrieved.

"No. We didn't know it until after he was dead."

"And there was a third time." Now there was nothing casual about Macready's question, his voice was sharp.

"Not for Hotzendorff, there wasn't. Not long after he died his wife—his widow—got out of East Germany with her three children. She came to us to enquire about his pension. Or at least his gratuity—"

"She got out? You mean we didn't get her out?" Macready cut in quickly.

"We didn't—she did."

"On her own, with three children? She must be a woman of considerable initiative. The East Germans don't like losing children—did she say how she'd done it?"

"She had friends, she said. And some money saved—it can be done with that. She also said that her husband had placed some money in Italy on his last trip. With a bit of a pension it would be enough to bring the family up, if we could drop a word here and there." Sir Frederick looked from one to the other of them. "She said they'd always planned to retire there one day. We had no reason to doubt her story. . . ."

Oh, brother! thought Richardson—a woman of considerable initiative!

"I suppose Little Bird really is dead—or that he hasn't just migrated to sunnier climes?"

Sir Frederick looked at him a little reproachfully. "I said we didn't doubt her story, Peter—I didn't say we didn't check on it. Although it might have been better in this instance if we hadn't."

The obvious question hung in the air between them for a moment, unasked.

"We checked his death in the hospital files in Moscow, and we closed down his contact network—that was all routine. And then we ran another check on her eight months later in Italy, just to make sure he hadn't been clever." Sir Frederick looked from one to the other of them bleakly.

"And it was David Audley who had the job of setting up the checks."

"Okay—that does it." Macready turned away from the desk to stare directly out of the window into nowhere, nodding spasmodically to himself.

"You mean David had the necessary information to spark him off?"

"More than that—he had enough to guess he'd been taken for a ride by someone." .

There was no need to expand on that : it would bug David Audley to hell and back to find out that—it would light his blue touchpaper as nothing else would.

Richardson turned back to Sir Frederick. "So Little Bird sold us out to Narva—he went private on us?"

"That's not important." Macready swung back again, the excitement rising in his voice. "It isn't the first time something like that's happened. A little bit on the side for a rainy day, put away somewhere nice and safe abroad—it's much safer than defecting, and Italy's a darned sight more comfortable than anywhere behind the Curtain, especially when it's your old age you're thinking of. . . . And he was getting on, Hotzendorff was—this wasn't his September Song, he was well into October. . . ." Macready trailed off, head cocked on one side, half smiling to himself as though suddenly taken with that thought, his excitement of a moment earlier apparently quite forgotten. "Where do flies go in the wintertime? Nobody knows. They just disappear—once they're gone nobody cares where they go. Same with spies. But if they survive they've got to live somehow, just like the flies."

Well into October, and Little Bird had been a small, unimportant creature, thought Richardson. A delivery agent for second-class mail, a pedlar of second-hand facts. Useful, but a foreigner and not irreplaceable, as his very code-names seemed to suggest.

And yet a human being, with a wife and a family—maybe

more of a human being than the super-bright, egocentric Macready—and with human plans for his old age that didn't include risking his neck on second-class mail.

No wonder it wasn't the first time!

"What is important, Neville?" said Sir Frederick coolly recalling Macready to reality.

"Yes!" Macready snapped awake again, looking around him with a curiously distracted expression. "You'd do better to ask David, of course."

"If he was here I'd do just that," said Sir Frederick with a touch of asperity. "As it is I must make do with you, Neville."

Macready looked at him sharply. He was still not in the least overawed, but it seemed to Richardson that he was already regretting the brief flare of excitement which he could not now leave unexplained.

Then he shrugged. "I can only guess, naturally."

"Guess then."

Macready bowed to the word of command. "So long as you realise it is a guess—the Russians are no damn business of mine, any more than oil is David's."

He stopped.

"Get to the point."

"That is the point. Oil isn't David's speciality. He wouldn't understand all the angles."

"You underrate him."

"Oh, I know he's well informed. But technology isn't his *thing*. And the Russians are."

He stopped again. He was wrapping something up, thought Richardson; but wrapping up what—

The North Sea, Narva, Little Bird—the Russians?

Forecasting where the oil lay was impossible, or a ruddy miracle. But the Russians seemed to have done it.

And for Little Bird to lay his hands on a piece of knowledge as hot as that was a miracle too—but he seemed to have done it. (It didn't matter what he had done with it afterwards—that was no miracle, certainly.)

So—two miracles.

The light dawned like a flash of morning sun through a wind-blown curtain revealing bright day outside.

"They gave it to him," said Richardson. "He couldn't have got it on his own, Little Bird couldn't. So the Russians gave it to him—on a plate."

Macready raised an eyebrow in surprise. "*Someone* gave it to him anyway. But that's only the half of it."

"What's the other half?"

"I'm still only guessing—"

"For Christ's sake—" Richardson exploded.

"Okay, okay! I mean I'm trying to see it through David's eyes, that's all!" Macready sounded quite alarmed at encountering consumer hostility. "It's there in the file— Hotzendorff never complained of any heart trouble. I know people do go out like a light sometimes, but there's usually a couple of warnings. So it looks to me as though someone gave him the information and then snuffed him out the moment he'd passed it on so he couldn't split on them—"

"Which means—" Sir Frederick paused, "—if that is it, then it was an unofficial leak, because they'd never have needed him for an official one."

"And at a high level, too." Macready nodded quickly to emphasise his point. "That's what's grabbed David—not the oil."

Someone at a high level: someone who knew about Hotzendorff—they must have got on to him after all, even if they weren't ready to pick him up. And that meant someone with access to KGB surveillance lists.

And someone who knew about the North Sea bonanza and for some reason, some convoluted political reason, wanted to make sure the British and the other Western nations knew about it too.

And someone with the resources and the ruthlessness to stop Hotzendorff's mouth once he had served his purpose.

Except the irony of that had been that Hotzendorff had passed on the information to the wrong address after all, even though it had added up to the same result in the end.

Always supposing that had been the design.

"And you really think that was how David put it together?"

It was odd : he had tried to make the question sound casual, but it came out abrasively, as though he not only questioned Macready's ability to get inside David's mind, but also objected to it. He had already had his knuckles rapped for letting friendship influence him, and he'd do better to remember an older piece of advice : *Gladiator, make no friends of gladiators.*

"Eh?" Macready blinked at him defensively. "I tell you I'm guessing. I don't know what goes on in anyone's head, least of all David Audley's. I'm not claiming to." He stared at Richardson for a moment, then rounded on Sir Frederick. "It's the questions he asked. It wasn't just Narva he was interested in—he knew about him, I told you. Or about the North Sea. It was the Russians he kept coming back to."

"What about them, Neville?"

"Mostly questions I couldn't answer off the cuff. He wanted to know what their future projected fuel consumption was, and their percentage increase rate. And where they planned to make up the difference—things like that. . . . And who would be in the know, and how their policies were formulated. But it was the Russians he was interested in—I don't think he gave a damn for the North Sea."

Richardson now saw the encounter in the Reading Room in much clearer perspective. Faced with the same piece of information Audley and Macready had reacted according to their own specialist knowledge, each flying off on his own tangent, oblivious of the other's obsession.

Mention of the North Sea had been enough to launch Macready on his hobby-horse; and if he had disbelieved the first miracle he had been none the less bugged by the unresolved mystery of Narva's investment. But Audley was already ranging beyond the second miracle to its possible explanation: the existence of someone high in the Kremlin who was prepared to leak valuable information to the West in pursuit of his own ends.

And it was no ruddy wonder David found that possibility irresistible: if there was such a man, and his identity could be established, he would be wide open to every pressure from genteel suggestion to outright blackmail.

Or would have been if David and Macready had been more discreet—and less unlucky—in their behaviour.

"Whoever it was, the Russians'll get him now before we can, damn it," he muttered.

"Via Hemingway?" Sir Frederick had evidently advanced along an identical line of thought. "I'm afraid that seems all too likely, Peter. Though I find their behaviour a little strange all the same. We shall just have to see what Cox turns up there. In the meantime—"

He stopped abruptly, frowning down at the intercom.

"—Yes, Mrs Harlin?"

"I have a call from Rome for you, Sir Frederick." This time there was no apology in the voice, and no hesitation.

"They've got through to Dr Audley?"

"It isn't from Mr Cable, Sir Frederick. This is an official call from General Montuori. He is using the NATO scrambler line, priority green. He is on the line now—"

XI

THE WORST OF the sweltering day was over at last, but that brought no consolation to Boselli: the concrete perimeter strip of the airfield had baked for hours and now it was restoring every particle of stored heat to the atmosphere around him.

Also his head ached abominably, as though the racket of the rotor of the *Pubblica Sicurezza* helicopter which had brought him south was still revolving noisily in his brain; it had been just another of the day's awful ironies that those two hours of relative coolness had been an agony of incessant din in which neither thought nor comfort had been possible.

And now there was also the unseasonable humidity to contend with, more enervating than the dry Roman heat to which he was at least resigned. He had expected blue Campanian skies—the General's secretary had made the trip sound like a holiday jaunt—and instead he was enclosed by a haze which obscured the hills in the distance.

But the heat and the ache and the humidity were all in the natural order of things, the old conspiracy of his feeble body and hostile environment against his unclouded mind. It was fear now that dominated him, both the sick stomach fear of physical danger and the chest-tightening panic of professional failure.

The two hard-faced PS plainclothesmen behind him in the car did nothing to alleviate the physical fear. Sergeant Depretis had obviously been an officer of vast experience and proven ability to have made one of the special squads, but that had not prevented him choking in his own blood in the dust of Ostia; and even Villari's miraculous reflexes had not been fast enough to duck a bullet.

The very thought of Villari clouded his mind with confusion and guilt. The man had saved his life and taken his bullet, and the uncontrollable inner wish that the wound might prove mortal was therefore ungrateful and dishonourable as well as an act of treason and a mortal sin.

But Villari's survival would bring humiliation, because everyone from the General downwards now believed that he, Boselli, had gunned down the assassin.

"One shot—straight through the heart, too! I didn't know you could even use a gun, Pietro."

"Sir—I—I—"

"It's all right, Pietro, you don't have to tell me about it, not yet—Porro's already told me how it was. And I know it was bad, don't think I don't know. The first time is always bad. It was bad for me just the same—it was a Tommy in 1940, just outside Tobruk, and I was sick as a dog afterwards. But until then I didn't know whether I'd measure up. You can't tell until it happens—remember that, Pietro."

Oh, God! It had been ordinary temptation first—the admiration in Porro's eyes and the General's voice. And he had suddenly become *Pietro* to the General after all those years of being *Boselli*—that was temptation doubled and trebled.

But after the General's homily on the moment of measuring-up the true explanation had stopped dead in his throat and then it was suddenly a thousand years too late for any sort of truth at all, and he was stuck with the lie like a hit-and-run driver who had run too far to turn back.

If only Villari had not been hit! Or, more impossibly, if only what everyone thought was the reality, and he had measured up!

But he had not measured up, and now God was punishing him in the most subtle way imaginable: in his day-dreams he had always yearned for the chance of proving himself in the field, in charge of some important operation where no one else could steal the credit, but directly under the General's eye; and now he had his wish and with it his only chance of redeeming himself.

It was exactly as Father Patrick had always maintained—when God punished He always built a second chance into the punishment, that was the nature of His Grace.

So now he must carry out the General's instructions to the very last letter or be doubly damned as a liar and an incompetent. There would be no third chance.

But then, when he had once more come round to that inescapable conclusion, the self-doubts began again—the doubt that he could deliver even half that the General wanted.

"You heard the tape of what Clinton said—it was very convincing—that note of surprise was a small touch of genius. I think there is no liar in the world like an English gentleman, Pietro, no liar in the whole world. They are absolute masters of the half-truth. But I must know the whole truth. . . ."

No liars in the whole world—Boselli could believe that because he had been convinced that the news of the Ostian blood bath had genuinely surprised Clinton.

But the General was right, of course: to send such a man as Audley to interview Eugenio Narva about his investment in the oil discoveries in the North Sea made no sense at all. It was a technologist's assignment, and a routine one at that. Nor was it likely to be of great interest to the Russians, the more so because it related to the past.

And above all it ought not to be a killing matter.

But at that point the second and more terrifying requirement obtruded.

"And I want Ruelle, Pietro. One way or another, alive or dead—I want him."

A small sound registered in the world outside Boselli's private turmoil, the distant sound of aircraft engines. He raised his hand to lift the dark glasses which had slipped down his nose, remembering guiltily as he did so to whom they belonged. They were beautiful, expensive glasses, self-adjusting to the degree of sunlight : he had always wanted such glasses, and it had seemed a crime to leave them lying where they had fallen.

He sighed. If Villari lived he would have to give them back too.

There was nothing as yet to see, only the increasing sound in the north-west to be heard. But it would not be long now before the Englishman arrived.

Captain Peter John Richardson.

Nothing could be more English than that, except that Captain Peter John Richardson was no more and no less English than George Ruelle—Captain Peter John Richardson was another bastard half Italian Englishman.

No, that was inaccurate : he was no bastard of a passing foreign soldier and an ignorant peasant girl, the dossier was clear on that point : the girl had been of good family and the wedding in Amalfi Cathedral was a matter of undoubted record.

Unfortunately those were almost the only undoubted things in the dossier. The man had trained as a soldier, had been seconded to army intelligence in Cyprus and had then been sent on a language course at a provincial English university. Conjecturally, at some stage in that process he had been diverted into Sir Frederick Clinton's department

—it could have been even before he had gone to the university or during his studies (the famous guerrilla leader Lawrence had spied on the Turks while still a student, Boselli recalled with a mixture of outrage and admiration. No doubt it was neither the first nor the last time the English had played that game).

What was certain was that he had never returned to the Army, but as the facts ran and re-ran through Boselli's memory he could reach no conclusion beyond that he had reached on first encountering them: the man was young, but he would be clever and tricky—and doubly tricky because that mixture of English and Italian blood was traditionally a bad one, prone to bring out the worst of each.

That was true of George Ruelle, certainly; it remained to be seen whether it was true of Captain Peter John Richardson.

When it came at last, it came quickly, out of the haze and straight down on to the runway, a compact little executive jet of RAF Air Support Command.

Once down it swung quickly to the right, directly towards the group by the perimeter fence, set its passenger down accurately and quickly no more than seventy-five metres away, and then swung back again on its direct path towards the main buildings.

The first warning was the man's grace. Boselli was always a little suspicious of too much ease of movement, too much physical confidence. That had been what Villari had had, and this man had it too: he gave the pilot a wave and then, as the aircraft left him, took one slow look around him before he started towards Boselli, a small leather travelling bag in one hand and his jacket, slung negligently over his shoulder, in the other. He looked as if he owned everything he could see.

A small pain hammered just above Boselli's left eyebrow.

a sickening migraine-like pulse. Already he did not like the half-Englishman.

"Signor Boselli?" The toothpaste-white teeth lit up the good-looking brown face, a totally Mediterranean face without a single Anglo-Saxon feature.

"Captain Richardson?"

"Not captain any more." The smile remained in position as Richardson stared into Boselli's dark glasses. He breathed in the heat appreciatively. "Thank God for a little warmth at last. It was raining when we took off."

Boselli ignored the pleasantry. "Your identification, if you please."

"Of course." Richardson handed over a plain black little folder. "The mug-shot's not a bad likeness, don't you think?"

The man's Italian was as faultless as his face, there was even an irritatingly added perfection in the hint of Neapolitan in it. He was smiling in the photograph, too.

"A formality," said Boselli coldly, handing back the folder.

"Of course." Richardson nodded. "And yours?"

The request caught Boselli by surprise; he had never, in his entire career, been asked for his official card by anyone other than the guards on the department, and that only in the dim past. But although the half-Englishman's intention of putting him in his place was perfectly clear he could see no way of refusing it without a direct confrontation, and the insolence beneath the smile was too well-hidden for that.

He fumbled for it in his wallet, but unfortunately it had long settled in the innermost fold and in extracting it he dislodged a dog-eared collection of small private objects, including the appalling snapshot of his wife and mother-in-law taken during the previous summer's martyrdom in Viterbo.

The snap fluttered down between them and Richardson bent effortlessly and gathered it up, offering it back as though in exchange for the card while Boselli hastily gathered up the rest.

"A formality also," said the half-Englishman. "Shall we go, then?"

Boselli followed him to the car seething with the knowledge that he had allowed himself to be overawed, even though it was the English who were in the weaker position. Yet he knew also that it was not the English who mattered, but the General. If he could only obtain results by seeming to abase himself to this nonchalant pig, then that was how the game must be played. At least it was a role he knew how to fill to the last humiliating syllable. Revenge could come later.

Nevertheless it would be a mistake to surrender too tamely, and he must take the initiative to start with.

"This is a serious business, Captain Richardson," he began heavily.

"You're telling me!"

"I am telling you, Captain Richardson. One of our agents has been killed and another lies gravely wounded."

Richardson chewed on that for a moment before replying.

"I wasn't aware that we were responsible for any of that, signore."

"It occurred as a direct consequence of the actions of one of your operatives."

"An indirect consequence. That would be a fairer description."

"Direct or indirect—the incident occurred and General Montuori is extremely angry about it."

"So is Sir Frederick Clinton."

"But General Montuori did not initiate this affair. He wishes to remind you further that Italy and England are treaty allies and that such actions as this could have grave repercussions within NATO."

That sounded good, Boselli decided happily, because it

sounded official. It was beside the point that it was exactly the opposite of what the General had said: *But we don't want any political trouble with the English. We're going to need them to keep that wild man Mintoff in line if he gets to power in Malta.*

"In fact he expects the very fullest co-operation now, Captain Richardson."

"Not 'captain', if you don't mind, signore," said Richardson. At last he was no longer smiling.

"Signor Richardson." Boselli smiled. He might not have to surrender after all. "The fullest co-operation."

"By that I take it you mean a two-way exchange of information?"

"We have no information to exchange. We did not initiate this affair, as I have already pointed out."

"I see." Richardson nodded, regarding Boselli reflectively. Then he turned away to the left as the car came out of a cutting through the dark-grey volcanic rock. "Monte Vesuvio's hiding himself today, I see. But he's still there all right. He's still there."

Boselli frowned at him, nonplussed.

"You know my family—my mother's family—came from these parts?" said Richardson conversationally.

Boselli nodded as Richardson turned to him.

"Of course you would. A big family it was, but not so big now. Too many of the men developed the bad habit of getting themselves killed. But we once had vineyards from here to Ravello—red and white Vesuvio, and Ischia and Avellino. Now only the Ravello vineyards are left, I think. And a pottery at Salerno. . . . And one of my second cousins has a machine-tool works at Torre Annunziata on the right there somewhere. It was his father who used to say that Monte Vesuvio sometimes hid himself, but he was always there." He turned back towards the mist-shrouded volcano. "Have you picked up David Audley, then?"

Boselli thought quickly, but could find no objection to answering.

"Yes."

Richardson nodded. "Where did you pick him up?"

"Does it matter?"

"I'd be interested to know. At one of the autostrada toll stations, I'd guess—near Naples, maybe?"

"Salerno."

"Salerno! He must have been pushing it, but that figures. . . . So in effect we gave him to you."

"There was a general call out for him, Captain Richardson."

"Signor. But we told you—Sir Frederick told your boss—where he was heading, so we gave him to you. That's what I call full co-operation. And you know who he was going to see?"

Boselli nodded cautiously. He had the feeling that the haze was about to lift from Monte Vesuvio—and that there might be smoke coming from the crater.

"Narva. Signor Eugenio Narva. Pillar of the Establishment and the Christian Democrats and the Church. Founder and master of Narva Enterprises from the Persian Gulf to Bonnie Aberdeen. Chief shareholder in Xenophon Oil and Singer and Bailey and Enfield Alloys and other companies too numerous to mention, plus a finger in North Sea off-shore block allocations 311/26, 312/6, 315/4. A very busy fellow, Signor Narva is—I'm sure you've heard of him, Signor Boselli."

Richardson grinned again at Boselli. "You know what happens to Romans who come South, signore—they're no good to the Calabrians because the Neapolitans have taken all their money from them as they pass through. That's why Calabria is so poor. But I'm only half from these parts, so I'll be nice to you—I'll tell you why we are so interested in Narva.

"You see, I'm afraid your General has gone off at half-cock—we didn't initiate this affair, as you put it. We were only very gently enquiring—and Dr Audley was doing nothing more than that—about a bit of industrial espionage in which Signor Narva indulged a few years ago. And a very nasty bit of industrial espionage, too—you could even drop the 'industrial' part of it if you liked. The sort of thing that'd raise unpleasant questions in our Parliament."

Boselli experienced a queasy feeling below the belt.

"The sort of thing—your boss was quite right there—the sort of thing that could have grave repercussions, not just in NATO but in the Common Market negotiations. In fact you're dead lucky that *my* boss is a Common Market man, otherwise our anti-marketeers would be having a field-day now."

We don't want any political trouble with the English: the sick feeling worsened. Between them Narva and the General represented an appalling range of political and professional problems, never mind Ruelle and these English, who between them personified danger.

"So just don't go on thinking you can call all the shots just because you've got Dr Audley," Richardson went on coolly. "I want to see him—and quickly."

Boselli nodded humbly. 'We are on our way to see him now, signore."

"Good. And I hope you haven't roughed him up, either."

Boselli tried to look shocked.

"It was just a thought." Richardson gave a conspiratorial nod towards the two men in the front of the car. "Some of your *Pubblica Sicurezza* special squads can be a bit heavy-handed, especially when they want to show off in front of the *Carabinieri*."

"I assure you there has been nothing like that. We have merely detained him."

"I'm glad to hear it. Because we're going to need him,

Signor Boselli—you and me both, since we're about to give each other the fullest co-operation, that is."

No smile this time, Boselli noted. Perhaps the half-Englishman also required a success for his record.

"You can rely on me, signore." Perversely, he was not wholly forging the sincerity in his voice. His brief, false moment of power had been heady, but followed by self-doubts even before Richardson had bitten back as he realised that he still didn't know what course of action to follow next. But clearly the half-Englishman knew what to do, and by hanging to his coat-tails he, Boselli, might yet salvage something, taking the credit for success and at least sharing the blame for failure.

And already he had learnt something to tell the General: the English were angry about Narva's interference in their North Sea and desperately worried that it should not become an issue of their domestic politics. In such circumstances even the General would wish to move cautiously.

"You can rely on me," he repeated, "Signor Richardson."

"Fine. And Peter is the name—I'm Pietro in these parts."

"I too am Pietro."

"Well I'd better stick to Peter, then. And the first thing you can do for me, Pietro, is tell me about this shooting of yours. What the hell happened?"

"It was in Ostia, signore—Peter. Ostia Antica."

"The old ruins? What was David Audley doing there?"

"We hoped you could tell us." Boselli shrugged. "Could he have been meeting someone?"

"It's possible. But who started the shooting?"

"We followed him, but—we were ambushed. One of our men was killed, another wounded, as I have told you. And one of theirs."

"Killed?"

Boselli nodded, looking past Richardson at a small family

saloon they were overtaking. It was piled high with boxes and battered cases on the roof-rack and bulging with children : they had passed many such cars already, families travelling southwards—homewards—from the northern factories for their annual holidays.

He remembered the ant which had stopped, bewildered, at the edge of the pool of blood in the dust. He thought he would never see an ant again without remembering that moment : ants and blood were linked together forever now.

"Yes."

"Identified?"

Boselli had already faced this question, and nothing had happened since to change his decision. It was high time the two half-Englishmen were introduced to each other.

"Yes. His name was Mario Segato. Aged fifty-six. Foreman plumber on a construction site in Avezzano—that's about a hundred kilometres east of Rome."

"I know where it is. You mean he wasn't a pro?" Richardson frowned. "A foreman plumber?"

"He was a foreman plumber." Boselli hugged the full story to himself for one final second. "But there was a time when he had a different occupation."

"Which was—"

"Bodyguard to George Ruelle."

"George—George Ruelle?" Richardson sat up. "You don't mean Bastard Ruelle?"

"You know him?"

"Know him? I thought he was dead! I thought he'd been dead for years."

"But you know him."

"No, but I've heard of him. My first cousin—my second cousin's father—knew him before he moved north. He said that was the best thing that happened to Campania since the Krauts retreated—the Bastard heading for Rome where the action was. He really was a bastard in the fullest sense of the word. The Italian Stalin, that was his ambition, Enrico said. But you mean to say he's alive—and—?"

Boselli nodded sagely. "Alive, Signor Richardson, and positively connected with this."

"But I thought the Bastard was drummed out of the Party back in the fifties?"

"So he was. And Segato with him. That is what worries us now—he does not fit the pattern."

"You mean your Communists have gone respectable?"

Boselli snorted. "They will never be that! But they pretend to respectability, and Ruelle—he is a creature from the Dark Ages, a man of violence. A Neanderthal."

"Phew!" Richardson scratched his head. "And old David's in the middle. I'm damn glad you've got him safe and sound." He stared at Boselli suddenly. "He ducked you both at Ostia, then—just like that?"

"So it would seem, signore. There was some—some confusion, you understand—"

He stopped, at a loss for a moment as he realised how grossly he was understating the nightmare situation which had developed in the aftermath of the shooting.

In spite of Porro's best efforts they had been quite unable to contain events. First the local police had arrived, their zeal apparently strengthened by a determination not to let the *Pubblica Sicurezza* hog any of the limelight. Rumours of a clash between Fascist and Maoist student factions had quickly blossomed into a Roman gangland battle, and then into a terrorist-anarchist bloodbath, which in turn had drawn crowds of sightseers, squads of journalists and a convoy of screeching ambulances. Two busloads of German tourists who had just entered the excavations added a dimension of babel to the confusion.

Confusion was a totally inadequate word for it, and it had taken no special talent for either the assassins or the Englishman and his wife to make their getaway in the last precious moments before it had descended; ironically it had been Boselli and Porro who had been first trapped and then humiliated. . . .

Boselli just managed to control an involuntary shudder at the memory of it as he became aware that Richardson was still staring at him, curiosity and puzzlement mixed on his face.

"There was—some confusion," he repeated mechanically.

Richardson smiled, but wryly this time. "I can imagine it." He paused. "I wonder what the devil he was up to?"

"Ruelle?"

"Him too." The half-Englishman nodded. "Perhaps him most of all. But I was actually wondering what Dr Audley was doing in Ostia Antica in the first place."

Boselli watched him sidelong. In repose, now unsmiling again, the brown face was too long, the jaw too angular, for good looks. But more than that there was an underlying worry in the expression which had escaped him until now. So the English too did not know everything, or did not know quite how to control what they had set loose in Italy.

It was a timely reminder that they were not to be trusted. Even in the days of their power and glory that had been true; now, in their age of decline, they would be as dangerously unpredictable as an old bull. In that respect at least George Ruelle and his fatherland were now disturbingly alike.

·XII·

LITTLE RAT-FACE BOSELLI had spoken the truth about Audley's detention, anyway.

The villa was new and surpassingly ugly, its salmon-pink tiles and bright red ironwork at odds with the colours of nature all around it. But if it lacked elegance as a home it was a decidedly superior temporary jail, the more so when its prisoner was established comfortably under a gay awning at the far end of the terrace with bottles on the table beside him.

Audley did not get up as they approached him.

"Well—hullo, Peter."

It was a low-key welcome, at least when coming from a man who had been plucked off the autostrada by the cops, no matter how well they had behaved or how comfortably they had bestowed him; there was more resignation in it than pleasure, and no surprise at all. But that was pretty much to be expected: Audley had had time since his arrest to compute most of the angles, with the arrival of someone from the department figuring in at least one of them. And being Audley he could be relied on at least not to play the guiltless innocent.

"Hullo, David."

He looked tired, though, thought Richardson. And also there was something else he had never before seen in the big man's face, an obstinate blankness like a safety door closed against him.

"This is Signor Boselli, of General Montuori's staff in Rome, David," he began cautiously.

"Signor Boselli," Audley nodded. He gestured towards the

table. "You'll join me? The drinks here are on the house, it seems."

He turned up two fresh glasses and splashed wine into them, topping his own up afterwards. But the wine bottle had been hardly touched before, Richardson noted, while the *aqua minerale* was almost empty.

David lounged back in his chair. "So you've come to bail me out, young Peter. I'm very grateful."

"We have to work our passage first, David."

"Indeed?" Audley murmured blandly. "Go on, Peter."

"After what happened at Ostia you're not the most popular Englishman in Italy, you know."

"At Ostia?" Audley glanced briefly at Boselli. "I'll tell you something for free, Peter : whatever may have happened at Ostia was none of my doing. I'm not responsible for homegrown Italian talent."

There was an element of truth in that, thought Richardson irritably, but it hardly accounted for Audley's lack of co-operation when it must be obvious enough to him that the Italians had the whip-hand.

Boselli drained his wine and stood up self-consciously.

"Excuse me, signori," he mumbled. "There are things I must do—excuse me. I will return shortly."

Audley watched him off the terrace, then turned towards Richardson, one eyebrow raised ironically.

"Now you're not going to tell me he's gone for a quick pee, are you, Peter?"

"Not unless you twist my arm."

"Good. So you both agreed on how to handle me." He nodded to himself. "But just because he's got you frightened that doesn't mean I have to get talkative."

"Him—? Got me frightened? Him?"

"You aren't? Well, don't be deceived by appearances, boy —although I admit they certainly are deceptive." Audley stared reflectively in the direction Boselli had gone. "Unless

167

I'm very much mistaken that little fellow is one of Montuori's top guns, specially imported for the occasion."

Richardson goggled at him, and then down the empty terrace wordlessly.

"I could be wrong, of course." Audley stood up. "He's a new one on me I admit. . . . But let's take a turn among those olive trees down there by the cliff. They didn't mind me walking there—there isn't anywhere you can get out, but it's a little more private."

Richardson followed him obediently down the white steps into the sparse little grove of olives until they came to a low stone wall. The roar of the traffic on the coast road far below rose to meet them. Away to the left Salerno spread out invitingly, and he remembered the last time he had been there, with a delectable Swedish girl he'd picked up at Amalfi—

"I want you to get me out of here, Peter," said Audley in his ear urgently. "I don't care how you do it, but just get me out of here quickly."

Richardson faced him. "It can't be done, David. They've had a man killed, maybe two. Montuori phoned Sir Frederick, person to person. He's out for blood. In fact they're both ruddy well out for blood—only it's yours Sir Frederick would like and Montuori isn't so choosy. I rather think it's someone else's he wants more than yours, anyway."

Audley studied his face for a moment, then shook his head. "Nobody'll get anything unless you get me out of here. Without me you haven't got a prayer of a chance. You just don't understand what's going on—neither does Fred."

Richardson looked at him in momentary surprise: this was the old Machiavellian Audley right enough—on the scaffold, but ready to bargain that what he had in his head was too valuable for anyone to dare cutting it off. It had worked well in the past, and it had been allowed to work, because in his own way Audley had always delivered the goods. But from the moment old Charlie Clark had pulled the trigger too much had happened, and too much was known, for it to work this time.

"You're dead wrong there, David." It was brutal, but it would be quicker this way. And anyway, he owed Audley something like honesty for old time's sake. "We know ruddy near the lot."

In spite of the noise from below there was a silence between them for a moment.

"The lot?" Audley measured the word.

" 'Near', I said."

"How near?"

"Ian Howard. Eugenio Narva. Neville Macready." Richardson paused. "And the Little Bird from East Berlin, of course—the Little Bird who sang in the wrong ear."

Not Joseph Hemingway or Peter Korbel or Bastard Ruelle—not yet. They were the second wave of attackers, ready if the shock troops failed to break through. Old times' sake didn't go all the way.

"I see."

Audley turned away, staring out over the bay.

"So . . . Neville Macready," he murmured to himself as though that one name accounted for the rest. Disquietingly he seemed almost relieved by it but still unbowed: the shock troops were not through yet.

"David, you've got to come clean with us now. There's no other way."

"Come clean?" The sudden anger, cold and bitter, deepened Audley's voice. "Come clean? Of all the goddam bloody stupid meddling fornicating *idiots*—blundering, fourth-rate, sanctimonious *twats*—"

"David—" Richardson was shaken by the sudden loss of control. On occasion he had heard Audley swear before, and more foully, but it had always been for effect, never from despair.

"Not you, Peter—not you." Audley shook his head quickly. "They couldn't trust me—just this once—and they've blown it because of that, blown it sky-high."

"It wasn't like that at all—" Richardson cut in desperately "—nobody blew it for you. There was a leak in the department, in the Reading Room where you had that talk with Macready."

"A leak?" Audley said incredulously.

"The Librarian—Hemingway. We traced his contact just before I flew out—

"The same old story—you've heard it all before." Cox had sounded bored. "He lived in Orpington—stock-broker belt— and he wanted to keep up with the Joneses. Only the Joneses in Orpington were too rich for his blood, with his army pension and what he was paid by your lot. You're not exactly good payers, are you? But his neighbours thought he was a senior civil servant and he had to live up to what he'd let them think. He was easy meat, Captain Richardson. Easy for an old hand like Peter Korbel—"

"Peter Korbel? Good God—I thought we'd expelled him with Protopopov and the Moscow Narodny Bank man. Months ago!" Audley's surprise was unconcealed.

Richardson grimaced. Their reactions had been identical.

"Protopopov and Adashev went, but we let Korbel stay on for a bit." Over the phone Cox hadn't even the grace to sound apologetic. "He wasn't considered dangerous enough—one of the hewers of wood and drawers of water, Captain. Besides, there's going to be a big clear-out in a couple of months' time if the Cabinet agrees. We'd got him on that list. We were rather hoping the Russians would save us the trouble, actually—he's long overdue for retirement. Must be all of sixty. . . ."

"Retirement is right!" Audley snarled. "But you've picked him up now—and Hemingway, I take it?"

"Hemingway's dead." Richardson decided that it was not the time to elaborate on the circumstances of the Librarian's death. Audley had quite enough to worry about as it was.

"And Korbel?"

"Gone—vanished."

Richardson waited for Audley to swear again, but the big man only stared at him in silence for a few seconds and then turned away once more, his self-discipline clamped back tight again.

"But listen, David—" Richardson felt aggrieved that Audley had still managed to ask all the questions instead of answering them—and that he still seemed set on playing both ends against the middle "—there's still a damn good chance the Russians haven't been able to put two and two together. Maybe Hemingway didn't hear everything. After Ostia. . . ."

The affray in Ostia was the awkward piece in the pattern, the very example of bloody public scandal which men on both sides risked their skins to avoid. It could only have happened because the Italian PS men and the Communist agents who were dogging Audley's footsteps had collided head-on and had panicked—that was Boselli's explanation, and if Korbel had been unable to warn his Italian opposite number about Hemingway's death it was an explanation that made sense. But, even more significantly, the presence of those incompetent Reds surely meant that the opposition didn't yet know what Audley was up to.

That thought roused another one, much closer to home: the opposition weren't the only ones in the dark about Audley's actions there—

"Just what the hell *were* you doing in Ostia this morning?"

Audley didn't reply. He didn't even appear to hear the question, but seemed totally abstracted in the great sweep of land and sea.

"For Christ's sake, David!" Richardson's sorely-tried cool finally slipped. Only a few hours ago he'd fixed a date with little Bernadette O'Connell of the Dublin Provisionals to meet in Mooney's bar next day and eat at Donovan's place in Balbriggan and end the evening strictly non-politically in her flat off Clanbrassil Street. She'd be waiting for him now, her passionate Anglo-Italian boyfriend with his sales list of Belgian sniperscopes and American rocket-launchers that would never see the soft light of Irish day.

"David—there have been some of your bloody stupid fornicating meddling idiots who've stuck out their bloody stupid fornicating necks for you this last twelve hours, including me for one. If you clam up now the Italians'll turn nasty, and then we've really had it."

Audley met the appeal stone-faced. "If I don't get out of here smartly, Peter, I agree with you: we've all had it. So just get me out."

"Man—you're crazy!" Richardson stared at Audley in bewilderment at his obtuseness. "I tell you for the last time, it's impossible—not after Ostia. And I tell you this too, David: I damn well wouldn't do it now if it was. Either you work with me and little Rat-face or you rot here until Montuori decides what to do with you. It's shit or bust this time."

Audley blinked. One corner of his mouth dropped and twitched, though whether in anger or despair Richardson could not tell. He had never before seen quite this look on this face.

"I'm sorry, David. But that's the way it is."

"Sorry?" Anger and despair, and bitterness too. "Yes, Peter, I think you very well may be."

Richardson accepted the bitterness with bitterness of his own at Audley's lack of understanding that he was sorry already. Sorry for the end of old times' sake, the end of advice and the exchange of ideas, and of evenings and weekends at the old house in Steeple Horley. . . . Sorry for friendship's end even where friendship was a luxury, and maybe a dangerous one at that.

Not that there was any choice, because it would be fatal for Audley to have been set loose while the Bastard was at large.

"You know who we're up against?"

"I'm permitted to know, then?"

Richardson ignored the sarcasm. "You've ever heard of George Ruelle?"

"I've heard of him, yes."

It was a flat statement: evidently the Bastard didn't frighten Audley.

"Those were his men at Ostia. David—you were damn lucky to get out of that." He grasped childishly at the obvious justification of his refusal to connive at Audley's escape. "You could have got Faith killed there, never mind yourself."

Audley showed no reaction at the mention of his wife.

"Where is she now, incidentally?" asked Richardson.

"Back in Rome, of course."

Another flat statement: it was none of anyone else's business what Faith Audley was doing, least of all now ex-friend Peter Richardson's—the message was plain enough.

Richardson sighed. "What were you doing in Ostia?"

Audley looked down his nose at him. "Unlikely as it may seem to you—" the blandness was insulting, "—I was showing my wife the ruins."

The simple logic of the answer was embarrassing. He had fallen into the trap of assuming that everything Audley had done was significant, forgetting that the big man had also been unaware of what had been happening in England, and had no reason to suspect that anything could go wrong. If he had he would never have hazarded his wife by keeping her at his side, but as it was there had originally been no particular urgency about this journey southwards; indeed, the whole Italian trip had probably been planned as a holiday, with the descent on Narva as a surreptitious side-expedition.

Richardson swore inwardly, recalling his pleasure only a few hours earlier at the sight of the familiar signpost to Upper Horley. Even the wild unpredictability of the Dublin IRA was maybe preferable to this, which already had the smell of disaster about it.

"And now you're heading for Narva?"

Audley nodded a little wearily. "I was. Until your new friends picked me up."

"No friends of mine." He emphasised the words hopefully, offering them like an olive branch. "We've got to work with them—they've got us by the short hairs at the moment. But if we can get the name of Little Bird's contact without their getting it, maybe it'ud put Fred in a better mood. They're not on to the real thing yet, I don't think, David."

Audley shook his head. "Don't kid yourself. Montuori's nobody's fool. When he gets to thinking about this he'll work it out right the way through."

"Maybe. But I've an idea it's Ruelle he wants more than anything else, the way Rat-face tightened up at the mention of him."

"Rat-face?"

"Sorry—Boselli. He sounded nervous when he spoke of him, like he was scared. Which I don't wonder at if the Bastard still has his touch after all these years. . . . But you say he's a gun too—?"

"That's right."

"But a new one? New to you?"

"I don't know him."

The Mediterranean had once been Audley's stamping ground, and his encyclopaedic memory was much admired. So Rat-face must be either very new or very special, or both.

"You know he's a gun, though?" Richardson persisted.

Audley shrugged. "Two of the PS guards here were talking about him below the terrace—I didn't encourage them to think I knew Italian, and they were careless. . . ."

"Yes?"

"It seems they knew the man who was killed at Ostia—the PS man. But apparently it was Boselli who got the killer. One shot straight through the heart at twenty metres. Whatever he looks like that makes him a pro, I'd say."

Richardson nodded thoughtfully in agreement: that sort of practice ruled out amateurs, sure enough. Which meant he had been dead wrong about Signor Pietro Boselli, because fussy little men didn't use one shot at twenty metres. And if he'd been nervous it would not have been with fear, but with a craftsman's excitement at the prospect of demonstrating his special aptitude again.

He shivered at the magnitude of his error of judgement, which was all the more unpardonable when he set this new information in perspective: if Montuori wanted Ruelle so badly he would naturally put one of his best men on the job. Also, Boselli was one good reason why Audley had been so intractably determined to get away again. So long as he was with them there'd be precious little chance of holding out on the Italians.

"Well, we'll have to make the best of him for the time being," said Richardson philosophically. "And at least he'll have an eye cocked for Ruelle."

"True." Audley still didn't sound unduly worried about the Bastard—a little surprisingly in view of his Ostian experience, Richardson thought.

"You know he operated in these parts in the old days?"

"Ruelle? I thought Latium was his province?"

A flicker of interest now.

"Not to start with. He led a partisan group up Avellino way in '43."

"Indeed?" The flicker brightened, steadied. "Well, that might account for it—"

"For what?"

"Eh?" Audley looked at him. "Oh—I mean it might account for the presence of old Peter Korbel."

"For Korbel?"

"The art of deserting and surviving—Korbel could write a book about that, and it would take the form of an autobiography." Audley grunted. "You know where he came from?"

"He was born in the Ukraine. The Germans captured him in '41—he came to England as a DP after the war, I thought?"

"Yes and no." Audley regarded him donnishly over his spectacles. "He started from the Ukraine right enough, but he came to us the long way round—via Italy."

He paused smugly. "Jack Butler did a rundown on him a few weeks ago, as a matter of fact, after that business of ours in Cumbria. . . . More out of curiosity than necessity, really, because everyone thinks they know everything about Korbel, and none of it matters anyway. But Jack has a more orderly mind than most—he likes to be sure.

"According to him Korbel deserted to the Wehrmacht, he wasn't captured. Told 'em he was a Volga German and made his story stick—or stick well enough for them to recruit him and ship him off to the Italian front. The whole world was fighting here anyway, so he'd fit in whatever he was."

That was true enough, reflected Richardson. The armies which had descended on poor old Italy had been absurdly polyglot. On the Allied side there had been everything from Maoris and Red Indians to Berbers and Japanese Americans, and the ex-Red Army men fighting under the German banner had even included two bewildered Tibetans who strayed across their Himalayan frontier accidentally years before. He himself was a living testimony of that racial confusion, with an Amalfitan mother and a father from Tunbridge Wells.

"Butler reckons he'd aimed to join the winning side, but when he got this far he realised he'd miscalculated. So in '43 he mustered out again—and became a Ukranian again too—and joined up with us after the Salerno breakout."

Again Audley paused. But the drift of his information was clear enough: Korbel had been here in Campania, changing allegiance again, at the exact moment when Ruelle had started operations—

Richardson frowned as the curious contradictions in this coincidence began to occur to him. Even if Korbel and Ruelle had known each other all those years ago their connection now was still very odd indeed. If the Russians had, for reasons which were still totally obscure, decided to investigate Audley's Italian mission, then it would not have been Korbel's job to start things moving—and even if it had, he would never have called on a bloody-minded old has-been like Ruelle to undertake the job.

In fact, the more he thought about it, the stranger it seemed, because the Russians hadn't even recruited Korbel until the mid-fifties—and by then the Italian Communists had already dumped Ruelle.

"David—" he tried to sound half-jocular, "—you wouldn't be putting me on, would you?"

"Putting you on?" Audley looked at him questioningly. "About Korbel?"

"About Korbel getting through to his old pal Ruelle."

As he stared back at Audley the sheer copper-bottomed absurdity of it mushroomed: not just the idea of Korbel suggesting the recruitment of Ruelle, but of the London

KGB *resident* listening to him, getting through to Moscow Centre . . . and then Centre calling up the Rome *resident*— damn it, the thing required simultaneous brain-storms in London, Moscow and Rome: it was like piling the improbable on the unlikely, all on a foundation of the incredible— and no one should know that better than David Audley himself: perhaps that was the strangest thing of all.

Richardson was glad he hadn't sounded too serious. It left him room for a touch of stupidity.

"Well, it's one hell of a coincidence, David." He grinned. "And the Russians don't go much on the old boys' network, either, surely?"

"Old boys' network?" Audley blinked. "No, they don't . . . in fact there's probably nothing in it—"

And that touch left Audley room to wriggle out. Which he was promptly doing.

"—You're quite right, Peter. But either way it doesn't matter, because we can leave Korbel to Sir Frederick and Ruelle to General Montuori, anyway. They don't concern us, thank God."

If there was one sure thing now, thought Richardson, it was that Korbel and Ruelle concerned him very much indeed.

"We concentrate on Narva, you mean."

Two sure things, rather: Audley still knew one hell of a lot more about Korbel and Ruelle than he was admitting.

"Right." Audley bobbed his head in agreement.

"And 'we' means me, David."

"Right."

"And Boselli comes along for the ride."

Shrug. "If that's the way you must have it."

'It's the only possible way."

Audley raised both his hands, fingers spread, in acceptance. "So—we all go to see Narva. Right!"

And thirdly and sadly: ex-friend David was one big ruddy liar.

XIII

AT LEAST THE General's new instructions made things easy—that was one good thing: all he had to do was to make sure the Englishmen didn't make a run for it, which under the circumstances of the General's conversation with Sir Frederick Clinton they were most unlikely to attempt.

Nor was it the only good thing, by any means. One had to beware of optimism, particularly as Villari had not yet regained consciousness after his operation. But there was hope even there, for if he survived his memory might well be vague about that last split-second: the farther the whole episode receded into the past in Boselli's own mind the more vague the truth became and the more he felt disposed to believe what was now the official story. That was the way history was formed after all—by the acceptance of what people wanted to believe.

The important thing was that the General was pleased with him so far. Admittedly, some of that approbation was founded on his edited account of the interview with Richardson, whom he had represented as shrewd and tough and unco-operative, but from whom he had none the less extracted useful information about Narva and the political implications of his industrial espionage activities.

Privately Boselli was convinced that Richardson was by no means as formidable as he had suggested, but that like all the native inhabitants of these parts he was merely untrustworthy and overweeningly sure of himself—and his English blood had merely reinforced those defects of character.

The man Audley was a very different proposition. He had

watched the fellow during dinner and had gained very little enlightenment beyond the confirmation of what had been recorded in the dossier : that superficial appearances were deceptive, and that behind the bulkiness of the athlete running to seed—that had been Villari's assessment—there lurked the sort of intellectual he instinctively feared.

Yet Audley was undeniably nervous, where Richardson was smooth and relaxed. While both had been noticeably careful with the wine, the older man had merely picked at his food while the younger had gorged himself, scorning Boselli's warning that the local seafood sometimes tested foreign stomachs with the boast that his was the least foreign stomach at the table. Indeed, the two seemed to draw away from each other during the meal, the pure Englishman becoming more English, more monosyllabic, and the half-Englishman becoming increasingly Italian.

Boselli had been so fascinated with his study of them that he had forgotten his own hunger, and now as they snaked along the coast road its pangs were already gnawing at his delicate stomach. However, in the circumstances this was probably just as well, for though lack of food had never sharpened his wits—that was a lie spread by the satisfied to appease the starving—too much of it invariably dulled them. Moreover, on this particular journey he would have had difficulty keeping any respectable quantity of food in its proper place, for the road was carved out of the side of the cliff along a tortuous coastline and the police driver seemed desperate to impress his passengers with his skill : on every hairpin bend the black emptiness of the seaward edge was hideously close.

"How much farther?" The big Englishman lapsed into his native tongue, then quickly corrected himself into Italian by repeating the question.

"We must be nearly there now." Richardson swung round

in the front seat and Boselli picked up the garlic on his breath once more. "That was Praiano we just passed—"

They had all seemed identical, the little towns and villages through which they had come in the darkness, with the same people, the same houses and the same scenes momentarily illuminated. But for Richardson every place was distinguished by some anecdote, or restaurant, or person (usually a girl, but often enough a blood relative). And most of what he said was now coloured with the conviction that his mother's native Amalfi was superior in every respect to the rest of Italy.

"—met this guy Mac—MacLaren, MacSomething—I can't remember but he came because he'd read we'd got St Andrew's body in the cathedral—"

Boselli's headache had gone, dissolved by the General's approval, but the flashing lights and the motion of the car made it hard to think constructively.

"—and he suffered from piles, only being an idiot he thought they were boils—"

The continuous narrative confused him, as perhaps it was intended to. It reminded him again that they were lying, despite their apparent frankness when he had returned to the terrace.

"—and there he was, squatting over a mirror on the floor, trying to put a hot poultice on his—"

Boselli tried to shut out the end of the tale, doubly grateful that he had not eaten too much at dinner. Whatever happened he had been the one to see the reason for their smokescreen of co-operation, anyway, and it was up to the General now to trace that missing piece in the jigsaw.

"—married his nurse in the hospital. And I was his best man." Richardson's voice cracked with the memory. "So you could say it all came right in the end—"

The car was slowing down at last.

"The Castel di Ruggiero, signori," said the driver. "Please hold tight."

He brought the car first through a full right angle to the left, directly over the cliff edge so it seemed to Boselli, and then, almost in its own length, through another right angle, until they were parallel to the coast road again, but facing the way they had come. Only now the car was tilted alarmingly downwards.

"That bastard," said Richardson.

Boselli, who had been trying to brace himself against the angle of descent, jerked back, striking his head against the side of the car.

"I wouldn't have called him that," murmured Audley. "A great man by any standards, I'd say he was."

"A bastard by any standards, you mean."

"Who—?" Boselli began, bewildered, only to be cut off instantly by Audley.

"Ah, but that's because of what he did to Amalfi, so you're biased. He was the greatest ruler of his time—the greatest ruler of the greatest kingdom. God help us, we could do with a few King Rogers today," Audley grunted. Then, turning to Boselli he continued more courteously: "King Roger II of Sicily, signore—he conquered all this coast and half the central Mediterranean in the twelfth century."

Boselli had made the mental adjustment one second earlier, but too late to forestall the explanation. It was humiliating to be informed about one's own history by a foreigner, though their sudden shedding of eight hundred years to argue about a dead king on the very threshold of Eugenio Narva's house was utterly inexplicable to him at the same time.

The car stopped suddenly in its descent as a figure looked up in the headlights. A powerful flashlight ranged over them, pausing at each face.

"Carry on!" A voice outside commanded.

"So Narva takes precautions," murmured Richardson. "And we're expected, too."

"We are expected," said Boselli primly. "But the precautions are ours, signore. There has been a guard here ever since we learned of Signor Narva's—involvement. For his protection, of course, you understand."

"Against Ruelle?" Richardson nodded. "That's why they let us come halfway down the cliff, eh? They'd just love him to come calling, wouldn't they!"

Boselli shrugged off the observation, deciding that he too could show his coolness. He addressed Audley: "I had forgotten for a moment that you are an authority on the Middle Ages, professore. And on the Middle East, too—and did not King Roger use many Arab soldiers in his conquests?"

"Ruddy Normans would use the devil himself if it suited them," said Richardson hotly, as though that old conquest of his beloved Amalfi had happened the week before.

"That's your Catholic upbringing doing your thinking for you, young Peter," replied Audley patronisingly. "The Norman kings of Sicily practised religious toleration in these parts somewhat before it became fashionable—if it ever has."

Boselli's feeling of unreality was now complete: it was as though they were deliberately playing some game of their own, talking about anything but the matter in hand, in order to confuse him.

He dredged into the cloudy memories of his own historical education, which had mostly been at the hands of an aged priest whose views of King Roger, as he now recalled, had exactly coincided with those of Richardson, though perhaps for very different reasons: it had been that wicked Norman, surely, who had not only opposed the policies of the great St Bernard, but had also driven an entire Papal army to muddy death in the Garigliano and had taken the Holy Father himself prisoner—

He was saved by the car's sudden emergence through a great bank of oleanders into a brightly lit forecourt. The twisting drive down the cliff in the darkness, coupled with the historical argument which had risen between the Englishmen like a summer storm, had served to disorientate him. He opened the car door quickly and hopped out on to the pavement gratefully.

As he did so the iron-shod doors in the blank stone wall beneath the lights opened with a clang, framing a white-coated manservant beyond whom Boselli could see a fountain playing in a green-fringed courtyard, like something out of the Arabian Nights.

"Signore." The servant bowed deferentially to Audley. Boselli hurried round the car to take charge.

"I am Signor Boselli," he snapped. "Signor Narva is expecting me."

The servant eyed him coolly, then inclined his head forward in what was little better than a nod.

"Signore—signori—if you will please follow me."

They passed under the arched doorway, through a short passage and into the courtyard Boselli had glimpsed earlier. Cascades of bright flowers tumbled down the walls out of the night sky, half obscuring the gaps between the slender columns on three sides of the square. The jet of the fountain in its centre sprang from a shell held aloft in the hands of a beautiful bronze nymph whose breasts glistened wetly through the sparkling droplets of water. It was deliciously cool, almost cold, and Boselli had the impression that it would always be cool here, even on the hottest and brightest day.

This was what wealth was all about, this privacy, this secret elegance designed to sustain no one but its master. The opulence of the scene pressed down on him, overawing him against his will, for although he was here as the representative of the State, with theoretical powers far beyond that of any individual, he had too often seen the way wealth and influence, wielded with more single-minded determination than the servant of some distant bureaucratic agency would dare to exert, could nullify those powers.

Nullify them—and maybe ruin the career of the servant in the process. Even as it was, Narva would be angered by the intrusion of policemen into his privacy, so it would be prudent for Boselli to maintain a low, apologetic profile, letting the Englishmen do the talking.

The servant led the way through a gap in the colonnade, down a broad stone stairway, and, turning sharply to the right at the foot of it, along another broad stone-flagged walk. On their right the house—the castle, Boselli supposed—rose up sheer; on the left, beyond a low parapet, was more of that black emptiness from which he had cringed in the car, with the smell of the sea rising up from below.

The walk continued into a vine-covered loggia, set with wrought-iron chairs sharply picked out in the light which shone through wide-open French windows. Here the servant halted, gesturing them into the light. Boselli paused momentarily, gathered his courage, and then followed the gesture into the room, screwing up his eyes against the brightness.

Eugenio Narva was like, and yet unlike, his picture in the files.

Like, because the big, aggressive nose and strong mouth, the high forehead and the thick iron-grey hair were all a matter of pictorial record.

But unlike, because when you'd documented everything and recorded everything, you still only had a two-dimensional portrait. Over the years Boselli, who lived in the midst of thousands of such facts and figures, had learnt that in the end. Partly it had come from his own observation, but most of all from his attendance on the General, who always seemed to set greater store by what men didn't say, or wouldn't say —or couldn't bring themselves to say—about others.

He had sometimes felt that the General expected his operatives to have the eye of an artist and the tongue of a poet in addition to their other attributes. Certainly, the compiler of the Narva file had not dared to describe how the man stood, squarely and solidly, as though he had roots in the rock under his feet . . . and that consequently anything made of flesh and blood which collided with him would very likely come off a poor second.

"Signor Boselli?"

Boselli started, gulped, bowed.

"I am—Boselli, Signor Narva."

Narva's dark eyes shifted towards the Englishmen.

"May I present Professore Audley and Cap—and Signor Richardson, of the British Ministry of Defence."

"Gentlemen—" This time Narva inclined his head. "You are not from the Embassy, then?"

"From England," said Audley.

"To see me?"

"To see you, Signor Narva."

"Then you have come a long way just to see me." Narva turned back to Boselli, and back into Italian. "And for this reason I have policemen in my grounds?"

"Indirectly, signore—for your protection."

"So it was said. But it was not said from whom I am being protected. And I would like to know, Signor Boselli."

"From the Communists, signore."

A small frown creased Narva's forehead. "I have the most cordial relations with the local Communists. And with the Communist Party. I certainly do not need protecting from them."

"The Russian Communists, signore."

"Indeed?" The frown was replaced by raised eyebrows

and bland disbelief. "That is surprising, since I have never had any dealings with them."

"Not directly, perhaps," said Audley.

"Nor indirectly, professore."

"You don't think the late Richard von Hotzendorff qualifies as a middleman, then?"

It was the opening move, and an attacking one even though it was mildly executed. Almost imperceptibly the big Englishman had come forward until he stood beside Boselli, while Richardson had drifted to the left.

"Richard—" Narva paused, "—von Hotzendorff."

"Your little bird from East Berlin, Signor Narva."

"And our little bird, too," murmured Richardson lazily. "Our busy little bird flying from tree to tree!"

Narva regarded Audley steadily. "I was acquainted with Richard von Hotzendorff, that is true."

"Acquainted?"

"He once advised me on certain business matters."

"Her Majesty's Government is very interested in those business matters."

Narva's lips tightened. "They were private transactions, professore—transactions made in Italy between an Italian subject and an East German citizen."

"Who happened to be one of our agents in the Soviet Union." This time Richardson's voice was curt.

"That was of no concern to me, signore."

"But the information he gave you is of very great concern to us, Signor Narva," said Audley heavily.

"I find that surprising—in view of the fact that I last saw von Hotzendorff in . . . 1968, it was. More than three years ago, in fact."

"Nevertheless it still concerns us."

"And it concerns the Russians too, signore," added Richardson. "Which is why Boselli's merry men are in your shrubbery. You should be grateful we got here ahead of the

187

KGB, you know. They seem to be in a rather disinheriting mood."

Narva stared at Richardson coldly. "Whereas you intend to say 'please' before you ask the same questions?"

Richardson shrugged. "We like to think there is a slight difference, you know. But if you're in doubt I suggest you ask Signor Boselli."

"I shall do better than that." The cold eye settled on Boselli. "Under which of our innumerable ministries do you come, Signor Boselli?"

Boselli quailed at the thought of the Minister on the telephone to the General. Anything was preferable to that, even the most shameless falsehoods.

"This—mission has been cleared at the very highest level."

"I don't doubt it."

"We have promised the British Government our fullest co-operation."

"You have, perhaps. But I haven't."

Boselli cleared his throat. "Signor Narva, I assure you—I will take full responsibility—"

Full responsibility! The very words stopped him in his tracks. He had heard them before—the General happily bulldozed through his subordinates' doubts with them—but never, never from his own lips. Indeed, he had risen from nowhere to what had been until this awful day a comfortable and satisfying position by the judicious avoidance of those dangerous words, against which his instinct had always warned him—the same instinct which now groaned in anguish.

"Responsibility for the discretion of two foreign agents?" Narva dismissed the grand gesture with contempt. "My dear Boselli, oblige me by not treating me as a fool!"

"But I assure you—"

"No! It is I who will assure you, signore! It is of no

consequence that you will not tell me to whom you are responsible—of no consequence to *me* that is. I know the man I want well enough."

Boselli stared helplessly as Narva hooked the ivory and gold receiver from the telephone on the table beside him. Of course he knew the man he wanted; someone like Narva would be on more than nodding terms with half the government. What was surprising was not that he knew exactly where to bring pressure to bear, only that he had not acted the moment the security men had invaded his privacy. But then he had the reputation for being a careful man never given to precipitate actions, a man who waited until he had the exact measure of every danger, every opportunity. It had been an assessment which hadn't fitted Boselli's conception of an industrialist—one more appropriate to a peasant than a man of great affairs. But looking at this granite personality now he understood it at last, and despaired.

"Salvatore—" Narva commanded the receiver, "—get me—"

"It won't do," exclaimed Audley.

Narva paused. "Professor?"

"I said—it won't do."

"One moment, Salvatore." Narva lowered the receiver to his chest. "What will not do, professor?"

"Foreigners."

Narva looked at him quizzically. "You are not foreigners?"

Audley considered him in silence for five seconds. "We are all foreigners somewhere. Here, in this house—in this country, I am a foreigner, certainly."

Narva matched the five seconds before replying. "Go on."

"Do I need to?"

"No . . . not if I take your meaning accurately," Narva spoke slowly. "In England I am the foreigner, eh?"

"We are all foreigners somewhere, as I said."

"But I am a bad man to threaten anywhere."

"But I am not threatening you—I am asking you for help . . . just as you may need help in Britain." Audley smiled. "You had better get used to calling it 'Britain', signore—to call it 'England' only offends the Scots and the Welsh and the Irish. If you want to make your fortune out of us then you must get used to our little ways. And there has to be a measure of mutual trust."

Narva replaced the receiver.

"You are trusted in your business transactions, Signor Narva," continued Audley more gently. "Your word is always enough, I have been told. . . . And tonight you are keeping faith with a dead man."

Narva inclined his head fractionally. "You honour me, professore."

"No. Trust is part of your stock-in-trade."

The Italian's face hardened. "But not, I would think, any part of your's."

"You'd be surprised how many people trust me," said Audley evenly. "And not with money, either."

Boselli examined each face in turn, fascinated. So the threat to telephone Rome, though real enough, had been also calculated to draw the Englishman. And the Englishman, in accepting this, was nevertheless taking the initiative.

"I was generalising, naturally, professore."

"Naturally. Because we both know that trust brings in information. . . . . In fact it was trust that brought you Richard von Hotzendorff."

"You think so?"

"I'm certain of it."

"I think you would find that difficult to prove."

"I'm certain of that, too. But proving it is really not important."

"Because I will break whatever confidence—whatever

business confidence—I had with Herr Hotzendorff of my own free will?"

"I wouldn't put it quite like that."

"Indeed? Then I would be most interested to know how you would put it."

Audley considered the question for a moment. "Well ... I suppose I would say that unforeseen circumstances might cause you to break the letter of your agreement in order to adhere to its spirit."

"My agreement?" Narva echoed the word with obstinate indifference.

"Hotzendorff sold you information about the discovery of oil in the North Sea, Signor Narva. Are you denying that?"

Narva shook his head. "I am neither denying it nor admitting it, professor. Neither do I deny or admit this agreement of yours—the words are all yours so far."

"Not quite all. You have admitted meeting him."

"I meet a great many people in the way of business. But I do not make agreements with them all."

They were back to square one, thought Boselli; the Englishman seemed to be losing the initiative.

"Nevertheless, there was an agreement," said Audley patiently. "And it didn't simply concern money."

It was a statement, not a question, and this time Narva did not reply to it. So the initiative hadn't been lost after all—

"Hotzendorff had a family in East Germany, Signor Narva," Audley continued in a matter-of-fact voice. "A wife and three young children. After he died they came to the West."

Still Narva said nothing.

"It isn't easy to get out of East Germany. Especially with three young children. Not for a widow—and not for a widow in a hurry. And especially not for a widow named Hotzendorff, I'd say—wouldn't you?"

Silence.

Narva shrugged. "But not impossible, evidently."

"No, not impossible. The West German Government could manage it. So could the Americans, and so could we, with a bit of extra effort."

"But you didn't?"

"None of us did, no. . . . But there are four private groups who would try it if the price was right—two in East Germany and two in West. When Frau Hotzendorff came out we reckoned it had to be one of the East German groups. At the time it hardly mattered, anyway."

"Professore—"

"But later on we got curious, signore. And in the end I—we—found it was one of the West German teams that did the job. To be precise it was the Westphal Bureau."

"West—" Richardson bit off the name so quickly that his sudden reaction almost passed unnoticed. And yet in that instant Boselli gained an equally sudden insight into the younger man's relationship with the older. A moment earlier he had been reflecting bitterly that he was the mere onlooker here, but now he knew that he was not alone; much of this was going above Richardson's head too.

"You know Joachim Westphal?" Audley cocked his head, knowingly. "A Gehlen graduate before he went private—and Gehlen never had a better man. Very good—very reliable—and *very* expensive. . . . And very choosy about his clients, so don't tell me that Hotzendorff had this all set up in advance, Signor Narva. Westphal wouldn't have touched Hotzendorff even if Hotzendorff had his sort of money, which he hadn't."

"No . . ." Narva nodded slowly and thoughtfully. "No, I will not insult you by arguing with you, Professore Audley. You are telling me that I arranged for the escape of Herr Hotzendorff's family from East Germany after his death?"

"Exactly that, yes."

"But you have no proof of this, of course?"

"Westphal never reveals a client's name, as you well know

—that's part of the deal. But I'm not concerned to prove anything, as I said before. Knowing is quite enough."

"Knowing." Narva chewed on the word. "And this was my 'agreement'—Herr Hotzendorff would trade information in exchange for safety?"

"And money—and secrecy."

"But naturally!" Narva nodded again. "The one would be of no use to him without the others. Not with the risks he proposed to take."

There was no argument about that, thought Boselli grimly, watching the two poker faces. By indulging in such a private deal the East German was not simply double-crossing his British paymasters by passing valuable information to a third party, but was also jeopardising their operations behind the Iron Curtain by taking on additional risks of his own. General Montuori's sphere of activity did not extend beyond the curtain, but in broadly similar situations Boselli knew how incensed he became. And vengeful too, for his punishment, when the moment for it finally came, invariably fitted the crime. Which of course was never very difficult with double-crossers, once their original master had tumbled to them and their usefulness had ceased to protect them.

"Perhaps it is fortunate for him that he is beyond your reach," Narva said blandly, "if that is what you think occurred."

Beyond everyone else's reach too. And that, no doubt, was why Narva felt so strong : he had paid his money and had his money's worth, and the one man who might have compromised him with the British Government was safely out of the way.

Safely and conveniently. If it had been anyone else but Eugenio Narva one might be tempted to suspect that so convenient a conclusion to a politically dangerous business deal had been a little too convenient. But Narva's reputation for honourable dealing was as rock-firm as the man himself

—there Boselli disagreed with the big Englishman's character assessment even while accepting his version of the alleged "agreement"; trust was not simply part of his stock-in-trade. Much more simply he was a man of honour. It might be a dying breed, and it might already be dead in the Englishman's decaying island, but it was not yet extinct in Italy.

Indeed (Boselli warmed to the thought) the very fact that Narva had spared no expense to extricate Hotzendorff's family after the man's death—

The man's death! That was the point, the whole point that made the agreement doubly binding in honour for a man like Narva if it had been in getting that information for him that the German had died. Information so valuable that even after three years both the British and the Russians were desperate to trace its source.

That was it. He felt the conviction of it blossom inside his brain. That was it.

"Beyond everyone's reach, Signor Narva," said Audley heavily, echoing Boselli's thought. "But his family isn't."

"His—family?" For the first time Narva showed something like genuine surprise. "What makes you think his family can help you, Professore Audley?"

"I didn't say they could."

"But you think his wife may—" The surprise gave way to sudden explosive distaste, "—tchah! But you think you can threaten me again, through them!" Narva's hand came up in an exact, economical gesture, stabbing first towards Audley with the fingers held stiff together like a broad cutting blade. "Well, I tell you this—" the hand moved abruptly sideways to include Boselli, "—and you also—that I do not tolerate such threats. Not to me, and not to them! And that is not a threat, signori. It is a promise."

After that brief flare of surprise and disgust Narva's voice had returned at once to its cool, almost conversational level. Anger, the brittle wall behind which doubt and fear so often tried to hide, would have been much more reassuring to Boselli; but here there was only determination and confidence —a confidence so strong that it permitted Narva to admit implicitly that he was aware of the Hotzendorff family. And—

Audley was nodding in agreement.

Boselli clamped his jaw shut quickly for fear that his astonishment should make him look foolish, even though no one was looking at him.

"Good—excellent." The Englishman's quiet confidence matched Narva's own. "Now we may have two common interests."

"Two—?" Narva frowned.

"The North Sea and the Hotzendorff family," Audley nodded. "Profit and responsibility."

"Since when did the British accept any sort of responsibility for Frau Hotzendorff and her children?" said Narva scornfully.

"We pay her a pension."

"A pittance."

"No doubt you augment it. But that's neither here nor there. We don't want the KGB calling on her—not if someone like George Ruelle is on their payroll."

Narva looked sharply at Boselli. "You have arranged protection for Frau Hotzendorff I take it?"

Boselli looked helplessly from Narva to Audley for support. He could hardly admit that until ten minutes ago he had never even heard of the wretched woman—or her double-dealing husband.

"Well?" snapped Narva.

"Frau Hotzendorff is in no danger at the moment," cut in Audley reassuringly. "But she will be very soon. And then you will be vulnerable whether you like it or not, Signor Narva—as vulnerable as a woman with three children. And that's why you have to tell me what our Little Bird whispered in your ear."

XIV

NARVA WAITED UNTIL the servant had gone before raising his glass to his lips, sipping the wine, then staring at them each in turn as though he had thereby completed a ritual gesture of hospitality which transformed them from invaders into guests.

"You could have saved yourself much time by coming to the point directly, professore," he said.

Richardson was surprised how dry his mouth had become. It was all he could do to prevent himself gulping the entire glass like a schoolboy, and the temptation to do so told him how unaccountably nervous he had become. The little Italian gunman next to him had evidently been as dry, if not as nervous also, but was less inhibited by it: he guzzled the delicious Capri bianco thirstily, like an animal at a desert waterhole.

"We have enough time—now," replied Audley, his own wine still untasted.

"You are very sure of yourself."

"Of that, certainly."

"But not of me?"

Richardson stared at Audley, uneasily. He had never seen the big man more apparently relaxed, or more confident, and yet beneath this armour there was still that coiled-up tension he had sensed in the olive grove. It went beyond the lies Audley had told, and far beyond the bitter anger he had shown momentarily at the department's intervention. In retrospect it came down to a strange contradiction in his reaction to events: for all that he had beaten down Narva's defences with the threat of the KGB, and above all with the murderous presence of Ruelle in that threat, he himself did not seem in the least frightened by it. And yet at the same time he was, Richardson could have sworn, absolutely terrified of *something*—something which had transmitted itself in that urgent appeal among the olives—*Get me out of here*—

"But not of me," Narva repeated.

"Of your reputation, shall we say. I couldn't be sure that you still recognised an—obligation to our Little Bird's nestlings." Audley's expression didn't change, but he raised his glass in graceful acknowledgement.

A rare bird indeed, thought Richardson—they had all said that and it now pleased Audley to believe it too. But it was possible to see self-interest in having Frau Hotzendorff still tucked under his wing rather than at risk in East Germany, just in case she knew too much. And it was equally possible, even likely, that Audley had planned this sequence of events with that very thought in mind.

"I see . . ." Narva digested the explanation coolly, with no indication that he took it as complimentary. "But—pardon me, professore—what I do not see even now is how you propose to protect them better than I can."

"From the KGB?"

"Even from them—in this place. It has been held before against enemies, you know. Once even by an Englishman—one of King Roger's mercenaries."

Audley cocked his head. "That wouldn't be Robert of Selby, would it?"

"You are an historian—?" Narva seemed surprised, then suddenly gratified. His hand came up again in that curious slicing gesture of his. "But of course! You are *that* Audley! I knew I recalled the name from somewhere. . . ." He regarded the big man with renewed curiosity. "Yes . . . it was not actually Robert, professore, but his nephew, John of Scriven. He held this castle for eighty days against the German emperor Lothair in the year 1137."

"Successfully?"

"The Germans went away in the end—they usually do. The sun is not good for them, I think."

"I'm afraid it won't drive away the KGB, signore. And it certainly won't stop George Ruelle."

"But you can?"

"I can do better than that."

"How?"

"By taking away their reason for coming here in the first place." Audley paused. "And I can do that if I know the name of Hotzendorff's contact in Moscow, Signor Narva."

Narva stared at him for a second, then shook his head decisively. "But I do not know that name. I have never known it—it was the one thing the Little Bird would never tell me."

The Little Bird: Narva's use of the code name meant that they were through, really through, at last. But, ironically, it looked like being a barren success.

"What did he tell you?" There was no disappointment in Audley's voice, however, only urgency.

Narva thought for a moment, as though marshalling his memories the better to bring them over in good order.

"First, you must understand one thing, professore—and you—" Narva included Boselli, "—that I did not suborn this man, I did not bribe him. He came to me of his own free will, unasked."

Audley nodded. "We accept that."

"He told me that he was a courier working for the British. He told me his code name—he said there would be ways for me to check up on that if I wanted to. . . . He said that he had discovered a source of information which I might find valuable. It had nothing to do with his work as a courier. He regarded it quite simply as his own property, to be exploited for his own benefit."

"What made him come to you?" asked Richardson.

"He trusted me, Signor Richardson," said Narva tightly.

"I'm sorry, signore—I didn't mean that. I mean—when he came to you in '68 you weren't involved in the North Sea. But Shell-Esso and BP and Xenophon and Phillips already were, so the information was worth much more to them than to you."

"The North Sea was not mentioned when he came to me."

"Not—mentioned?" Richardson gaped.

"He did not say one word about it, signore. He said he had a source of confidential information about Russian oil policies. Nothing more."

"But that interested you?" said Audley.

"Mildly," Narva shrugged. "As you know, this country imports substantial quantities of oil from the Soviet Union. It was running at about 16 per cent of our total needs in '68, and the figure is a good deal higher now. But what was interesting me at that time was the possibility that at some stage the Russians would approach the West for assistance in developing their oil industry."

"Is that likely?" asked Richardson.

"I think it is more than likely. In fact I have been buying stock in the Occidental Petroleum Corporation of Los Angeles steadily this year because I believe they will be the first beneficiaries of such a move."

"Because of what Little Bird told you?"

"No, signore," Narva shook his head. "The Little Bird did not send me any such valuable information at first. What he sent me was what I could just as easily have taken from the Petroleum Ministry hand-outs and the Russian technical journals, with a little gossip thrown in. He was a disappointment."

"But you kept him on."

"It was not like that." Narva nodded towards Audley. "We had what you would call 'a gentlemen's agreement'— you are a good guesser, professore—that I would pay only for results. The Little Bird himself insisted on that. He said it would take time, but he was confident in the end it would pay off for both of us. He said he was quite content to wait."

"And you waited."

"No. He sent regular messages."

"How?"

"I do not think that is any of your business."

Possibly through someone in the Italian embassy, thought Richardson. It might not be too difficult to put someone on the payroll there.

"From the nature of his messages it is possible that his man was in the West Siberian fields—the 'Third Baku'—to begin with," went on Narva thoughtfully. "But if that is so he moved to Moscow fairly quickly."

"The nature of the messages changed?"

"There was a time gap first . . ." The Italian paused. "I remember thinking then that maybe this would be the end of it, and there would be nothing more. But then they started again, only not with Siberian information any more."

"The North Sea?"

"Not at first. To begin with there were details of projected oil exports to the Scandinavian countries—and to Great Britain—" he nodded at Audley, "—countries with a North Sea littoral, it is true. But there was no mention of that."

It was beginning not to fit, thought Richardson uneasily. Or at least not to fit Macready's hypothesis of a calculated betrayal by a highly-placed official. It looked like a genuine piece of active intelligence by Little Bird.

The trouble was that that didn't fit either—it didn't fit the German's image of a careful operative who ought to have been able to calculate the risks against the possible profit.

"And then suddenly he put through a question," went on Narva. "He wanted to know whether I was interested in North Sea oil."

"That was—when?" asked Audley quickly.

"Early spring. April—or maybe late March."

Richardson looked at Audley. That was well before even the Cod Condensate strike.

"And you were interested, naturally."

"I was interested . . . intrigued might be more accurate."

"Because at that time some people were beginning to have their doubts?"

"That is true." Narva nodded slowly. "The natural gas experts were pleased enough. The oilmen were not—that is true."

"Did it surprise you that the Russians had information of value?"

Narva's shoulders lifted. "I knew they were interested in off-shore exploitation like everyone else. . . . But I was not aware that their exploration methods were ahead of the Americans. I did not expect anything spectacular, I will say that."

"But then you got it?"

"Not exactly."

"How—not exactly?"

Narva frowned a little, as though searching for the right word. He grunted to himself. "You knew this man—this Little Bird?"

"I never met him, if that's what you mean, signore."

"Hmm. . . . He was not an impressive man physically. Not one of those big blond Germans, the *herrenvolk*. He was—" Narva carefully didn't look at Boselli, "—a short person . . . grey-faced, older than his years—he gave that impression. He put me in mind of the Herr Dr Goebbels a little, to be frank. But he was impressive to me nevertheless."

"How so?"

Narva remained silent for a moment. "I think it was his confidence which moved me. And I had the impression that he was a very careful man at the same time. It is a good combination, that—confidence and care."

"And he trusted you."

"That too," Narva agreed. "He was prepared to place himself entirely in my hands, and to be paid by results only."

"And you undertook to get his family out?"

"That was to be the final payment."

"If things went wrong, you mean?"

"No. He did not believe things would go wrong—"

They always believed that. Although with his experience Little Bird ought to have known better.

"After he had satisfied me he was resolved to retire, and he wished his children to grow up in freedom." Narva nodded at Audley wisely. "I think it was for them that he did this thing, professore, for his wife and for his children more than for the money. He came close to saying as much. But in any case, I myself have no doubt of it."

Richardson examined Narva closely. The man had no son himself, the wife whom he adored—so the record stated with a flash of sentiment—having died childless. But that did not mean he was without those family feelings which ran ocean-deep in every good Italian; even watered down in his own veins Richardson had felt this unEnglish characteristic tug at his affections.

More to the point, however, it helped to account for Narva's curious feelings for the Hotzendorffs : by the purest accident the little Kraut had found a chink in the tycoon's armour. And Audley too had found the same weakness, though not by accident.

"Yes—" Audley coughed apologetically "—but things did go wrong."

"Not at first. In fact not until the last."

"Exactly how did they go wrong?" asked Richardson, inflecting the question carefully so that it should not be apparent that this was the first certain intimation he had received that Little Bird's death had not been from natural causes.

"No—" Audley raised a finger "—let's take one thing at a

time. You said a moment ago that what he sent wasn't so spectacular. I don't follow that, frankly."

Narva gave a short, understanding grunt. "Yes, I see that might seem contradictory . . . but I will try to tell you how it was—"

"After that first mention of the North Sea?"

"That is right—and after I had indicated my interest. He said then that his contact had seen a top secret memorandum forecasting Western European oil requirements during the next ten years. The figures were substantially as one would expect, taking into account the development of natural gas and atomic power stations, and allowing for some protection of coal industries. Nothing in the least unusual, there was.

"But in the section on sources of supply there was an extraordinary discrepancy. And what it amounted to was that by 1978 half of it would be coming from a new source —something in excess of 200 million tons."

Richardson caught Narva's attention. "But they're finding oil all the time. Couldn't this be Alaska and Canada—the North Slope, or whatever they call it?"

"No." Narva shook his head. "All the other known potential sources were listed—Australian and African as well as American. And Hotzendorff said there were strong indications that it was the North Sea which was the new source."

"So what did you do?"

"I sent three of my best men out—one into Shell-Esso, one to Xenophon and one to Phillips. And I asked Hotzendorff to get more precise information."

"You didn't believe it?"

"Let's say rather I was not prepared to reject it, professore. I know the Russians are very interested in European power sources, they have their surplus production to market, just like any poor capitalist nation."

As an Italian, Narva would know that better than most, thought Richardson. Ente Nazionale Idrocarburi's dealings with the Russians since the mid-fifties had been a source of considerable annoyance to some of their NATO partners.

"Not to mention the political aspects," murmured Audley helpfully.

"That is precisely what he did mention next," Narva agreed quickly. "Apparently the Russians foresaw a period during which the Middle Eastern producers would attempt to increase prices as much as possible—that would be maybe until 1975. Then there would be a happy time, when the European nations would be no longer vitally dependent on foreign sources. And finally there would be an increasing chauvinism against the big American companies operating here, particularly as U.S. home production dried up."

"All of which any halfways competent political economist could tell you," observed Audley dryly. "And none of which was what you really wanted to know—eh?"

"It wasn't quite as simply stated as that."

"But you wanted facts, not politics or strategy?" Audley persisted. "You pushed him a bit?"

Narva compressed his lips, as though he had reached an awkward point in his recital of the Little Bird saga. "The men I had sent reported back that there were no signs of any major oil strike. Rather the opposite—Xenophon was even thinking of selling its new rig and pulling out altogether."

"Then what made you half-believe Hotzendorff?"

"There was a difference between what my experts told me and the information he supplied."

"Namely?"

"*Certainty*, professore—that was the difference! My men said nothing had been found *yet*—they would not say it wasn't going to be found. But these Russian reports weren't simply hypothetical, they were policy decisions founded on something that was evidently a fact, with no ifs and buts."

"It didn't occur to you that they might be taking you for

a ride, signore?" cut in Richardson. "Because there isn't one damn bit of evidence that anyone else knew better than your chaps, you know."

"But why should they take me for a ride, Signor—Richardson?" said Narva. 'My success or failure is not important to them—they had no reason, they could have no reason! And I was not taken for a ride, either. That is the fact of it, is it not? We have not reached the figures that Little Bird gave me, I know. But they are going up all the time now—already they are talking of 150 million tons a year. That is 40 per cent of European needs in 1976. And that is not being taken for a ride, signore—or if it is I would like to be taken on more such rides, I can tell you!"

Narva's vehemence, compared with his usual cool, was interesting. Hitherto only the threat to the Hotzendorff family had aroused him, with its implication of strong family feelings. To this Richardson now added the likelihood that he disliked even the suggestion that he could be deceived. Or could it be that in this one instance he had taken an uncharacteristic risk, and was sensitive about it?

That was worth pushing further—

"But what made you rely on this fellow?"

"But I have told you! He—"

"Not Little Bird, signore. This contact of his—the Russian chappie he wouldn't tell you about. Didn't he want anything? Did he spill the beans simply out of love for the West?"

Narva stared at him, slowly subsiding. Then he shrugged. "There was no money in it, anyway, that I know. When I asked that same question at the beginning Hotzendorff said that no money was required. He said the deed was its own reward."

A political protester, thought Richardson. Or a disaffected technocrat. Or an admirer of some dead poet or persecuted novelist, or even a Russian Jew. If there was anything in this version of the impossible it could be any one of those.

Audley murmured something unintelligible to himself. "We're still straying from the point. You wanted facts and he didn't give them to you—"

"How do you know that?" interrupted Narva.

"Because you've been saying it all along." There was a sudden nuance of weariness in Audley's voice. " 'Nothing spectacular'—and the known facts were against him all the way. But you threw your money into the North Sea all the same." Audley broke off for one moment. "And for that he had to give you proof—just one bit of total proof."

The two men stared at each other over the word like dogs over a buried bone. One dog knew the bone was there, because that was where he had buried it; the other dog also knew it was there because other dogs' bones were what he lived on.

"Yes, Professor Audley—he gave me proof."

"What proof?"

"The best proof in the world: his death."

Not one bone, but two hundred and six of them. Tibias and fibias, big juicy thigh bones full of marrow and little crunchy finger bones. All the bones that went to make a man. So brittle that a chance blow might crack them, yet strong enough to lie in the earth for a million years.

Narva sighed. "You are once more a good guesser, professore—I pushed him. . . . It happened that I needed a new field for investment. One inside Europe, politically stable—that was very attractive. And this was the time to start if what he was saying was the truth, before the bigger companies totally committed themselves . . . before the stampede. . . ."

Now he was explaining himself, almost justifying himself, in a way that was equally uncharacteristic. It was almost as though he regretted making good : Richardson began uncertainly to revise his earlier conclusion.

"How did he die?" Audley's harsh question interrupted the process of revision.

"How?" Narva shook his head. "Officially—he had a heart attack. I have been able to find out no more than that."

"But unofficially?"

"Unofficially? There is no unofficially. I do not have the resources to investigate a man's death in Moscow. All I have is his last message, and there was no heart attack in that."

"What was there in it, then?"

"I will tell you first how it came about, professore. In the first place I pressed him for proof that this was not a mere precautionary plan. And then I said it was not even enough to know that the Russians were convinced there was oil there, I had to know how they knew this. And above all I had to have the locations of the fields—whether these were in the British sector, or the Norwegian or the Dutch. I told him that without this certainty his information was without value. And I told him there was very little time left.

"He replied that it would be dangerous to try to go too fast. I would have to be patient, but that he would do his best. In the meantime he asked me to get him a camera—something like the Exakta, which was the East German camera made for espionage work. He said that as a courier he had no such equipment, and couldn't get any without drawing attention to himself—"

Narva fell silent suddenly. Then he squared his shoulders. "I had a suitable camera sent to him. But—I told him that he had better use it quickly."

"You had begun to believe him?"

Narva looked at Audley for a moment without replying. "I would like to think so, professore. But I think also I had become greedy. The new Xenophon rig was almost ready for sea, and I had the opportunity of buying a large block of their shares at a competitive price. If what Little Bird said was true I could make—a killing. For me the time was exactly right."

"But not for Little Bird?"

"The Little Bird sent me one more message," said Narva. "It was very short, the shortest he ever sent. He said his contact had conclusive proofs—submarine survey methods, scientific data and locations in British and Norwegian areas. But there was a risk that someone was on their track, so they were both coming out at once. They would meet my representative in Helsinki in one week's time. But in the meantime I must get his family out of East Germany as fast as possible. His wife would be ready with the children."

There was no longer any hint of feeling, of emotion, in the Italian's voice, and by God there didn't need to be, thought Richardson—because everyone in the room knew too well how to dress that last message in the widow's weeds of reality.

It was a dead man communicating, a man who already knew he was as good as dead when he transmitted it but was still reaching against hope for life. Even now, long after the thing was over and done, Little Bird's despair was like a view of some distant star exploding—an event at once ancient history and immediate tragedy.

"I had already approached Westphal and we had a contingency contract. He took thirty-six hours to get Frau Hotzendorff and the children out of East Germany into Czechoslovakia, and another thirty-six to get them into Austria. And I had the Xenophon stock within a fortnight. Six weeks later Phillips found their condensate field in the Norwegian sector, next to the British block 23/37."

"But you never saw the Exakta film?"

"Since then Phillips has proved the Ekofisk field, and West Ekofisk and Eldfisk—" Narva ignored Audley's question "—Xenophon has Freya and Valkyrie, British Petroleum has Forties, Shell-Esso has proved Auk, Amoco has Montrose.

And there will be more, professore Audley, you can be sure of that. . . . And I made my killing. Or killings, if I am to include those who enriched me."

Again, a rare bird—even rarer than he had seemed before : a tycoon with a sense of sin. And of one sin in particular, and that the occupational sin of tycoons—greed! Clearly, whatever turned Eugenio Narva on, it wasn't the piling up of mere treasure on earth : he was driven by much more complex motives.

"So you have no idea about the identity of his contact?"

Richardson looked sidelong at Audley. Now, there was a man with no sense of sin at all . . . and a man now totally cured of that fourth sin of his which had set all the hungry cats among the pigeons again. The problem evidently absorbed him so much that it would never occur to him to be sorry for Narva's good Catholic conscience, only to gamble on its existence. The only real sin David Audley might recognise now was failure.

"No. I have told you so already."

"And the woman—the widow Hotzendorff?" Audley went on remorselessly.

Narva looked at Audley coldly for a moment, then shook his head. "She knows nothing."

"What makes you so sure?"

Narva was saved from replying by the click of the door behind him. Without turning away from them he inclined his head to listen to the white-coated doorman's urgent whisper.

Only in that concentrated silence the whisper was just that bit too loud for secrecy.

This was the second of the day's conversations which had been unexpectedly disturbed by General Raffaele Montuori, thought Richardson.

Only this time he was doing it in person.

XV

WHAT IMPRESSED RICHARDSON most about General Raffaele Montuori was neither his rank and beautiful uniform nor the fact that his arrival scared little Rat-face out of his cardboard shoes, but the simple white and blue of the British Military Cross embedded in his rainbow display of decorations. All the others might mean something or nothing, but the MC didn't come up with the rations.

That was what the book had said about Montuori, of course: he was an old timer close to retirement, but still a hard man, a throwback to days of the Roman legions whom even Sir Frederick had treated with a deference which wasn't purely diplomatic. But it was still a good thing to be reminded of it by that ribbon.

Not that Narva conceded him any special treatment.

"General—this is an unexpected honour," he said formally. "But you are welcome in my house."

"Signor Narva—" Montuori bowed "—it grieves me that you have been disturbed in this way, at this hour."

"I understand the necessity for it, General."

"Nevertheless we are grateful for your co-operation."

Richardson had the feeling that the two men were communicating very different messages to each other than their apparent platitudes suggested.

"It is freely given."

"That is understood." The General paused. "Though I would expect no less in the circumstances."

So that was the way of it: Narva had served notice that he had talked because he chose to talk, and Montuori had indicated that he would have had to talk whether he liked it or not. But being practical men in temporary agreement neither was prepared to make an issue of the matter.

"Signor Narva has been extremely helpful." Boselli's head bobbed. "He has been helpfulness itself."

Momentarily the General's eyes left Narva's face. But they settled not on Boselli, but on Audley.

"In that case it would be unreasonable to take more of your valuable time, signore," said the General. "But if I might be permitted to speak privately with these gentlemen we may then be able to leave you in peace—"

Any similarity between Superintendent's Cox's retreat from Sir Frederick's room and Narva's retirement was purely accidental, Richardson decided as he watched the General pour himself a generous glass of Caprese. Anyway, what mattered now was the man who remained, not the one who had gone.

The General turned towards them.

"More wine, Dr Audley?" he said in almost unaccented English.

"Thank you." Audley held out his glass.

"Captain Richardson?"

"Thanks, General. But I don't use the rank now."

"Indeed? Why not?"

"I don't wear the uniform."

"Your mother must be disappointed."

Richardson held his glass steady. "What makes you think so?"

"She always intended you to follow in your father's footsteps. Assault Engineers—is that not so?"

"You know my mother, sir?"

"My dear boy—there was a time after the war when I might have become your step-father." Montuori smiled. "You will be so good as to remember me to her, perhaps?"

"Of course." Richardson nodded. "It's a small world."

"Yes, I have always found it so. And never more so than now. . . . Would you not agree, Dr Audley?"

"I think the probabilities usually even out the improbabilities in the end, actually."

"A somewhat unromantic view. But you may be right—I gather you usually are—stop hovering, Pietro!"

Boselli blinked nervously. "Sir—I—I was wondering about Villari—"

"And I am wondering about Ruelle. Did Signor Narva's helpfulness extend in that direction?"

Boselli shook his head. "No, sir. But we did not expect him to know anything—in that direction."

Richardson looked at the little Italian with renewed interest. He had kept as quiet as a church mouse during Audley's duel with Narva, almost as though he wanted no part of it. And his present nervousness was obvious. But they knew better now—that the quietness was a deceptive front and the nerves were those of the hunter at the smell of his quarry, Ruelle.

"That is true," admitted the General, eyeing Audley speculatively. "One of your probabilities, Dr Audley."

"And Signor Villari?" Boselli's voice sounded stretched and thin.

The General turned slowly towards him. "Armando didn't make it, I'm afraid."

Boselli drew a long breath.

"I—am sorry, General."

"Yes, so am I." The General straightened up. "The bullet was touching the heart. It was just too close, that's all—too close."

"I am sorry."

"Yes. But it was not your fault, Pietro." The General nodded. "Tell me, Dr Audley—how is your wife?"

Richardson looked at the General in surprise which was instantly transformed to dismay as it dawned on him that this was no social inquiry—the unexpected question was delivered with a cold precision which altogether precluded that. So it could only mean that the Italians' patience was exhausted and that they were prepared to turn the screws as ruthlessly on Audley as he had done on Narva only a few minutes before.

"For God's sake!" Richardson snapped. "Mrs Audley's got nothing to do with this, General Montuori."

"Indeed?" The General kept his eyes on Audley. "I'd like to hear you say as much, Dr. Audley."

"She's—"

"Shut up, Peter," said Audley quietly.

"Damn it, David—"

"Shut up!" Audley raised his hand. "You tell me, General—how is my wife?"

"I wish I knew." The General nodded slowly at Audley. "And I think you wish you knew too—eh?"

Richardson stared at them. "What the hell—?"

"Calm yourself, Captain." At last the General turned back to him. "I think perhaps you have misunderstood me, boy."

"I don't understand you, if that's what you mean—either of you."

"No, I believe you don't—I really believe you don't!" The General looked at him quizzically. "Where do you think Mrs. Audley is at this moment?"

"In Rome. With her baby."

"No, not in Rome, Captain. And not with her baby." The General paused. "We made an error, you see. After Ostia we looked for Dr Audley and we forgot to look for his wife. But we took it for granted that she was with him. Fortunately Boselli here had the wit to suggest that she might be engaged on some enterprise of her own when he found that she was *not* with him."

"Faith—?" Richardson made no attempt to hide his disbelief. The idea of David sending Faith on any dangerous enterprise—and of Faith agreeing to go—was plain ridiculous. "You must be joking!"

"No, Captain Richardson. I am not joking—even though Boselli was quite wrong, of course."

"Quite—wrong?" Richardson stared at Boselli, whose surprise now clearly equalled his own. "Wrong?"

"Our second mistake. No—I should say my mistake. And Dr Audley's in the first place, I'm afraid. To underrate the nature of the beast—"

"I made no mistake," said Audley sharply. "Except to assume the security of my own department—that was a mistake, I agree. But I didn't even know the beast was loose, as it happens."

"Good God Almighty!" exclaimed Richardson as the jigsaw pieces in his mind shook out of the old ill-fitting pattern into a new and hideously better-fitting one.

. David's extraordinary nervousness—his lies and his inconsistency. Even his urgent appeal *Get me out of here* . . . and Richardson had let friendship and bitter embarrassment confuse him, stopping his suspicions from crystallising.

"They've taken Faith!"

Audley gave no sign that he had even heard: it was Montuori who nodded.

Richardson's brain accelerated: a kidnapping . . . the oldest and crudest trick there was, although in high fashion now. And still the cruellest and most effective trick too—in the right circumstances.

Yet although the KGB was capable of it, the more so with someone like Ruelle at the helm of the operation, that still didn't make this thing explicable, pattern or no pattern.

"But—for God's sake, David—why? What have they got to gain?"

"I would have thought that was obvious, Captain," said Montuori. "Since they have not stopped Dr Audley from taking action, then they must want him to do some of their work for them."

"But they don't need him, sir. If they already know about Little Bird—"

"But they don't," Audley cut in.

"What do you mean?"

Audley sighed. "I mean the Russians know nothing about Little Bird—or about Faith."

"But Ruelle—and Korbel—?"

"Ruelle and Korbel—yes, they know.... But tell me, Peter, what do you know about Ruelle and Korbel?"

"They work for the KGB, damn it."

"Ruelle did once maybe, but a long time ago—and Korbel won't for much longer. They are two old men, Peter. Two failures who have outlived their usefulness, and they know it. And for that reason they have become very dangerous."

Where do flies go in the winter time? Nobody knows—they just disappear—

"You think Ruelle is acting independently?" said the General. "Without official sanction?"

"I don't think, I know."

"How?"

"Because he told me so, General Montuori. When he abducted my wife at Ostia he made it very clear to me that he was answerable to nobody, and that I was to deal only with him."

"And what does he want of you, Dr Audley?"

"He wants the name of the high-ranking official who leaked the North Sea oil strike to Richard von Hotzendorff in 1968. He also wants—or Peter Korbel wants—the details of the report Hotzendorff made."

"And just what does he propose to do with those items?"

"That he didn't say. I can only guess that Korbel believes the report is worth a fortune still. But as for Ruelle—"

Audley shook his head "—perhaps he thinks he can use that name to restore his own. I don't know whether it's power or mischief that he's after—maybe both."

So that was it, thought Richardson: not a deep laid Russian plot after all, but a stratagem by two twisted, embittered old men!

They had known each other once, and had maybe met again to curse the ill-fortune which had betrayed them, and the years which had left them high and dry, and which were now fast running out on them. So naturally they had jumped at the last unexpected chance which Hemingway the librarian had dumped in their laps.

And equally naturally, because they were old men and losers, the chance had gone wrong on them, first on the stairs at Steeple Horley and then in the hot, dusty streets of old Ostia. After that the stakes had become life and liberty as well as money and power.

"Mischief—yes, that is Ruelle," murmured the General. "And they used someone else to make you do what they know they are not capable of doing—that is Ruelle too. The Bastard still runs true to form." He looked at Audley shrewdly. "What exactly were his terms, then?"

"They will hold my wife until they have used my information. Then they will let her go."

"And you believe that?"

"No, not a word of it," Audley shook his head. "Until I give them what they want Faith is safe, I believe that. But after that we'll both know too much to be left alive—I know how Ruelle's mind works."

"He'd finish both of you, yes—I see you understand the animal."

"I understand him perfectly, General."

Audley sounded calm and collected now, as though the hideous problem of saving his wife's life was an academic one divorced from reality.

"That's all ruddy fine, David—understanding how the Bastard ticks. But he's still got Faith and you haven't got one damn thing to trade for her even if he was on the level."

"That's true, Peter."

"And you don't know where they've taken her, sir?"

"Regrettably—no." Montuori shook his head. "We have one witness who saw a woman answering to Signora Audley's description in a car with several men on the road from Ostia Antica to the autostrada to Rome. That is the last we have seen of any of them."

"Well, if Narva hasn't got the answers—and if Frau Hotzendorff hasn't either—what the devil are we going to do?"

"Peter, I never expected them to know. And even if they had, it wouldn't help Faith."

"Then why did you come here?"

"Simply to make sure that I had Hotzendorff figured out properly. Only Narva could tell me that."

"Okay!" Richardson's irritation splashed over. "So what are we going to do to save her?"

"We're not going to lose our heads—we're going to use them." Audley's voice tightened. "How badly do you want the Bastard, General?"

"Badly. I've waited a long time for him."

"They wouldn't let you have him?"

"The Party?" The General's lip curled. "Oh, they kicked him out, but they've kept him in view. Times have been known to change, Dr Audley."

"But now—things may be different?"

"They may be. But that will not save your wife, Dr Audley." The General eyed Audley closely. "I assume that you have a plan of action?"

"It depends very much on your help."

The General nodded slowly. "I can afford to wait a little longer—perhaps."

Audley gave the General an appraising look, as though calculating the odds.

"No state security is involved," went on the General smoothly. "So go on, Dr Audley—what do you propose to do?"

Audley looked at them both.

"Why, if you're going to help me—which I admit I'd hardly hoped for—we can go on with my original plan."

"Which was—?"

"So far I've only lied and bullied and cheated. Now it's time to start making dirty deals."

"With whom?"

For the first time, the very first time since they had met again, Audley smiled. But it was not a goodwill smile and the eyes behind the spectacles were not bright with anything remotely like happiness. Richardson found himself hoping that nobody ever had cause to smile at him—or about him —like this. If tigers smiled, as the poets alleged, then this was how they did it.

"Someone who'll know just how to find where Ruelle's gone to earth, General."

Montuori stared at him, stone-faced.

"You mean the Party?"

"They'd know his bolt-holes—you said yourself they've kept an eye on him."

"But I didn't say they'd give him up—not to me. They might not stand in my way any more, but they wouldn't help me, and they'd never let me lean on them. They wouldn't like the precedent."

"I'm sure they wouldn't. But I wasn't thinking of asking you to lean on anyone—and I'm not making the deal with them at all. After all, they don't really want anything that we've got—"

A dirty deal . . . and a dirty deal not with the Italian

Communist Party: premonition was like a punch in the gut. But would David really go so far?

"—but Moscow does."

David would.

"There's a man I know in the Kremlin—Nikolai Andrievich Panin. I think he might be persuaded to help us, if the price was right."

Richardson managed to control his impatience until the door had closed on the Italians, but only just.

"Will he come?"

"Panin?" The tiger's grin returned. "'I can call spirits from the vasty deep'—that's always the million dollar question, Peter—but will they come when I do call for them?"

"Well, will he?"

"Not in person. But of course he doesn't need to—and we don't need him to. Just a word from Comrade Professor Panin is what we want. A word from him would be quite enough to start things moving."

That was certainly true enough. Even a whisper from the very loftiest pinnacles of the Kremlin, which was where Panin now operated, would gather strength as it echoed downwards, like the small fatal sound on an avalanche slope. The trick was to stay clear of the disaster area thus created.

"They'll get through to him, anyway. No one'll dare stop a call like that."

Richardson nodded. Again that was well calculated. By selecting someone so far up the official ladder Audley had brushed away the danger that some officious bureaucrat would try to be awkward. Just as the name Montuori would clear the Italian lines, so would the name Panin clear the Russian. And night or day, the Kremlin switchboard would know where to put the call.

"So the answer is—yes, Peter, I think I can call this spirit from the deep. I think he'll talk to *me*."

That was the final element in the chain of reasoning: not only did Audley know Panin personally, but he judged himself to be of sufficient interest for the Russian's curiosity to be aroused. And judged correctly, thought Richardson, wryly remembering the flurry in the department dovecote at his unscheduled disappearance. David Audley was too unpredictable to ignore!

Audley was looking at him rather apologetically, though, as though that thought was catching.

"I'm afraid I may have made trouble for you, young Peter."

Understatement of the year: what this private call to Moscow would do to Sir Frederick's blood pressure, never mind Fatso Latimer's mischief-making tendencies, only God Almighty could compute. Not to mention Peter Richardson's career. It would be back to the 39th Assault Engineers on Salisbury Plain most likely.

But there was Faith Audley to think of ... and maybe Peter Richardson had learnt a thing or two himself these twenty-four hours.

"Think nothing of it, David. My main brief was to bring you back in one piece. And they did tell me to be nice to your hosts, so maybe we can blame the General—"

Richardson stopped as a less charitable thought struck him. There was in truth nothing he could do now, and Audley not only knew it, but had intended it to be that way from the start. First he had tried to get free and then he had struck a bargain with the General. But from the moment Faith had been kidnapped he had had this private deal with Moscow in his mind as being the only way he could track down Bastard Ruelle.

"Yes ..." Audley considered the lie with a professional's detachment, "we might confuse the issue that way, at least."

"But what I don't see still is what you've got to trade

with Panin, David. If the KGB got Little Bird then they must have got his contact, darn it—and as soon as Rat-face has briefed the General he'll realise that too."

"If I know Raffaele Montuori that's just what he won't believe, Peter," Audley shook his head knowingly. "You're being gullible now—you're believing what doesn't make good sense."

"I'm believing the ruddy facts, man. That's all."

"The facts? But there aren't many of those—and that's a fact to start with."

"Little Bird's dead. That's one you can't argue with."

"Peter, it's the key fact. Everything else is powered by it. Without it there's nothing—nothing at all."

"Sure—that's what convinced Narva, I take that point."

"But you're not taking it half far enough. Because why the devil should the KGB kill him and then fake it up as a heart attack—on their own patch? And if they picked up his contact, since when have they changed their policy on spy trials? Come to that, why didn't they pick up his other contacts—our contacts?"

Richardson remembered belatedly what Macready had concluded, which he had somehow forgotten: *someone gave him the information, and then snuffed him out the moment he'd passed it on so he couldn't split on them. . . .*

But—

"And you might ask how the KGB let his family get out too, Peter. I don't care how efficient Westphal is—they had the time to get her under surveillance first. And Westphal's men wouldn't have stirred a finger then—they'd smell an ambush a mile off, they're experts at it."

"But, David—Narva said—"

"Phooey to what Narva said. Narva was set up, just as Little Bird was set up."

"Set up for what, for God's sake? Why should they be set up?" Richardson tried not to let his impatience show.

"You're not going to tell me there's no oil in the North Sea, because there's a ruddy lake of the stuff."

"But has it ever occurred to you, my lad, why Narva never received that final report on it—the one that really counted?"

"Because the KGB got it first, of course."

"And then staged a false heart attack and let everyone else go home?" Audley shook his head. "That just doesn't wash, I tell you."

"Then what does?"

Audley stared at him over his spectacles for a moment, like an Oxford professor with a hitherto bright pupil suddenly afflicted with culpable intellectual blindness.

"Do you recall the Garbo network during the last war, Peter?" he said.

The professorial look was too much—after so much.

"A little before my time, that was."

"A pity." Audley chose to ignore the sarcasm. "Garbo was a Spaniard who worked for us—for the Twenty Committee. Masterman called him the Bradman of the double-cross world. He was a perfect genius at inventing imaginary sources of information—imaginary agents—to deceive the Germans."

"So what?"

"So Little Bird's Russian contact, the one who passed on useless information from Western Siberia—he has the smell of Garbo about him."

"The smell—?" Richardson screwed up his memory, trying to pinpoint the moment of falseness in Little Bird's tale.

"Garbo—"

"I—I have read about him, actually," Richardson admitted, already regretting the sarcasm. "But I seem to recall he passed on false information. And this certainly wasn't false—two hundred million tons of oil a year say it isn't."

"I never said it was."

"Then what are you saying, for Christ's sake?"

"I'm saying there has to be a man somewhere in the Kremlin who wanted to slip the word about the North Sea—someone high up. Why—well, maybe Neville Macready could answer that for us, but it doesn't really matter now. What matters is he wasn't a traitor. He just wanted to make sure that we kept drilling."

"Why didn't he tell us then? Why did he tell Narva?"

"Because we would have wanted to know too much, and he didn't want to give away technological secrets. To convince us he'd have to put himself in our hands and he'd be at our mercy then. But if he could get Narva to switch his investment to the North Sea he reckoned he would tip the balance without betraying his country or risking his neck.

"But his problem was to sell the truth without the proof, and that's where Little Bird served a double purpose, poor little sod—"

A double purpose—

"—Alive he sold Narva the truth. And dead he proved it."

The best proof in the world!

Richardson saw the plot in the round at last: Little Bird had been manipulated into conning Narva with a mixture of truth and falsehood, only to be conned himself. And if that was how it was, then Comrade X was a true cold-hearted bastard, who deserved to be sold down the river in his turn.

"The only thing that went wrong was—"

Audley stopped abruptly as a small figure burst through the French windows, skidded to a halt and stared at them in speechless surprise.

"Manfred! I told you not to run on the terrace—you will slip and then—"

The gently chiding voice tailed off as its owner appeared framed in the opening behind the little boy, to stare at them both with the same wide-spaced eyes.

Mother and son, as like as two flowers on the same stem, blue and rich honey and spun-gold.

It couldn't be—and yet it ruddy well had to be, thought Richardson, seeing the evident look of recognition on the woman's face as the cornflower blue eyes settled on Audley. Of course Richard von Hotzendorff had lost his first family in the war, and it was reasonable to expect him to have married a younger woman the second time round. But he had somehow expected a competent, muscular *hausfrau*, and Narva's description of the man had reinforced the expectation. Yet the real somehow was wholly unexpected: somehow the grey Goebbels-figure had captured this gorgeous Rhinemaiden.

"Dr Audley!"

"Frau von Hotzendorff—I—I—regret—"

Audley had the grace to sound genuinely regretful, at least. And with good reason, since this whole KGB scare was a thing of his own making to twist Narva's arm . . . except perhaps if Audley failed the Bastard Ruelle might indeed turn his attentions to the Rhinemaiden.

The door opened behind them.

"Sophie, my dear—" Narva went forward quickly and embraced the woman "—it is good to see you."

"Eugenio, I'm sorry I rushed away as we came in, but Manfred will go off to the ramparts—"

"Ah!" Narva swept Manfred into his arms, lifting him up high. The little boy's arms and legs wound round him affectionately. "So Manfred wishes to go on sentry duty on the ramparts!"

"Uncle, there should be cannon there. Why do you not have cannon to drive away the pirates?"

"Because cannon will not deal with pirates, my love—pirates do not attack castles, they are too cowardly. To deal with pirates you put your cannon in a tall ship and you hunt them and seek them out and blow them out of the water—

that is what you do with pirates—you blow them to bits!"

"I know! I know! It is all in that book you gave me, the one with the big coloured pictures."

"Good—so you liked my book?" Narva set the boy down. "Now there are many other books in your bedroom for you to see. Your brother and sister are there already, and there is a tall glass of fizzy orange for you, but if you don't hurry the fizz will have all fizzed away. So off you go and I will come and see you tucked up in bed and we will discuss pirates—"

"—And how to blow them out of the water?"

"Exactly!" Narva watched Manfred scuttle away, his eyes warm. Nor did their warmth diminish as he raised them to Manfred's mother, Richardson noted. What had once been a debt of guilt and honour was something more than that now, evidently.

Sophie von Hotzendorff's glance shuttled uneasily between Audley and Narva. "There is trouble, Eugenio—for you to want me to bring the children—?"

Narva nodded. "But you will be safe here, Sophie."

"Safe?" She looked at Audley.

"It concerns your husband, Frau von Hotzendorff," said Audley. "It is to do with what he was doing when—before he died."

"But I do not—did not—know in detail what he was doing. He would never tell me, apart from his work for the business. I told you so when we met, Dr Audley—and it was the truth."

"Yet you did not tell me everything that was the truth—there were things you didn't tell me."

The blue eyes turned in doubt to Narva.

"It's all right, Sophie my dear," Narva's voice was reassuring. "He knows about Westphal."

"Then there is nothing else to know. I didn't lie to you, or to the man I saw in London, except in that."

225

"Your husband told you what to say if ... if he didn't come out?"

Sophie nodded. "Yes, Dr Audley. If a man named Westphal—or giving that name—came to me I was to go at once with him, with the children. He said we were to take nothing with us, just to lock the door and go as though we were visiting the neighbours next door."

That was the Westphal trade mark. For every client everything was laid on, everything prepared. And paid for.

"But not to tell us?"

The delicate hair shook the answer.

"He sent that message to you?"

"No. He told me before he left ... for the last time."

"So you knew he was doing something very dangerous?"

"I knew he was risking his life for us." Sophie swallowed and her neck muscles tightened momentarily. "But I'd known that for some time, Dr Audley."

"How did you know—if he didn't tell you about it?"

"How does a wife know anything?" Sophie swallowed again. "The man—the man in London—he said Richard was a good agent, that he was always very careful. But I know even better that ... he was a good man ... that he was a good husband and a good father. Although he was older he never seemed like it to us—he used to say we had given him a second lease of life. And it was true. ..."

The emotions beneath the simple words were on a cruelly tight rein. But what was clear from both (unless she was a marvellously accomplished liar even when there was no need for lies) was that the little carrier of second-class mail, the limping salesman of agricultural machinery, had been a big man to his Rhinemaiden, and that he had impressed her every bit as much as he had impressed Eugenio Narva. And if that didn't fit the pictures in the file it was the pictures that deceived: like the poet said, it was all in the eye of the beholder—the cornflower-blue eye.

"But then he was different. . . ."

No one seemed to want to ask the next question, in the hope that the answer would come unasked.

"He was worried, he was terribly worried each time he went on a sales trip. And when he came back he was so tired—instead of taking the children out he pretended he was still getting over the 'flu—he'd just had a nasty bout of it in Moscow—"

"He pretended?" Audley repeated gently.

"He pretended he'd been to the doctor and got some little white pills he took, but he hadn't been at all—when I went to the doctor about Lotte's tonsils I asked him, and he said Richard hadn't been near him in ages. . . . He was sick—he wouldn't eat and so he lost weight—but it was worry he was sick with. And I knew it wasn't the business because Frau Krauss told me how well they were doing, and how pleased they were with Richard—she is the sales director's secretary—"

Sophie paused, taking a deep breath, as though she felt the reins slipping and needed time to grip them again.

"The lie about the doctor—I thought we had no secrets until then. So I asked him outright: I said if he had something bad on his mind I had a right to share it, just as I shared the good things."

"You thought it was something to do with his work for us?"

"It was what I was always afraid of, yes. But he said it was not that. And then he told me of his meeting with Eugenio—with Signor Narva . . . and of the plans he had for us to come to the West."

"You had talked about escaping before?"

"To the West?" Sophie gave Audley a bitter little smile. "Oh yes, Dr Audley—we dreamed of it. We dreamed—of one day."

"But he never told you what he was going to give in exchange for his dream?"

Sophie shook her head. "No . . . but he said that this time there could be danger. He said it would not be easy, as it was for you. And then he told me what to do when Herr Westphal came for me. That was all."

"Except you weren't to tell us about Westphal, eh?"

Richardson, watching her intently, could not decide how much lay still untold and how much had gone over her golden head—she was stunning enough to fog anyone's judgement. But if that *when* was genuine recall and not a slip of the tongue—*when* Herr Westphal came—it was the final dead giveaway that Hotzendorff himself hadn't banked on being around for the pick-up.

And even if her memory had played her false, or even if her husband had just been his careful self, preparing for the worst, it still amounted to the same thing. For if he couldn't yet decide about Sophie, whether she was a good liar as well as a good wife, he had decided at last about Little Bird.

After flying for so long in the safety of the woods, Little Bird had broken cover to soar high and free—where the birds of prey were always waiting for little birds. He had known the risk that they would swoop on him, but Sophie made the risk worthwhile; for someone like her the chance of a few rich years in the sun would be enough for any man. All the theories and counter theories were resolved in her.

"That is true, Dr Audley." Sophie regarded the big man gravely, as though she understood that the implied rebuke was fair. "But let me say this: my Richard never cheated you—he always served you honestly."

"I didn't say he didn't."

So Audley had succumbed to her too, or at least he was being gentle to her. For her Richard had undoubtedly placed other men in jeopardy by attempting his private coup, the men of his own delivery network in Russia and in East Germany.

"I didn't want him to go—do you think I wanted him to go back to Moscow?" Sophie's voice rose. "I begged him not to go back there. But he said it was all too far gone—he had his obligations. All his life he—he had obligations—he never let anyone down. But he said now he was just thinking of us—"

"Sophie, my dear—" Narva took a step towards her, uncertainly.

Poor old Eugenio Narva, thought Richardson, watching the pain and irresolution in the man's face, as out of place on it as flowers on a fortress. His sin had caught him out with this ultimate refinement of cruelty: not just his sense of guilt but the powerful ghost of a self-sacrificing husband lay between him and the woman. Ten billion lire and an infinity of Hail Marys weren't enough to beat that alliance.

"Ha-hmm—professore—"

Somehow little Rat-face had entered the room without anyone taking the least bit of notice.

"Professore—" Boselli began nervously.

But then unobtrusiveness was probably another of his skills. And, come to that, it was hard to imagine those rather timid eyes lining up an automatic—the whole weird deception of the man was remarkable!

"—We—the General has a line cleared to—" the eyes flicked over the others "—a line cleared."

So the two names had worked their magic.

Moscow was on the line.

XVI

THE BLEACHED STONES of the dry watercourse were treacherously unstable, as though the last of the winter torrents hadn't been strong enough to settle them firmly into their final positions. Already Boselli had nearly broken his ankle on one, saved only by his stout new country boots.

Unfortunately, the boots were also stiff and uncomfortable, and neither in shape nor colour did they match his city suit. But then the suit itself had come far down in the world in the last twenty-four hours: it was dusty and rumpled—it looked as though he had slept in it, which was close to the truth—and there were signs of serious damage to the knees and elbows, the souvenirs of Ostia.

Boselli wondered unhopefully whether he could add the suit to his growing list of expenses. The boots, he had already decided, were a legitimate charge on the state, being the result of a direct command from the General, but for the rest he would have to consult the appropriate schedule. Maria was always very hot on his recovering the most minute expenses, down to the smallest bus fare, insisting on checking them all herself before he submitted them. But he had never before had anything like the bizarre items now entered in his little book, so bizarre that he would never dare show them to her. He would have to pretend he had lost the book, meekly accepting the contempt that the lie would incur.

"Keep your head down, Pietro," snapped the General out of nowhere. "Keep your head down and put your coat on—and then come up here."

Boselli looked about him wildly, clutching the precious

tape recorder to his chest. Better a broken ankle than a broken tape recorder—it was small, but it had an expensive weight and feel to it even apart from its contents.

"My coat?"

"They're not blind, man. That white shirt of yours stands out like a surrender flag. Cover it up!"

The shirt blended in rather well with the stones, thought Boselli, and his jacket felt like an overcoat in the heat. But an order was an order.

The General lay full length in the dirt, half under a bush on the lip of the bank, a large pair of binoculars beside him. Boselli began to scramble up, his boots slipping in the loose pebbles. When he had reached the level of the General's feet he stopped, steadying himself with his free hand.

"Beside me—here," ordered the General, indicating a dusty patch just within the shadow of the bush. It was clear that he expected Boselli to prostrate himself similarly, which was all very well for someone in battle-dress and combat jacket, but which would put the finishing touch to the suit's degradation.

Unhappily he edged his way up the last stage of the incline and stretched himself alongside his master.

"Good. Now have a look at the place," said the General briskly, offering the binoculars.

It was just as hot in the shadow as in the open, but the General showed no sign of discomfort. In fact quite the opposite: he radiated an air of well-being and good humour —it was obvious that he was enjoying himself playing at being an operational commander again after so many desk-ridden years.

And so he might, thought Boselli, because no ordinary commander would have been able to cut through all the inter-departmental, inter-force rivalries so easily. When the General whispered, people moved; when he spoke they jumped; when he growled they broke the sound barrier. He had known this before, but he had never participated in it actively, and the memory of what he himself had achieved in the past few hours using the General's name steadied him now. There were morale-raising rewards in pretending to be a man of action, always provided one could keep out of the front line.

As if to support this conclusion came the distant sound of the spotter plane, making its second pass exactly on schedule. It droned high over their heads, corrected its course to pass directly over the hill and disappeared over the mountains beyond.

Boselli wedged his dark glasses above his brow, blinking for a moment in the harsh light, wiped his sweaty palm on his trousers, and accepted the binoculars.

It took him ten fumbling seconds to adjust them—the General must be as blind as a bat—and then the hilltop came up in focus, first the vines, then the outbuildings, and finally the dilapidated farmhouse itself. But there was not a sign of movement anywhere, and he could see nothing more in close-up than he had been able to see with the naked eye half a mile down the gulley of the watercourse, in the grove of trees where the cars were hidden.

He lowered the binoculars and stared at the landscape around. The ground directly ahead was bare and scrubby for perhaps half a mile, maybe more, until the first row of vines. Away to the right he could see the naked line of the track which must lead to the farm from the road. It was poor country and the wine from those grapes would be harsh—a land of bare subsistence living.

"Well?"

Boselli shrugged. "If this is the place—it looks uninhabited."

"It is the place."

"They could be lying."

He realised that he didn't know—would never know—

who "they" were. It had been just a voice calling the number they had given from a public callbox—at the *Stazione Termini.*

"Disobeying an order coming all the way from the Kremlin?" The General snorted. "I really don't think that's very likely. Besides, I know it is the place."

Boselli waited for enlightenment.

"According to the local police it is owned by the brothers Giolitti, but unless I'm very much mistaken their real name is Prezzolini . . . and they were both founder-members of the Bastard's execution squad in the old days." The General nodded up towards the hill speculatively. "This is the place."

He turned back to Boselli. "And now, Pietro—you have arranged everything?"

"Yes, General—" Boselli checked his watch, "—the helicopter will be here on the hour. The spotter plane—"

"That was on time. It has made two passes." The General nodded. "Just enough to alert them, but not quite enough to frighten them. The chopper will do that."

"And it is necessary to frighten them?"

"Oh, yes. That is the psychology of it—Dr Audley's psychology. You must remember that this is really his operation, Pietro. We have merely implemented it."

Boselli had been remembering little else in his spare moments ever since that first call to Moscow, and he was no nearer resolving the contradictions in the General's behaviour. For two things were clear to him beyond all else : the General wanted George Ruelle dead—and the General was proposing to let George Ruelle slip through his fingers.

Admittedly, any attempt to take Ruelle from his hilltop would almost certainly result in the death of the Englishwoman, which would be regrettable. But the English had only themselves to blame for the situation, and the deaths of Armando Villari and the policeman, never mind that old score from 1943, demanded final settlement. The General was an honourable man, of course, and would keep his word—Boselli had no quarrel with that. What he could not reconcile was that the General had agreed to give his word in the first place.

"General—" Boselli searched for a way of saying what was in his mind, or at least some of it, and came to the conclusion that it was probably written on his face anyway.

"We must let Dr Audley save his good lady first," said the General. "After that—we shall see how things develop. But now I would like to hear that tape of yours, eh?"

Boselli unzipped the black leather case and drew the recorder out.

"From the beginning, General?"

"I think so. I know you said over the phone that it was not exactly informative."

"Except where the Russian—Panin—said that he had given orders that the Party would find out where Ruelle was hiding, General. Otherwise he denied everything."

"No leakage of secrets? No traitor?"

Boselli shook his head. "He insisted that the German's death was due to natural causes—that the record was correct."

"And did Dr Audley seem surprised—or disappointed?"

"No, General—not at all."

"Of course he didn't, Pietro. He never expected the Russians to admit anything. Like all savages they are very sensitive about such things." The General's mouth twisted sardonically. "And frankly, if I was in their place I wouldn't have admitted anything either."

"And yet he trusted them to get him the information he wanted."

"And was not disappointed, Pietro—for here we are—" the General nodded towards the hill, "—and there the Bastard is."

Boselli frowned. The General's high good humour was

positively unsettling, but this was no time to suggest by further questions that he, Boselli, was out of sympathy with it because he was too stupid to understand what was going on. He had never thought of himself as stupid before, but it was clear that he had missed the significance of whatever it was that pleased the General.

He reached forward to the tape recorder.

"But of course he didn't trust them," said the General. "It is as well for you to understand that, because you may have to deal with this man Audley again and you must learn how his mind works."

The General paused thoughtfully. "He has a good mind, this Englishman—a Renaissance mind. He knows how to threaten without making threats."

"He threatened them—the Russians?"

"Oh yes. But not in so many words. What he did was to give them the blueprint of the threat—the materials . . . a— what do you call it?—a do-it-yourself kit. That is what he gave them—a do-it-yourself kit!"

He grinned boyishly at Boselli, as though his knowledge of such a plebeian thing as do-it-yourself was surprising.

"Don't worry, Pietro—your instinct was right. No one in his right mind trusts a Communist to trade honestly, they are worse than Neapolitans. But you must remember what Audley said to the man Panin that first time at Positano."

"He was—very frank."

"Indeed he was. He offered to trade one piece of information for another, and to show his good faith he offered his own information in advance. But what else did he give?"

Boselli thought back. At the time he had thought the Englishman had been unnecessarily talkative, both as regards events in England and in Italy.

"He made sure the Russian knew that he was personally involved—that his wife's life was at stake. He said there had been a shooting in England—" the General's manicured left forefinger marked off each item on the fingers of his right hand, "—and a worse one in Italy. He emphasised that he knew the KGB was not to blame—that the agent Korbel and the Bastard were no better than terrorists—and that the authorities in both countries were prepared to offer terms not only to save the woman but also to avoid unnecessary scandal. He said if the newspapers here got hold of it, with the elections approaching, they would make a feast of it, and nobody wanted that—it would only benefit the neo-Fascists and the trouble-makers. He—" The General stopped as he saw the light of understanding in Boselli's eyes, "—you see, Pietro?"

Boselli saw—and saw that he had been absurdly slow in catching on.

The deal—the trading of information—was a fiction to enable the Russians to take his orders and to give their own without loss of face. The traitor in Moscow was of no importance to the Englishman compared with his wife, and he had served notice that if any harm befell her he would blow the whole scandal wide open.

It mattered not at all that the KGB was for once blameless. Either the world would refuse to believe it, and they would be branded as kidnappers and murderers at a time when the civilised world was sick of such crimes; or they would be revealed publicly as the incompetent employers of kidnappers and murderers, incapable of controlling their own agents. And the fact that this was often true enough made not the least difference: what mattered was that it should not be seen to be true by the man in the street.

"You see, Pietro?"

Boselli nodded. But what he still did *not* see was why the General, as a life-time Red-hater, was so happy to go along with the Englishman's plan.

"Good!" The General looked at his watch. "Now you can play me the tape."

By the time they got back to the cars the Englishmen had arrived: they were sitting on the pine needles, talking quietly for all the world as though they were waiting for a picnic to begin. Indeed, they seemed more relaxed now than at any time since he had first met them, during which no immediate danger had threatened them. And since they might be both dead within half an hour this must be a conscious display of that celebrated British phlegm of which they were so proud, but which Boselli had always imagined stemmed from a simple lack of imagination.

Audley rose slowly, brushing the pine needles from his trousers before coming towards them.

"Good day, General—Signor Boselli," Audley gave the General a little bow and Boselli a curious glance as though he was looking at him for the first time. "Are we all set, then?"

"Everything is as you wished it to be, Dr Audley," said the General. "It's a typical Ruelle bolt-hole, with an escape route at the rear—he always boasted that his kennels had back doors to them. But we have the whole place covered."

"And the presence of your men in this area is accounted for, just in case?"

The General looked at Boselli.

"Yes, professor. There was an announcement on radio and television last night and again today—there is supposed to have been a breakout from prison at Naples. We have had roadblocks set up over half the province to make it look authentic."

"Excellent. And of course the roadblocks will have discouraged them from leaving the farm, eh?"

That bonus hadn't occurred to Boselli, but he nodded quickly and knowingly in agreement. He had worked hard enough on this operation to justify taking all the credit that was going spare. Besides, it was for the best that the Englishmen should have their confidence built up: they were taking all the risks, after all.

"Very well." Audley turned to the General. "But there is just one small change in plan. I'm not going to take Richardson with me. I've decided against it."

Richardson's brow creased with surprise. "What do you mean? We agreed—"

"—We didn't agree anything, so don't start arguing, Peter."

"Arguing? Man—I'm here to watch out for you!"

"Too late for that. And once we're up there, there isn't anything you can do to stop things going wrong—if I can't swing it."

"Oh, come off it! The Bastard's a real mean guy, David—"

Audley shook his head obstinately. "I know the score. You're not coming, Peter. I don't need you—and besides, it's better that one of us remain here."

Richardson turned hotly to the General, though why he was so keen to reject the chance of safety with honour quite escaped Boselli. It could only be bone-headed self-esteem: the fellow was as bad as Armando Villari.

"General—" Richardson appealed, "—you tell him!"

"No, Captain," replied the General, with a sudden flash of his old military decisiveness. "Dr Audley is right and you are wrong. I agree with him."

"My job—"

"—Your job, Captain, is to obey orders. If not Dr Audley's, then *mine*," snapped the General. "Now, Dr Audley—do you intend to go alone?"

The grove of trees was quite cool, really. And for once even the cicadas seemed to have given up.

"No. I need someone to deliver your bargain . . . to give substance to it, anyway."

"Again, I agree," the General nodded. "Then I shall go with you. I'd like to have a last look at the Bastard—I didn't get a good look last time."

"No, General—"

A fearful premonition stirred within Boselli.

"—that would be bad tactics. It might be like a red rag to a bull, and we don't want this bull angered—"

No General! Not you General—Boselli felt the stillness ringing inside his head, making his senses swim. It was like the moment in Ostia all over again—like the moment when the other car turned towards you and there was no time to turn the wheel and nowhere to go. The moment when the examiner said *I'm sorry, but*— The moment of total realisation and of no escape.

"—and your name will be enough, at the right time. I'd rather take Signor Boselli, if you can spare him—"

XVII

HE COULDN'T REMEMBER anything they had said, he could only see the dusty track stretching up the hillside towards the farm.

"Is there anything else you'd like to know before we start?"

Boselli felt the sweat beneath his palms on the steering wheel. He had the feeling that this was at least the second time of asking that question. But there was nothing else he needed to know, because he knew it all.

Maybe the big Englishman was doing what he thought was best and most reasonable in cold blood. And maybe he was right at that! But he, Boselli, the Boselli of flesh and blood, was here because the General liked to hedge his bets; because the General thought maybe the Englishman couldn't pull it off, and if he didn't then it would be better to lose the little clerk Boselli than the son of one of his old flames, the half-Englishman—

If you can spare him—

"I beg your pardon, signore—professore?"

"Is there anything you're doubtful about?"

"Doubtful?"

Mother of God, but that was an understatement!

Audley regarded him keenly. "You didn't seem very interested in what I was saying back there."

Not very interested? Well, if that was how he had appeared Boselli supposed he ought to be grateful that he had concealed his absolute dismay so well. It had certainly not been lack of interest, but rather the resignation of the bullock in the slaughterhouse yard.

"I was listening." That was true enough; he could even remember the Englishman's words exactly. The trouble was that they were now just a string of remembered sounds without the life-breath of meaning. "You are going to tell the truth."

"Pretty much, yes. The only thing I'm not going to tell him is that it's the KGB itself we've consulted. He mustn't even suspect that, or we're done for."

"I understand."

That was not quite true, either, since Audley had omitted to say what this miraculous truth of his was, or how it was going to change George Ruelle's plans. But the General hadn't seemed unduly curious about it, and neither was Boselli now. He was cast as an onlooker again, and the bullock's lethargy was overpowering.

Anyway, the truth was there, up in the farmhouse, waiting for him. And so was Ruelle. And he could escape neither of them.

Except for the bumping of the car on the potholes and summer-hardened ruts they didn't seem to be moving: it was the farm that was coming towards them, first on one side and then on the other, and finally on the last straight hundred metres dead ahead. He couldn't take his eyes off it.

"You're going too fast," murmured Audley. "Go slowly— we must do everything slowly now."

The tyres slithered as Boselli braked too hard. He hadn't been aware of his speed, and the Englishman was absolutely right: whatever fear he felt at coming to this place would be matched by the alarm their arrival must cause here. Fear made men trigger-happy, and these pigs had already shown themselves to be that.

The farm resolved itself into a tumbledown collection of buildings almost encircling them, with two other cars tucked in the shadow of a crumbling barn—a little Fiat 600, old and battered, and a larger pale green vehicle of a make Boselli didn't recognise.

"Stop here."

Obediently Boselli halted in the middle of the yard.

"Get out slowly—and for God's sake keep your hands in view. They'll be expecting something from you, if anyone."

Boselli couldn't understand what the Englishman was driving at, but there was no time to ask for an explanation. He knew only that his hands seemed to have become large and clumsy, and he didn't know where to put them for safety. In the end, as he came round the front of the car, he found that he was holding them loosely in front of his chest, as he did at home when he was looking for a towel to dry them.

"*Stop!*"

The voice was as loud as a pistol shot behind him.

"*Don't move—and don't turn round.*"

The second part of the command was superfluous: there was nothing in the world which would have moved Boselli one hair's-breadth from where he was standing, and for a moment he was afraid his heart was obeying also.

"Raise your arms—higher—now walk towards the‚ wall ahead—slowly—"

The wall? Up against the wall?

"You—*move*!"

Boselli's legs managed an unwilling shuffle.

"Stop! Now lean forward on your fingertips."

Boselli knew what to do: he had seen it on the films and in photographs—the helpless prisoners lined up without dignity against a thousand walls already pitted at man-killing height. Through the roughness of the walls he was joining this multitude of the half-dead.

A heavy boot struck the inside of his right foot without warning, kicking it farther away from the other. The sudden extra weight on his other leg made his left knee buckle, so

that for a moment he thought he would lose his balance.
"Stand still!"

Boselli froze while a rough hand explored his body, one
side at a time, from ankle to crutch and then from waist to
armpit.

"All right—you can stand up." The voice sounded farther
away, as though its owner had decided that they were still
dangerous even though unarmed. "Turn round."

Boselli turned slowly. It was not Ruelle, certainly, though
the age was about right, and not the confederate from
England either, the man Korbel. The stained working
clothes and the three-day beard suggested one of the
Prezzolini brothers, the ex-executioners. And so did the
machine-pistol in his hands: where the man was dirty and
unkempt, the gun was spotless.

"I want to talk to Ruelle," said Audley abruptly.

"What about?"

"About my business—and his."

"How did you know where to come?"

"You know who I am, then?"

"I said—how do you know where to come?"

"And I said I'll talk to Ruelle."

The man stared belligerently at Audley, then gestured
with the gun towards the house.

"Inside."

It was something to have survived the first encounter,
but the doorway of the farmhouse, with shuttered windows
on each side, didn't look inviting: it was like the opening of
a black pit.

As he passed under the low lintel—the Englishman ahead
of him had hunched his head to negotiate it—the smell of
savoury cooking was the first and strongest sensation to
register, rather than any impression of the room's contents.
And then there was no time to take in anything apart from

sordid litter on the table just ahead of him, a blackened saucepan, bottles and a half-eaten loaf.

"Ruelle—" Audley snapped.

They were to the right of the table, no mistaking this time, even in the slowly clearing half-light—no mistaking even though he had never seen these men in the flesh.

"How did you get here?" Ruelle echoed the Frezzolini brother's question, but with much greater menace even though he carried no gun to back it up.

"The Police brought me."

"*The Police!*"

It was the man alongside Ruelle who spoke, in a thick foreign accent which Boselli couldn't place until he recalled that it had been Southern Russia from which Korbel had set out thirty years before.

Ruelle was silent for a moment, then he reached inside his coat and drew out a large automatic pistol from his waistband. "Guido—cover the front. I'll call you when I'm ready. I'll deal with these."

The light from the doorway was cut off for an instant as Guido ducked outside without a word; the old habit of obedience hadn't lapsed with time. But it was Ruelle's last phrase which petrified Boselli.

Audley ostentatiously looked at his watch. "Peter Korbel —you know me. And you know I'm not a fool—"

"You brought the Police," Ruelle cut in fiercely. "I warned you—"

"No!" Audley bit back just as fiercely. "I said the Police brought me. There's a difference."

"Not to me."

"You idiot—they've been on to you from the start. They saw you at the airport. You brought the Police to me!" Audley turned back to Korbel, reaching slowly across his chest and taking the white handkerchief from his outside breast-pocket. "There's a little window on the north side of this house, a narrow one just above ground level. Hang this out of it."

Korbel stared at him, his broad, creased face still frozen with the shocked imprint of the word 'police' on it.

"Why?"

"Because if you don't they'll be swarming all over you in—" Audley looked at his wristwatch again, "—just under six minutes."

"By which time you will be very dead."

"I will have you to keep me company soon enough."

Ruelle's lips twisted. "Signore—the Fascists couldn't catch me and the Nazis couldn't catch me either. And they knew the score. Your fucking baby cops are still wet behind the ears. If they knew the way I operate they'd be here already—"

"You mean your kennel has a back door to it?"

Ruelle gaped. "Eh?"

"Yes, there's an old acquaintance of yours out there, Ruelle," said Audley conversationally. "His name's Raffaele Montuori. He was a major when you last met him, but he's come a long way since then. He's a general now."

"George—" Korbel hissed, "—Montuori is—"

"—I know what he is—shut up!"

"And he hasn't forgotten you," continued Audley. "In fact he wants you so badly his balls ache. And he's just hoping you'll put a bullet in me so he can come and take you—so badly he's had this place sewn up tight for the last fifteen hours just in case you made a run for it."

"George—"

"Maybe you heard on the radio about the Naples jail-break," said Audley remorselessly, shaking his head slowly. "But of course that was just for your benefit, so he could block this place off properly . . . just in case you still might know what the real score is."

In the moment of silence which followed, Boselli heard

the distant sound of an engine. He looked down quickly at his watch: the helicopter was one minute early.

Audley had heard too. He leaned forward across the table. "I'm the only thing that stands between you and Montuori, Ruelle—you talk with me or you take your chance with him. He doesn't want to talk."

The engine was louder now.

"And you've got ninety seconds to start listening to me."

The room darkened again as Guido Prezzolini appeared in the doorway. "There's a plane coming up the valley from the west—this way, chief!"

"Not a plane," said Audley. "A helicopter. The plane has already been over. The first pass will be just to pinpoint the target. There are armoured personnel carriers on the road, rocket launchers. For all I know he's got Alpini on the mountain behind you. You're getting the V.I.P. treatment today."

Korbel stretched across the table and snatched the handkerchief from Audley's hand. Then, as the sound of the engine increased to the point where Boselli could identify the distinctive racket of the rotor, he disappeared quickly through a doorway just behind him. There was a thumping noise and then a tinkle of broken glass: whatever the state of Ruelle's nerves, his partner was ready to talk.

The roar of the helicopter reached a crescendo as the machine clattered low over the farmhouse, and then diminished quickly as it passed over the shoulder of the mountain beyond. Korbel slipped back quickly into the room again.

"Go back and watch, Guido," ordered Ruelle. "Let me know the moment anyone starts up the track."

This time Prezzolini's reaction was not so quick. He looked at Ruelle half mutinously before grunting and slouching back into the yard.

"What are you offering?" said Korbel.

246

"First—I want to see my wife."

"She's not been hurt."

"Then she can tell me that herself."

Korbel nodded. "Very well."

Audley and Ruelle stared at each other silently for half a minute after Korbel had ducked back through the doorway again.

At length Ruelle spoke. "How did they get on to this place?"

Audley shrugged. "They haven't told me. Maybe they kept tabs on your friend with the gun. They're not so wet behind the ears as you think, anyway—not with Montuori behind them. And they had you spotted, as I've said."

Ruelle's eyes shifted to Boselli. "Who's he?"

Boselli's heart thumped. Those were butcher's eyes appraising a bullock, and he hoped desperately that Audley wasn't going to let slip that the bullock belonged to Raffaele Montuori.

But before Audley could reply the door at the back of the room swung open again.

"*David!*"

The woman was very thin—he remembered that the soft-drinks vendor at Ostia had said as much—and her long hair was so pale as almost to seem white in the gloom, half covering her face. She was not at all the sort of woman he would have associated with the heavily-built Englishman, and also much younger. He was reminded of the German woman back at Positano, though she was much more beautiful and feminine than this one.

Audley took three quick strides round the end of the table, sending a chair spinning.

"Love—it's all right—there, it's all right." The Englishman enfolded his wife in a bear-hug.

"Okay—so you've seen her!" Ruelle's voice was loud and harsh, and the automatic was raised and steady, as though he expected Audley to come at him. "You have a deal—I'll hear it. I promise nothing, though."

Audley didn't let go of his wife, but merely loosened his grip.

"You've got fifteen minutes to be out of here, and forty-eight hours to be out of Italy—you two. The others don't matter. They must leave here with you, but after that it's up to them."

"I said a deal. She goes with us."

"David—"

"I said it was all right, love." Audley's arm tightened round his wife again. He looked at Ruelle coldly. "With her you won't get past the first roadblock, I promise you that! They'll let four men through in one car—and then only after I've given them the next signal . . . which will be given the moment you drive out of here, not before."

"That's no deal at all—without her we have nothing!" Korbel said.

"With her you have nothing. Without her you'll be alive."

"No!" Ruelle filled the word with anger. "For your wife there was to be a name—I still want that name!"

"Would you believe any name I gave you now? I could give you a dozen names—good Russian names—and they'd all be false—" Audley paused, "—because there is no name to give you, and there never was. Except one, and you knew that already—Richard von Hotzendorff—Richard von Hotzendorff first and last and all the way through."

Boselli stared at the Englishman.

"He took you for a ride—the clever Little Bird—and me too, and Eugenio Narva. He even took his wife for a ride. He made everyone do what he wanted—he even made Death change his plans. He chose a hill in Moscow and threw his little white pills away, his chlorothiazide and his digitalis—they found them lying in the gutter—and he ran and he ran up the hill. Not very far, but far enough to get where he wanted to go. And there wasn't any KGB man at his back either, just death catching up on him as he intended."

He looked Ruelle full in the face.

"He was getting old and he had nothing to show for it, so he thought—he was dying and he had nothing to give his wife and children. He couldn't even give them freedom, it took too much money . . .

"So I think he sat down and he realised that he knew just one thing for sure—that one day soon his heart was going to give out on him and he was going to die. So he made a plan around that, so that he could use his death to make it believable—"

"But the oil? The North Sea?" Korbel interrupted feverishly. "He knew about the oil—he knew it was there!"

"He didn't know. Nobody knew—not the experts, not the oilmen. They just thought it was there—they were giving sixty to forty—but they didn't know, because there wasn't any way of knowing and there still isn't. . . . But that didn't matter to him because he'd worked it out so he couldn't really lose—because he'd chosen Eugenio Narva for his mark, and Narva's an honourable man. He reckoned even if he was wrong Narva would see his widow right—and whichever way it went she'd be out of the East with the children. . . . Maybe he even reckoned that she was good-looking and Narva was a widower who liked children—but at the worst they'd be better off. And if the oil was there—jackpot!"

"But how do you know this?" Korbel's voice was hoarse.

"I've talked to Narva, and to the woman—and the thing had the smell of a trick. Only I thought there was a Russian behind it somewhere." Audley shook his head slowly. "And then I talked to—a contact of mine who'd checked the man's death again. . . . I never could understand why it had been made to look like a heart attack, I couldn't accept that it really was that until he told me about the pills and the hill. And then I knew it wasn't a killing made to look like a natural death, but exactly the opposite—a self-induced natural death that no one would believe was natural."

The pills and the hill. Boselli had heard of them on the telephone tape, and they hadn't registered. And now he saw them in an altogether different sequence of events on the very margin of credibility, yet somehow more credible than anything he had heard before.

He could see incredulity in their faces, and then the dawning of bitter realisation.

And he knew instinctively why they understood, as the Englishman had gambled they would: *Little Bird was getting old and he had nothing to show for it. And neither had they!*

"The Russians haven't made a single big off-shore strike since '67," said Audley. "I tell you—we've been had, the lot of us."

They had grasped their opportunity just like the German, only with violence and without understanding. And above all without sacrifice.

And for nothing!

"But I've managed to make a deal for you." Audley pointed suddenly towards Boselli. "This is Signor Pietro Boselli—he represents the Ministry of Justice." He snapped his fingers. "The documents—"

Boselli reached hurriedly towards his pocket, and then froze as the gun came round towards him.

"Go on, Boselli—put it on the table!"

Carefully Boselli extracted the long envelope with his thumb and forefinger.

"A policeman was killed at Ostia, but his killer died too, so to save more bloodshed they're going to call that square—for forty-eight hours."

Korbel split open the flap of the envelope and emptied its contents on the table.

"Two passports," said Audley. "The pictures are from

their files, but the names are blank. Work permits for Switzerland and Germany. Swiss francs and Deutschmarks—not many, but enough to keep you for a few weeks. And a letter from the Minister putting your forty-eight hours in black and white."

Korbel stared at the table wordlessly, but Ruelle's glare was still fixed on Audley.

Life and death was balanced on Ruelle—they had known that from the start. And now Ruelle was balanced on the edge of despair.

"And one more thing," said Audley casually. "There's a letter."

He added a pale blue envelope to the other debris.

Korbel reached for the envelope.

"It's addressed—to you."

"Read it," said Ruelle.

Bastard—

He wouldn't read the superscription, Boselli hoped, remembering the General's face.

"*In exchange for the lives of the woman and the bearers of this letter you will go free. I am required to give you my word of honour to this effect and I hereby do so. You owe me nothing for this, since it is against my advice—the lives of my men, whom you betrayed, cannot be exchanged. It is my greatest wish that you will find these terms unacceptable—*"

XVIII

"AND SO YOU were there when it happened?"

Richardson stared out over the treetops. The rain had damped down the exhaust fumes, bringing out the damp leafy smell of the Park. England—even London—was so much greener than midsummer Italy, which now seemed such a world away. But no greener than Peter Richardson.

"Hardly that. . . ."

He recognised the signs. Sir Frederick was in the mood for all the ghoulish details, like an old rugby club buff sniffing the tale of an away win, and he would have to be satisfied one way or another.

". . . We'd pissed around a bit. It was maybe twenty minutes later that we caught up with where it happened. . . ."

Montuori had been laying down the ruddy law. Christ—he'd been working on the Bastard's epitaph, and the ink hardly dry on his word of honour—

"Which he kept, Peter—don't forget that. Not one finger did he lift against them!"

Richardson realised that he'd spoken his thoughts aloud. He must be losing his little grip at last, then.

"He didn't need to, did he?"

"Ah, but that was the whole point of it. He understood that."

The whole point.

Sir Frederick smiled. "Montuori is a soldier, but he's also very much a political animal, and David knew that. . . . He's been itching to get Ruelle for years, only the man was a partisan hero, and a communist one too. If he'd done it himself there would have been awkward questions. So he couldn't resist the deal."

"And Ruelle?"

"Ruelle was the danger—" Sir Frederick paused judicially, "—because he was much less predictable. But if you remind a man like that how much he hates someone else you do give him a reason for surviving. And that word of honour was a nice touch: Ruelle despised it, but he naturally trusted it nevertheless. I assume that was David's idea?"

Richardson nodded, poker-faced.

Sir Frederick nodded back. "Yes—David wanted his woman back, and he didn't much care how he did it. But he had to offer each of them something they couldn't resist in exchange. So of course he offered them each other."

Clever David. No word of honour for him, he played dirty just like Little Bird, and for the same driving personal reason. But that had been where Ruelle had underestimated his man: he'd reckoned David would do anything to get his woman back, but he'd miscalculated the vengeful limits of David's *anything*.

"David had a deal for everyone, in fact."

"But he also took the risk for everyone if it went wrong— and he was careful to cut you out of that, Peter."

Perhaps that had been part of the deal too, thought Richardson perversely: maybe David had calculated that what Sir Frederick himself couldn't resist was that ultimate acceptance of responsibility. Or was it more simply that he couldn't face surviving anything less than success this time?

Was that courage—or cowardice?

"And yet he took Montuori's man with him—instead of me?"

"That was to make it easier for Montuori if things went wrong, Peter. It would have looked bad if Ruelle had started shooting and there hadn't been an Italian casualty.... But you still haven't told me what actually happened on the road—"

On the road ...

The mountain road had been hot and bumpy, and the dust from the Police jeep ahead had blown in through the window.

And he had still not really understood, and hadn't wanted to travel with the General, only David had made it plain that he wanted to be alone with his wife. . . .

"A crude fellow, but fortunately rather stupid," murmured the General at length.

He made it sound like an epitaph, thought Richardson.

"Now the man Hotzendorff, your Little Bird, he was *not* a crude fellow—to make a killing by dying to order! In fact for a German he was a man of quite remarkable imagination and I'm sorry not to have known him. . . . But then the prospect of extinction is said to have a sharpening effect on the mind, although that doesn't seem to have sharpened the Bastard's wits, I must say!"

The Police jeep was slowing down : there was a confusion of cars on the bend ahead.

"I thought you'd pulled off the roadblocks, Pietro?"

Boselli peered ahead distractedly. "I gave the orders, General."

"Well, kindly go and see they are carried out. I have an appointment in Rome this evening."

Boselli slid out of the car and marched self-consciously towards the roadblock.

The General sat back. "Yes, a man of remarkable imagination. . . . You know, I wasn't going to tell Narva about him, but on reflection I think I shall. It will wound his pride, but that woman of Hotzendorff's is much too fine to waste—she has good hips—and I think he's inhibited by his conscience, poor fool. Once he knows the truth there'll be no holding him. Besides—I rather like the idea of completing your Little Bird's work for him."

The General in the role of Cupid was an arresting thought which sustained Richardson until Boselli returned.

He looked oddly flustered.

"Well?"

"General—it is not a roadblock. There has been an accident."

"Indeed?"

"A car has gone over the edge, into the gorge. A car with four men in it—a pale green car—"

"A road accident," said the General dismissively. "Then there's no reason for us to be delayed. Get back there and tell them to clear the way."

"But there is a peasant who says there was a lorry—" Boselli stopped as he saw the General's expression, swallowing the words quickly. "Yes, General."

For one elongated moment of realisation Richardson stared after him. Then he looked at the General accusingly.

"You gave them your word."

"I did," said the General.

"And now they're dead?"

"Very likely. But not at my hands, Captain—I gave my word."

The General was entirely relaxed, the very model of a clean-handed, conscience-clear General. Yet one who had somehow contrived to pay all his debts in full, damn it!

"But you ruddy well knew what was going to happen?"

"I was confident that the Russians would do my work for me, Captain—if that's what you mean." The General regarded Richardson with fatherly tolerance. "They have never found private enterprise—forgivable."

The Russians.

Not the General, not Audley—and not the *Pubblica Sicurezza* or one of Sir Frederick's tame psychopaths.

Nothing so messy as that: just the KGB settling everyone's account.

It was so obvious that it hurt—and so obvious why the General was smugly relaxed about it. In fact, all along he had been relaxed about it, ever since David—

"Kidnappers," murmured the General. "Kidnappers and murderers and troublemakers—they don't need anyone's tears shed for them. And we couldn't have saved them in any case, not from their own side."

Not after David Audley had carefully and deliberately told the Russians everything, right down to the moment when the troublemakers would be set free in exchange for Faith; he had fingered them as accurately as any Murder Incorporated contract, signed and sealed.

And the General had understood perfectly that the offer was being made to him as well as to the Russians. All he had to do was to flush the target into the open for the KGB to hit, with no awkward questions to ask before or excuses to supply afterwards.

Nor explanations either. The beauty of the two-way deal David had made—if beauty was the right word for it—was that its true substance wasn't even written in the small print at the bottom, but between the lines where only those who were meant to read it would do so. Probably the General was only talking now because he didn't want the son of an old flame to get the wrong idea about the durability of his word of honour.

"Listen, my boy—" the General gave Richardson's arm a confiding squeeze, "—don't think I didn't want to take him, because I've wanted George Ruelle to myself since before you were even born. But what I'd like and what I want are two different things—one must never confuse desires with objectives. . . . I wanted the Bastard dead, and he is dead at last. When you are my age you will learn to be content with such compromises."

SOME
BURIED
CAESAR

"It was what the Americans call a 'Think Tank,'" observed General Montuori. "They forecasted international trends, trouble spots, and likely reactions." He murmured the last words half to himself, as though he fancied the idea of a private Think Tank at his own fingertips.

"Quite so, sir," said Boselli quickly, hastily evaluating the note of envy in his master's voice and thoroughly disapproving it. Such a group of intellectual outsiders would tend to devalue his own importance more likely than not. "But there is a disadvantage in his system—a disadvantage and a temptation. And this man Audley exemplifies each of them."

"Indeed?"

"These men—" Boselli martialled his thoughts very carefully, "—they are difficult to control. There is a—a rogue factor in them. They pursue truth rather than policy."

"I see . . ." The General nodded thoughtfully. "And if the truth gets out . . ."

OCTOBER
MEN

ALSO BY ANTHONY PRICE

The Labyrinth Makers*   The Hour of the Donkey
The Alamut Ambush*   Soldier No More**
Colonel Butler's Wolf*   The Old *Vengeful***
Other Paths to Glory**   Gunner Kelly**
Our Man in Camelot**   Sion Crossing*
War Game**   Here Be Monsters*
The '44 Vintage**   For the Good of the State*

Tomorrow's Ghost**

*Published by THE MYSTERIOUS PRESS
**Forthcoming from THE MYSTERIOUS PRESS